Will of a Tiger

Best wishes !

Iris Y

Iris Yang

Open Books

Published by Open Books

Interior design by Siva Ram Maganti

Cover images © Nova flickr.com/photos/fox3nova and Ysbrand Cosijn shutterstock.com/g/ysbrand

ISBN-13: 978-1948598132

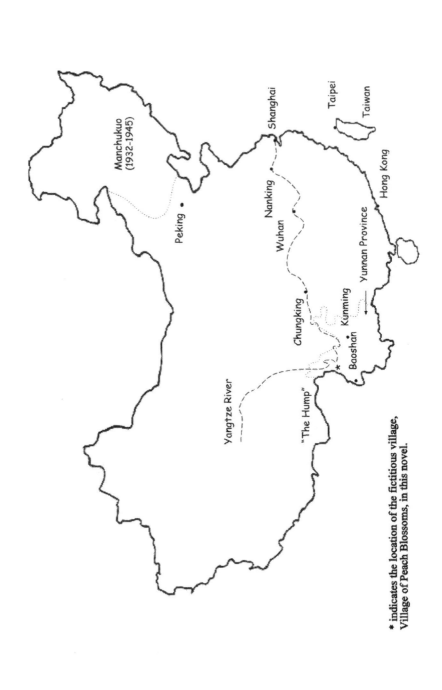

Manchukuo
(1932–1945)

Peking

Shanghai

Taipei

Taiwan

Nanking

Hong Kong

Wuhan

Yunnan Province

Chungking

Kunming

Baoshan

Yangtze River

"The Hump"

* indicates the location of the fictitious village,
Village of Peach Blossoms, in this novel.

Part One

Between Life and Death

Chapter 1

———————

Birch Bai was in trouble. Enemy fire had crippled his P-40, and he'd struggled, hoping to fly long enough to get out of Japanese-occupied territory. He was near Dashan, a mountain town in Yunnan Province, when the sputtering engine quit. The bullet-riddled plane plummeted into an uncontrollable spin, barely giving him enough time to slide open the canopy and tumble out.

A sharp wind rushed past him. Even wearing a helmet, he could hear the hissing of cold air as it blasted through his sheepskin-lined flight jacket. He pulled the ripcord and heard the parachute unfurl behind him. Jerked suddenly upward, the chute blossomed like an enormous white flower as the air filled it, and he began to float upon the air currents.

Despite his repeated calls for help, none of his squadron had replied. His radio had been silent since he was shot over the target—a Japanese airfield near the border of China and Burma. His P-40 had been hammered in the engine and the cockpit as he flew through a stream of deadly fire. Afterward Danny had followed in his fighter while the other planes returned to their base.

Having flown in combat for eight years, the thirty-year-old major was one of the top Chinese fighter pilots in the Air Force. *At least we've destroyed the base. Now, the Japs have no easy way to replenish their supplies.* Images of flaming airplanes, hangars, and runways still excited him.

Birch aimed for a meadow the size of a football field. Thick woods made up the southern and western boundaries. Around Dashan, ancient bamboo huts were perched on the lush hillside, blending naturally with the environment. If he hadn't been in combat, he would have enjoyed the scenery. But he didn't have that luxury. From his airy vantage point, he noticed two armored vehicles already moving toward his wreckage.

A sudden gust of wind pushed him to the edge of the meadow, and a tree branch caught his parachute. The cords stretched to their full length, leaving him tangled in his harness, dangling ten feet off the ground. Quickly Birch took stock of the surroundings. On the other side of the field, a Japanese ground patrol was snaking its way toward him. He had only a pistol and an extra magazine. With one swift motion, he withdrew the hooked knife from his pants pocket, stretched his lean arms, and sliced through the cords.

Struggling to free himself, he heard the roar of a plane overhead, and a split-second later, gunshots. *Danny must have seen the Japs, too.* Birch looked up. The tiger-faced plane zoomed toward the enemy patrol at treetop height. The American airman's bullets surprised the Japanese, who dove frantically into the undergrowth for cover. Dirt and rocks flew everywhere.

"You're too low," Birch shouted at the top of his lungs even though he knew that Danny couldn't hear him. "Dammit! Get the hell out of here, Danny."

But the P-40 didn't retreat. It swooped low, its guns rattling. The trees quivered and the ground shuddered. The fighter plane made strafing runs and pinned the patrol down, forcing the Japanese to deal with the airplane rather than pursue the downed pilot.

Anti-aircraft fire from the vehicles and the patrol's machine guns sprang skyward. The explosive shells burst around Danny. Soon the sky was studded with small black puffs of smoke. The sight and sound sent chills up Birch's spine.

It took no more than a minute to untangle himself, but it felt like an hour. Cutting the last cord, he dropped to the ground, made a forward roll, and sprang to his feet. He unbuckled the straps from around his legs, let the harness drop, and headed toward the forest. In just a few steps, his athletic frame was swallowed by the dense woods. Soon it would be hard for the Japanese to find him.

Before Birch had time to catch his breath, he heard a dreadful noise—a motor cutting out. Without the slightest hesitation, he spun around and rushed back. His eyes widened as he watched the P-40 crash land at the far end of the meadow. Smoke poured out of the fuselage. The deafening impact made his heart drum in a frantic rhythm.

Danny!

Birch sprinted toward the crash site. Danny Hardy was his best friend and his sworn brother. *I'll never leave him alone in the hands of the devil!* He didn't think he could reach Danny before the Japanese. But he had to try.

After a few steps Birch yanked off his helmet and thick jacket. Anything slowing him down had to go. Other than his long, powerful runner's legs, he didn't have any advantage to win this race.

He ran, dodging and weaving from side to side. His hand reached for his pistol. With several bursts, he raked the Japanese. His bullets hammered the enemy. One of the soldiers spun; his rifle flew off. Another doubled up.

But there were simply too many of them...

Dozens of Japanese chased after Birch like a swarm of killer bees. Some ran diagonally across the field, trying to block his path to the crash site. Others rushed to the downed plane. Tracers whizzed over his head. He understood their intention—to slow him down and capture him alive.

Before long, Birch ran out of ammunition. The enemy stopped shooting, too. For a moment, the battlefield became eerily quiet. The only noise was his heavy breathing and pounding heartbeat. The Japanese surrounded him. Their rifles and bayonets glinted in the sunlight.

The plane was still a hundred feet away. Dark smoke continued to belch from the nose of the aircraft. There was no sign of the American. Where was he? Birch's eyes went wide before a look of panic twisted his features. *Is he still inside? Injured? Dead?*

———————

Dozens of Japanese engulfed Birch. Even without a proper weapon, the Chinese pilot wouldn't give up without a fight. He clutched the knife so tightly that his biceps bulged. Sweat glistened in his dark hair as adrenaline coursed through his body.

Birch was taller than most of the Japanese. He twisted and turned. His leg kicked one soldier full in the chest and sent him flying. His arm shot out and smashed another attacker's face, who slumped to the ground with a yelp of pain.

In the interim, though, a bayonet stabbed Birch's right thigh.

A heavyset man on his left tried to restrain him from behind. He jabbed his elbow into the enemy's face, giving him a bloody nose. The hands around Birch's body loosened their hold. Meanwhile, another bayonet slashed a cut on his left arm.

Ignoring the pain, he pounced on a skinny soldier and shoved him so hard that the little man stumbled and crashed into another Japanese soldier. As they toppled together, Birch thrust the knife into the enemy's chest. Blood surged from the poor soul, smearing Birch's uniform. At the same instant, the butt of a rifle smacked into the side of Birch's head. He saw a blinding light, and then blackness swept over him. The impact threw him off the dead man and knocked him to the ground. He lay sprawled on his stomach, head ringing. Despite throbbing pain and blurred vision, he worked to push himself up, using both hands and elbows.

It was too late. The surrounding soldiers kicked him from all directions. Air rushed out of his lungs as he collapsed onto the ground. They shoved his face into the dirt and twisted his arms behind his back, tying his hands with a thin leather strap. Then they patted him down and confiscated the pistol and his favorite leather gun belt bearing the Nationalist emblem. Finally they blindfolded him and hauled him to his feet.

Unable to see, Birch yelled Danny's name. Warm blood oozed

from his temple and dripped down his dirt-smeared face. He was pulled by the arm, away from the crash site. He kicked hard, trying to stay in the area, hoping against hope to hear from his brother.

More punches landed on his stomach, and a boot reached behind his knee. The sharp pain forced him to bend down. Birch clenched his jaw. He wouldn't give his enemy the satisfaction of hearing him cry out again.

He was dragged and shoved forward. He yanked, trying to get free from the hold. Instead, sharp fingernails dug deeper into his opened flesh. He stumbled along, trying not to focus on the pain in his arm and leg, and the ache in his head and throughout his body.

Minutes later they stopped. Before he knew it, he was lifted by several hands and flung upward. *Thump.* He collided with a metallic surface. He scrambled to sit up. Holding his breath, he listened. There was a commotion in the distance and footsteps nearby. A few men climbed on board.

His ears were now on high alert, and moments later he heard a loud thud. Someone else had been thrown onto the truck. "Danny?"

"I'm...here." The voice was barely a whisper.

Birch's breath eased but his heart was still pounding in his chest. He leaned closer. "Are you all right?"

"Still kicking."

Birch could tell that Danny was hurt. "Where are you hurt? Is it serious?" But he heard no response this time. Panicked, he inched closer. "Hey, are you okay?"

A couple of hands landed on his shoulders, wrenching him away. He jerked, shaking the ugly claws off. "Danny?" he called out, straining to hear any word from his companion. "Hang in there. Don't give up!"

"Shut up," one of the Japanese growled in broken Chinese.

"You shut up!" Birch snapped. Anger burned inside him, twisting his bruised features. Even the blindfold couldn't obscure his rage. "Kill me if you want. That's the only way you'll stop me."

Oddly, the soldier stopped.

It was June 1945. The Allies were winning. The Germans had

already surrendered. The war against Japan was drawing close to an end. The Japanese seemed to know it was a matter of time before they would be conquered.

Birch kept talking to Danny. Every so often he heard a short answer, but most of the time he didn't get a response. Time stretched on and on as the truck crawled over the bumpy, serpentine road. His worry dragged him into an abyss.

Chapter 2

The truck came to a squeaking halt after what seemed like an eternity.

Hands seized Birch under the arms and yanked him to his feet. Two steps later, they pushed him off the back of the vehicle. With eyes blindfolded and hands tied behind his back, he managed to half-jump and half-tumble off the truck. As he landed on the ground, he screamed, worrying about Danny being thrown from the truck, "Let me help him." Birch scrambled to his feet, but unable to see or to reach out, he couldn't do anything for the American. "Please! Let me give him a hand."

No one listened to him or cared about his plea.

Then he heard a thud followed by Danny's bellow of agony. The American had taken pain before; he'd been injured several times, but Birch had never heard him complain.

"Danny?" he yelled again.

No answer.

Pushed and shoved, he staggered forward. He had no idea where they were taking them. *Are they going to shoot us? Cut off our heads? Bury us alive?* He'd heard enough horror stories to know that these were not far-fetched possibilities. Many airmen captured by the Japanese had been brutally murdered. *Maybe they will stage a public execution to bolster their morale. They need it. They're losing the war.*

"Danny?" Birch called over his shoulder.

"Still here…"

Danny's voice was faint, but he wasn't far behind.

A few more steps and Birch heard the noise of heavy metal and creaking wood. A door opened and he was shoved inside a room. The leather strap around his wrists was removed. Ignoring the tingle from his numb fingers, he yanked off the blindfold.

Whirling round, he tried to catch sight of Danny, but his blindfold had been on too long. Squinting, he lifted his arm to shade his eyes from the light and watched in horror as the American was tossed to the floor like a sack of trash. Then the Japanese left, locking the door behind them.

"Danny!" Birch dropped to one knee and took the American's right hand in his. "Where are you hurt?" He stared at his friend, checking him up and down.

Danny lay slumped on the ground, semi-conscious. His forehead had a nasty laceration along the hairline. Dry blood matted his brown hair and trickled down his temple. Dark spots spattered two scarves around his neck. On the left breast of the flight suit, a few droplets of blood blemished the image of a winged tiger leaping out of a Victory "V." His face was a mess—split lips, broken nose, a black eye. Midway between his left knee and ankle, a hole larger than the size of a hand was burned in his pant leg. Through the opening, the flesh was mostly pink and yellow, covered with blisters; a few small areas appeared leathery brown and black.

"Are you…okay?" Danny's voice was too hoarse to find much volume. His gaze shifted from Birch's blood-smeared uniform to his battered face.

"He's an American?" someone said as people in the room gathered around them.

"Yes." Birch looked up for the first time to survey the room.

It was a small prison cell. The unpleasant smell of dampness and unwashed body odor filled the air. A dozen prisoners stood around them, several in Chinese Nationalist Army uniforms, the rest in plain clothes. They looked haggard and gaunt. Their clothes were dirty; some were ripped and tattered; others stained with dried blood.

"Major Danny Hardy." Birch motioned with his hand toward the American and switched to speak in Chinese. "He's a Flying Tiger."

The nickname enthralled the men. They huddled closer.

The Flying Tigers was a feisty group of young pilots called the American Volunteer Group, formed under President Roosevelt's executive order in 1941. In less than eight months, they'd destroyed almost three hundred Japanese aircraft and over half a million tons of Japanese shipping. With sheer determination and courage, the American Volunteer Group had turned the tables on Japan in China's skies. Their bravery and vital contribution had gained such respect from the Chinese that they were called the Flying Tigers, since in Chinese culture, the tiger was a symbol of extraordinary strength and vitality.

"Wait!" said Zhou Ming, a lanky officer. He was wearing an ill-fitting Nationalist uniform. "You are Major Bai Hua? I saw your photo in a newspaper not long ago. In fact, there are several reports about you and this Flying Tiger."

Birch nodded.

Zhou Ming placed a hand on Birch's shoulder. "It's an honor to meet you, Sir. I only wish it were in a different place." Enthusiastically he told the inmates, "These two are fighter pilots in the Air Force. They probably killed more Japs than all of us combined." He clicked his heels together and fired off a salute. Several men in the Nationalist Army uniform followed suit.

Birch returned the salute. Then his gaze dropped to Danny.

"Where is he hurt?" asked a man as thin as a stick. His voice was rough as sandpaper, contrary to his youthful appearance. He was dressed in a formal outfit. The blue one-piece garment extended to his heels. One lens of his eyeglasses was missing.

"Not sure. His leg—"

"Let me take a look." The young man moved forward and squatted. Others stepped away, giving him more light. "My name is Ding Fang. Everyone calls me Mr. Ding. I'm a teacher, not a doctor. But I know a little bit about herbal medicine." He leaned over for a closer inspection of the American's leg. With care, he tried to bend it.

Danny made an involuntary sound.

"The burn is nasty. And very painful. But it will heal." Mr. Ding frowned. "Something else is wrong. I'm afraid his leg is fractured."

"What can we do?" Birch asked.

"Not much. We have no medicine, nothing with which to make a splint. I'm afraid that it'll be up to him to recover on his own."

"Let's move him to the bed," ordered a man with the eyes of an eagle. He was in ragged peasants' wear. Despite his shabby appearance, he exuded an air of authority and self-confidence. A long scar down one side of his face and a full beard made him seem dangerous. In fact, he'd been a fearsome man to the Japanese for years. Captain Zhang was a Communist guerilla leader.

The men around Danny lifted his tall frame from the hard packed ground.

The American moaned again.

"Steady," Birch called out as they moved.

"The bed" was just a layer of straw running along either side of the narrow room. There wasn't anything else in the cell except two wooden buckets.

"How about some water?" Zhou Ming offered after they set the wounded man down.

"Yes, water..."

The officer dipped a canteen cup into a bucket and handed it to Birch. Threading his left arm under Danny's neck, Birch lifted his upper body to allow him to drink. Even this small movement made the American cringe.

"Too bad we don't have a stick," said Mr. Ding. "It'll help it to heal faster if his leg is immobilized."

"Where can we—?"

"Wait until tomorrow. It'll be School Boy's turn. He might be willing to find a couple of sticks for us," the captain cut in.

"School Boy?"

"A young guard. He's not as mean as the others," Mr. Ding explained. "He just graduated from high school. I overheard him talking. I understand some Japanese."

"Meanwhile, is there anything to reduce his pain?" Birch asked. Everyone shook their heads.

"I know a bit about acupuncture, but we don't have a needle." Mr. Ding hesitated. "I can try…." Picking up Danny's left hand, he pressed on the valley-like depression between the thumb and index finger. "This meridian point is good for releasing pain, particularly in the head and the abdomen." He applied gentle pressure with his thumb, holding it flat on the spot, and then kneading in a circular motion. "It won't be as useful as a needle. I hope—"

"Jasmine used needles," mumbled Danny.

"Does it help?" Peering through his damaged glasses, Mr. Ding addressed his patient.

"Like a charm."

But Birch knew that it really didn't help, at least not much. He could feel Danny's hand clutching his as tightly as before. "Tell me how to do it," he asked the teacher.

Mr. Ding showed him where the meridian point was located. Birch applied pressure on the spot until their dinner arrived—if gray-colored watery rice could be called dinner.

As soon as they finished eating, Birch grabbed Danny's arm again.

"No need," the American whispered. "It doesn't help much."

Birch stared at his best friend. He knew how it felt because he'd broken his leg while rock-climbing. It had taken him two months in a cast before he could put weight on the fractured leg. "Mr. Ding says it's good for a headache." He gestured to the wound on Danny's forehead. His own temple bloomed with a livid bruise from the butt of a rifle; the rest of his face was mottled with bumps and contusions.

Danny closed his eyes. He was drained. The injuries had sapped his strength.

Birch held his brother's hand and never stopped kneading the meridian point, even after Danny fell asleep. Only in the wee hours did he surrender to his own exhaustion and doze off. In his slumber, he heard explosions and wondered whether it was real or just a dream.

Chapter 3

— — — — — — —

Birch was jolted awake by a loud commotion. He sat up from the pile of hay on which he'd slept and made circles with his head to work out the stiffness in his neck. His temple had stopped throbbing, but it was still sore and would probably remain discolored for days. Rubbing his eyes with the back of his hands, he strained to see. The first light of dawn barely lit the room.

"*Ike. Ike.* Go! Get out. Now," a short Japanese barked in passable Chinese as he herded the prisoners out of the cell. Dark bushy brows shaded his slanted eyes. A well-trimmed toothbrush mustache hovered between his stubby nose and thin lips.

In a daze, Birch took hold of Danny's arm, trying to lift him.

"Not him. He is useless," yelled the Japanese. He stepped closer, yanking Birch away from the American. When he encountered resistance, he hissed a vile curse and tugged harder.

A feral gleam in the eye of the Japanese put Birch on guard, but he kept his tone neutral and stood his ground. "I have to take him with me."

The Chinese pilot's statement enraged the little man. After bellowing and pulling a few times without success, he drew his pistol from his holster and pointed at Birch's head. His eyes opened wide, and there was madness in them. Disobedience wasn't tolerated in prison. "If you do not go, now, I will blow a hole in your face."

Birch didn't flinch. "I'm not going anywhere without him." He tried to lift Danny again.

"*Baka*," bawled the Japanese, waving his arm and cursing, his thin lips shiny with spit and saliva. The prisoner was trying his patience, and he wasn't a patient man. His flat face twisted as he switched his aim and placed the ugly black muzzle on the center of Danny's forehead.

"Don't!" said Mr. Ding, speaking Japanese. "He's new. He doesn't understand you. We'll go now." He bowed to the Japanese officer.

"Go!" Danny urged Birch.

"They're just taking us to work," said Zhou Ming, dragging Birch toward the door. "Danny can't do it. Don't worry, Major. We'll be back."

Reluctantly, Birch moved as he kept his gaze fixed on Danny.

Three years ago, along with his sister and cousin, he'd rescued this Flying Tiger. The life-and-death experience had bonded them, and they'd become best friends and sworn brothers. Leaving his wounded brother lying on the prison floor was the last thing Birch wanted to do. Only Danny's firm nod gave him strength to keep moving.

———————

The Japanese soldier forced them outside where sixty other prisoners milled about. Surrounded by a barbed-wire fence, this small camp looked bleak—the ground was covered with dirt and loose gravel without a single tree or plant in sight. Near a wooden gate, a watchtower loomed. On top of a wooden pole, a Rising Sun flag flapped in the chilly breeze.

"What are we going to do?" asked Birch in a low voice. Mr. Ding raised his narrow shoulders in a shrug as they passed through the gate.

Amid a crowd of dreary-eyed, haggard men, Birch took stock of his surroundings. They were walking on an uneven road just wide enough for vehicles. He could see no landmark, only dense forests and hills that dominated the mountainous area in Yunnan Province. The sun was barely above the horizon. Except for a few wispy pink clouds, the sky was cobalt blue. The June morning was fragrant with the rich odor of earth and wildflowers. A chorus of birds sang in the woods.

For twenty minutes they trudged along. Then Birch let out a low whistle. He'd spotted patches of blue flowers, their petals covered with dew drops lit by the warm sunlight like hundreds of sparkling diamonds.

"Forget-me-nots are pretty." Mr. Ding covered his mouth to muffle his voice.

"No," Birch blurted out, and then corrected himself. "I mean yes. But it's more than that. It can heal wounds." Danny had been saved by Jasmine Bai, Birch's cousin; one of the herbs she'd used was the precious forget-me-nots.

Slowly, Birch edged toward the side of the group. A few steps later he turned, scanned his surroundings to make sure that no guard was watching. But before he could pick the flowers, he heard a sharp cry.

He whirled round. In disbelief, he saw Mr. Ding being beaten. The young teacher crouched down, his hands protecting his head, as a stocky Japanese guard punched and kicked him. A few blue flowers lay scattered at his feet.

Birch felt responsible. He took several huge steps forward and, bending down, he tried to shield the young man. Just then, something hissed behind him. Before he could react, he felt a blistering pain down his back. It took his breath away.

He spun round, assuming a fight stance. His hands curled into fists, ready to strike.

"Don't!" someone shouted. The low but firm voice bolted Birch into place. "No fighting! He'll kill you."

Birch caught sight of Captain Zhang standing behind the Japanese who raised the whip again. The captain stood still, his face stern, head shaking slightly. His hands balled into fists at his sides as he forcibly suppressed his rage.

With all the willpower he could muster, Birch dropped his hands but stood defiantly facing the mustachioed Japanese. His fiery stare remained on the enemy's eyes.

"Bow!" The Japanese sent the whip whizzing through the air. "Do not look at me in the face, you pig!"

Birch sucked in a sharp breath. The whip cracked across his face, neck, and chest, setting his flesh on fire and cutting a bloody gash under his left eye. The unexpected power caught him off guard, and he fell on one knee.

Born in the Year of the Tiger, Birch had been trained as a warrior. His instinct was to fight back. Not being able to do so violated his soldierly pride. He struggled to stand.

"*Baka! Baka!*" The Japanese growled and slapped Birch across the face with an open palm. The Chinese pilot's defiance infuriated him. Again and again, he struck Birch with both hands. The hostile intensity behind his eyes was more than evident. He was determined to teach this new prisoner a lesson.

The humiliation was too much to swallow.

Although his father, a general in the Chinese Air Force, had never spoiled him, Birch was born a respected young master in the upper class. No one had ever raised a hand to him. Even though life as a fighter pilot was tough and many of his missions were death-defying, an airman belonged to a prestigious group—only highly educated young men, some with impressive family backgrounds, had the chance to join.

To a proud fighter, the maltreatment was worse than death. He struggled to stand up again.

"Stay down, you fool! Don't give him an excuse to kill you." The captain's sotto voce warned him again. So Birch clenched his fists and dug his nails into his palms. It took all his strength to tolerate the ill-treatment.

I could strangle this midget with my bare hands. He was more than a foot taller than the Japanese and had the lean and powerful build of a natural athlete. *But then what?* Plenty of armed soldiers surrounded them, sabers drawn and rifles fixed with bayonets. If he were alone, he would fight to the death. But he wasn't alone. He couldn't let Danny face a senseless death.

Grinding his teeth and setting his jaw, Birch fought to stay on his knee. His cheeks were swelling with red and purple welts. His ears were ringing. His nose was bleeding, and he could taste the blood, bitter and sharp.

Steeling himself for more pain and degradation, he suddenly heard Mr. Ding crying. Then the teacher's husky voice spoke in Japanese. Birch didn't know what Mr. Ding was saying, but it sounded like the man was pleading. A few more hits, and the guards stopped. "*Ike. Ike.* Go!" they yelled at the prisoners and waved their arms.

Birch stood up, wiping the blood from his mouth and nose. He spotted Mr. Ding slumped on the ground. Stepping closer, he pulled the young teacher to his feet.

The blue flowers scattered around them were tempting, but Birch curbed the impulse to pick them up. The short Japanese gave him a hefty shove in the back, and as if reading his mind, stepped on the delicate forget-me-nots. His thin lips pressed together in a smirk. Fixing his stare on Birch's eyes, he dug the sole of his boot into the ground and crushed the flowers. "Go!" he barked again and jabbed his index finger forward.

By then the rising sun had spread its glow over the mountainside.

Chapter 4

■ ■ ■ ■ ■ ■ ■

They marched for another twenty minutes. A number of large craters in the middle of the road blocked their path. Birch guessed that either the Nationalist Army or the Communist guerillas had done the damage. The Japanese ordered them to repair the road. A vehicle covered with camouflaged netting brought the tools. Some prisoners received handmade baskets. A few older men got spades and shovels, but the others had to use their bare hands.

Birch secured the basket full of rocks with both hands. The weight bent his upper body forward. The rough basket made of twigs and vines scraped the welts on his back, opening the wounds. Blood stained his uniform. Before long, he was drenched with perspiration. The salty sweat stabbed at his wounds like a thousand pinpricks.

Once a crater was filled, they were ordered to smooth the road using a heavy stone roller, which was normally pulled by oxen. Now two dozen men were forced to tow the roller with straps fastened over their shoulders.

Birch leaned forward, pushing on the balls of his feet. With the guards breathing down their necks, he struggled to get the heavy wheel turning. The rough strap bit into his chest. The pain was impossible to ignore, but he ploughed onward.

The chilly morning gradually grew warmer. The prisoners worked non-stop for hours under a broiling sun that leeched their energy and made Birch feel like his skin had been lit by a torch. By noon they'd repaired half the damage and were allowed a fifteen-minute break. Lunch was a cold rice ball the size of a small onion.

Birch was hungry; his stomach grumbled. And he was dying of thirst; they had not been given any water. His lips were split and chapped, his throat parched. His left cheek was inflamed so badly that it had turned his eye as narrow as a sewing needle. He winced as he nibbled the rice ball.

"You'd better eat it. The only meat you'll ever have here." Sitting next to Birch on a rock, Mr. Ding pointed to the yellow maggots in the rice. "Welcome to hell's dining room."

"What did you say to the Jap earlier?" Birch asked, moistening the cut on his lip with the tip of his tongue.

"I told the bastard that the flowers were for him." The teacher gave a lopsided grin, one corner of his lips split. His forehead was discolored with bruises.

"I'm sorry."

Mr. Ding waved a hand. "You know, there are plenty of forget-me-nots in our backyard."

"Really?"

The young teacher bobbed his head, then his mouth curved into a frown. "Too bad we don't have a way of getting them."

"No fighting back." Captain Zhang interrupted the conversation. He was sitting on the other side of Birch. "No heroes here," he reiterated. "This is hell. No hero will ever walk out of here alive, only survivors. Understand?"

"Captain Zhang is right," Mr. Ding agreed. "Jackal killed a couple of officers in cold blood just a month ago. One of them picked some wild berries. He was hungry. He didn't even get a chance to eat them. Jackal beat him ruthlessly."

"Jackal?"

"The one who hit you. We gave him the nickname. Unfortunately, he's in charge here."

"That midget?"

"Don't think less of him because of his size. He's the cruelest of the cruel. I overheard that his father and two brothers died during the war. He's taking his revenge on us."

Birch nodded.

"Anyway, another officer stepped up, trying to protect his colleague. They were buddies. Jackal shot the officer in the face right before us then turned around and continued to punish the hapless fellow. The poor guy died the next morning."

Birch closed his eyes for a moment as anger gnawed at him.

"Do whatever you must to survive. Subdue your soldierly pride. To the Japs, we're nobody." Mr. Ding cited a proverb. "'A great man knows when to yield and when not to.' Don't rebel every chance you get. It's like an egg striking a rock, only to cause its own destruction."

Birch stuffed the last bit of rice ball into his mouth. "What happened to your nails?" he asked, regarding the captain's hand holding the food. The guerilla leader had no nails on his fingers.

Captain Zhang shrugged.

"Japs pulled them off, one by one, with pliers," said Mr. Ding. "Captain Zhang has never told the Japs anything, no matter how much they tortured him."

Brutality like this wasn't news. Birch knew how the Japanese had tortured and raped Jasmine after she refused to give up Danny. If they'd treated an innocent girl with such cruelty, they were capable of anything. Pulling out nails shouldn't shock him, yet he felt chilled.

The victim was a communist, and Birch worked for the Nationalists, yet he couldn't help but feel sympathy for the bearded captain. In an instant, the guerilla leader gained Birch's respect. Captain Zhang was famous. Years ago the Japanese had put a price on his head after he and his group had conducted many skirmishes, ambushes, and moonlight raids.

"They forced hot spicy soup down Mr. Ding's throat," the captain grumbled. "They know he's a teacher and his voice is important to him."

"Yes, they know how to hurt a person." Mr. Ding scowled.

Birch sat upright. He let out a gasp. "What might they do to Danny?" He regretted leaving his wounded brother behind. But what could he have done? If he'd insisted on staying, the only outcome would have been a beating or even death, probably his and Danny's.

"Don't worry too much, Major," said Zhou Ming. "I've been here for a month. They've never interrogated me." He seemed both relieved and embarrassed. That explained why his clothes were cleaner and he looked healthier than the others.

"So no one will know where we are?"

"That's right. This is a secret jail for political prisoners." Except for a few Nationalist Army officers, most prisoners were in plain clothes.

"Then why bother to keep us here?"

"Maybe they'll need information from us later. Perhaps trade us for their POWs one day. Or use us as human shields…"

With a sinking feeling in the pit of his stomach, Birch spent the rest of the afternoon worrying about Danny and praying that his brother would be okay.

Chapter 5

━ ━ ━ ━ ━ ━ ━

As soon as they returned to their cell, Birch rushed toward the American. "Danny?" he called out. "Are you all right?" He checked him up and down to find a sign of further injury.

Danny opened his eyes, a wide grin breaking the craggy angles of his bruised face. Then his smile vanished. "What happened?"

Ignoring the question, Birch asked again, "Are you all right?"

"I'm okay."

"They…they didn't hurt you?" Birch was afraid to use the word "torture" as though it would be true if he verbalized it.

"No." Danny gave an adamant shake of his head. His smile came back. "In fact, you won't believe it." He drew a small bottle from his pocket. "A young guard, School Boy—I guess that's what everyone here calls him—came in and chatted with me for awhile. He speaks broken English. His uncle moved to the States years ago. Look what he gave me." He handed the medicine bottle to Birch.

"What's this?"

"For pain, he said,"—imitating the guard, Danny tilted his head, placed his palms together and put them on his cheek—"and for sleep."

"You believed him?" Birch looked incredulous. "It could be poison for all we know." A gummed label with Japanese writing was stuck to the side of the bottle.

"If they wanted to kill me, they wouldn't go to this much trouble.

Look at me. They could have me any way they want." It was the sad truth. The Japanese could kill them anytime, anywhere, using any method they chose. "At any rate, I slept like a log."

Birch let out a breath of relief. Tension drained from his shoulders as he rocked back on his haunches.

"He also gave me—" Danny pointed to the two sticks by the side of the door. "It took him a while to understand what I wanted."

Mr. Ding picked up the sticks. "Great!" He positioned them on Danny's fractured leg, away from the burn wounds. "We need something to tie them." His eyes searched the room and landed on Danny's blood-stained white scarf. "We can tear that in half—"

"No," Danny refused without hesitation.

"But we need—"

"Forget it!" The American's tone was imperative.

"Hold on," Birch ventured. "We don't have to destroy it." He understood that the white scarf was an invaluable gift—Jasmine had given it to Danny on his birthday three years earlier. "His red one should be long enough." He was referring to the shorter, square scarf, which had also belonged to Jasmine. Birch had found it after she died, and Danny had asked for it as a remembrance of the girl with whom he'd fallen in love. Ever since her death, the American had worn two scarves wrapped around his neck.

Reluctantly, Danny took off the scarves.

Birch threaded the long white scarf under Danny's injured leg above the knee. Carefully, he wrapped it around the sticks and the leg a few times, tying a knot.

Meanwhile, Mr. Ding used the red scarf to secure the lower part of the splint. "That's all we can do. I hope it will help."

"Your left leg is cursed, isn't it?" sighed Birch, shaking his head. Danny's left leg had been injured when Jasmine, Daisy, and Birch had rescued him three years earlier.

"On the bright side, I've already practiced hopping on my right leg." Danny made a face. Then his levity vanished, and with all seriousness, he asked, "What did they make you do today?"

Birch recapped their day, skipping the beating. As an afterthought, he added, "I believe I heard the blasts last night."

"Can you tell where we are?"

"No particular landmark." Turning around, Birch asked, "Does anyone know?"

Everyone in the room shook his head. Most sat on the floor, resting; only a couple stood near the trio.

"We were blindfolded," Mr. Ding clarified.

"How long do you think it took to get here?" Danny asked Birch. He'd passed out on the way.

"About thirty to forty minutes, less than an hour." Time had seemed very different when he was blindfolded.

"Let's say the truck traveled at thirty miles an hour. The mountain road isn't good. So we're about fifteen to twenty-five miles from the town. Too bad we can't tell which direction. Thirty miles west or south of Dashan would take us out of China. For all we know, we could be in Burma."

Birch shook his head. "We're still in Yunnan, north or east of Dashan."

"How do you know that?"

"There were ups and downs, but mostly we went downhill. I noticed the pressure change. There are taller mountains in the west and south. So it can only be north or east."

"Good call!"

They were encouraged that they'd figured out roughly where they were, though it seemed useless considering that they were locked up and surrounded by barbed-wire. Still, any information, no matter how trivial, might later become crucial.

———

Danny took another pain reliever before he went to sleep. He handed the small bottle to Birch. "Take one."

"Nothing I can't handle."

Danny paused, his eyes focused on Birch's battered face. "What happened, anyway?"

Birch raised his broad shoulders in a shrug.

Danny heaved a heavy sigh. Rolling on his back, he closed his eyes.

Birch lay awake for hours, even though he was exhausted from lack of sleep the night before and the day's hard work. His head was pounding. Blood pulsed in the flesh surrounding the welts. Because of the punches and kicks he'd received the day before, he was aching all over. He tossed and turned, trying in vain to find a less painful position. The hard floor covered by a thin layer of straw made comfort impossible.

A horde of hungry mosquitoes descended upon him. He tried to ward them off, but they were so persistent that he was severely bitten. The itchy welts on his face and hands added to his discomfort. *How can the others sleep*, he wondered?

Noise was another nuisance: several people in the room snored; one man stirred and twitched in his dreams; and a guard walked back and forth in front of the cell, his boots pounding against the hard ground.

Occasionally, the bark of a dog rippled through the night. Birch had seen several German shepherds walking with the guards. Ever since the massacre three years earlier, he'd despised those huge, aggressive dogs. Whenever he heard a bark, a teenager's torn belly appeared in his mind. A German shepherd had mauled the village boy.

For a long time Birch watched the moonlight pour through the bolted windows. In the pale light, he clenched his teeth until his jaw hurt. Yet not once did he consider taking the pain reliever. He would rather have a sleepless night than take the precious medicine.

Birch was only a couple of months older than Danny, but his youthful appearance made him look a few years younger. Nevertheless, he'd always taken pride in being the Big Brother. Daisy and Jasmine, his younger sister and cousin, had perished before him. It was the young women's death that had brought the two men together and forged their unbreakable bond. Intuitively, Birch had replaced his affection for the girls with this newfound brotherhood.

A restless night was a small price to pay for being *Da Ge—Big Brother.*

Chapter 6

Wincing from aches and pains, Birch rubbed the sleep from his eyes. After a breakfast of soggy rice, he plodded to the rear window. Twirling around, he angled his head toward Danny. Delight wiped away his drowsiness. "I wish you could see this." His bloodshot eyes brightened with excitement, although his left eye was still smaller than normal from swelling.

"Give me a hand," said the American.

"But—"

"I have to move, or I'll rot here."

Birch turned to Zhou Ming. "Help me, will you?" The two men wrapped the Flying Tiger's arms around their shoulders and lifted him to a standing position.

Danny cringed as he took a small jump forward. The sticks held well as a splint; his injured leg dangled an inch above the floor.

"Not a smart idea," frowned Mr. Ding. "You shouldn't do this."

In traditional Chinese medicine, healing required bedridden rest. But in Danny's dictionary, recovery meant vigorous exercise. The Flying Tiger couldn't sit around waiting for his wounds to heal on their own.

"Easy," Birch called out as they inched forward.

The distance to the rear window was a matter of steps, but it seemed longer than the Great Wall. Every movement caused Danny more agony. He grimaced and gasped. But he didn't stop, and took time only to catch his breath, waiting for the stabbing sensation to subside, before subjecting himself to another.

For over fifteen minutes they struggled to travel those few yards. Danny's chest rose and fell with labored breathing. Perspiration flowed in tiny rivers down his face when they reached their destination.

Although the window was nailed shut with heavy planks, the openings between them were large enough to see through. The view wasn't much—only a small meadow backed by dense forests—but it was revealing.

"By golly!" exclaimed Danny. Grabbing the window frame, he hungrily took in what was in front of him. Tiny blue forget-me-nots dotted the field, their vibrant color highlighted by the brilliant sunlight. Industrious bees buzzed among the blooms. A yellow butterfly with black lines and dots darted in front of them.

The beauty lay in stark contrast to the dark inside, and it transported Danny to another world where two gorgeous young women had lived. For a long while he said nothing, lost in his thoughts, immersed in his fond memories. Then he closed his eyes and took a deep breath of the sweet fragrance. "I can't believe she never told me what happened that night."

"Jasmine was modest, you know, like most Chinese women," said Birch.

"I know. I just wish she'd told me. Now I'll never find out."

Birch nodded.

After the girls had found Danny unconscious in a meadow, Jasmine had spent the night with him while Daisy went to a village for help. No one knew how Jasmine had safeguarded the injured Flying Tiger. All she said was that she'd used forget-me-nots and another herb.

"You'll laugh at me." A soft smile crossed Danny's lips, but it was hollow. "Crazy as it seems, I think she kissed me. She was an angel. Her kisses brought me back to life."

His smile faded, leaving only sadness in his eyes. "It's absurd, I know. Who am I fooling except myself? No Chinese girl would kiss a man without marriage." His head drooped, hanging between his hunched shoulders.

With a flicker of sympathy, Birch stared at his friend.

"To this day, I still have trouble wrapping my head around it. How could a girl like Jasmine protect anyone? The pain she took—"

"Danny, don't go there." Birch clapped the American's forearm. "Jasmine wouldn't want you to feel this way. She did it willingly."

"I know. I—" Danny paused to clear the emotional knot from his throat. His eyes had lost their usual glimmer. His vision was blurred by the haunting image of a young woman with three long, bloody cuts on her cheek. "I miss her. And Daisy, too!"

"I miss them, too."

"Will the pain ever go away?"

"I don't think so."

They looked at each other, and in that single glance, unspoken sorrow flowed between them. Side by side the two men stood before the barricaded window, dreaming the impossible dream of being with the ones they loved.

Danny shook himself out of his reverie. His gaze shifted to the woods. Birch and pine forest stretched endlessly beyond the meadow. "The birch trees seem short here."

"They are much taller in the north. Actually, I'm surprised to find them this far south. It must be the high elevation."

"Well, it may not be the tallest tree, but it sure stands straight." After a pause, Danny added, "You know what? I wouldn't name my child Birch."

"Why not? It's a good name."

"The tree is beautiful. Clean-cut. Graceful. But look at those eyes! Every time I see it, I wonder if a tormented soul lives inside."

"You'd better lie down. You've been standing long enough." Birch waved at Zhou Ming, and the two men helped Danny back to the pile of hay.

Facing the American, Birch sat down, cross-legged. "So, what name would you give your child?"

"Jack. It has a down-to-earth feel."

Birch dipped his head. Jack Longman had been Danny's childhood friend, Susan Hardy's fiancé, and another Flying Tiger. He'd been killed three years earlier. "What about a girl?"

Danny opened his mouth but made no sound. He seemed startled by the question. Then he cracked a sheepish smile. "No clue. I guess I thought I'd have a son one day."

"As if you can control it," Birch said with a chuckle.

"What about you?"

"If it's a boy, he'd be Dan Ni."

"That's swell." Danny's famous smile was evident. "A girl?"

"Phoenix."

"Bai Feng Huang. White Phoenix. That's a cute name."

"I hope she'd rise from the ashes of this damned war and become an incredible woman like Daisy and Jasmine."

"That's something else. Hey, may I name my girl Phoenix, too? Phoenix Hardy."

Birch burst into a carefree laugh, but then grimaced. His palm went to soothe his left cheek. "Don't you know a Phoenix is a female ruler of the avian world?"

"I do."

"Well, remember the saying I taught you? 'One mountain cannot accommodate two tigers.'" Birch shook his head with a wink. "We can't have two phoenixes in the same household."

"Sure we can. Daisy used to say that both of us are the best."

"She had probably forgotten that both of us are Tigers." A shadow of sadness passed over Birch's face. "Daisy also said I wouldn't promise anything I wouldn't do. She trusted me." He swallowed a mouthful of acrid saliva. "And look what I've done…?"

Maimed and embittered, Birch lowered his head. His eyes became empty. Daisy was his sore spot. It had been three years, but the loss was still an open wound. The sheer horror on her face before she'd been killed by the hand grenade—his hand grenade—was etched permanently into his memory and never failed to bring a lump to his throat.

Danny put his hand on his wingman's arm, waiting patiently for him to collect himself. The silence was broken by a dripping noise. Captain Zhang was urinating into the waste bucket. A stench permeated the already smelly room.

Birch pulled his shoulders back and gained a measure of control. Clearing his throat, he changed the subject. "What would you like to do after the war...if we get out of here?"

"Go home for a while. Then I'd like... Hey, why don't you go with me?" All at once, Danny lit up with vigor. "Mom, Dad, and Susan will be thrilled to meet you."

"I'd love to meet them, too!"

"We'll go hiking in the Sierra Nevada Mountains, just like Jack and I used to do." Danny's eyes brightened with the memory.

In their musty prison cell, Birch felt an unexpected surge of energy. He'd been to America once during his training. Danny's words painted a bright picture and provided a temporary reprieve from the dire situation.

Just then a guard walked past their cell. His boots made a clomping sound against the hard ground. Last night the thump-thump of the footsteps had bothered Birch, but now they didn't deter his high spirits.

"Afterward, I want to come back to Yunnan," said Danny. "I'd like to go back to Tao Hua Cun to search for Jasmine."

Danny and Birch had tried to locate her remains near Tao Hua Cun, Village of Peach Blossoms. A girl who had seen Jasmine jump took them to a place on the ridge, but when they searched below they found nothing. After witnessing the massacre of the entire population of the village, and then gang-raped, the teenager might have been too traumatized to identify the correct location.

"Then, I'd like to find Jack," continued Danny. "It will be even harder; he went down in a remote area."

Birch nodded.

"I'd like to bring him home." Danny swallowed twice before continuing. "And I think we should look for those who died along the route to the Hump."

"You must be joking."

"Remember the reflections from the wreckage that we saw? They were our colleagues. There must be more than a thousand, don't you think?"

"Probably more," said Birch. Leaning forward, he planted his elbows on his knees. With his left fist supporting his chin, he tapped his lips with his right index finger. "That's a long stretch in the remotest and roughest part of China—or in the world, for that matter."

"I know. But we both love the outdoors. What could be more rewarding?"

"That's some forward-thinking." Birch slammed a fist into his palm. "I've only thought about Jasmine and Jack." His eyes lit up, translucent with zeal and hope.

Both Birch and Danny were born in 1914, the year of the Tiger according to the Chinese zodiac. Tigers were brave fighters. They would stand up to the bitter end for what they believed was right. They were passionate yet calm, warm-hearted yet fearsome, courageous in the face of danger, yet soft in other areas.

Being a Tiger, Birch, like Danny, always had a thirst for adventure. "If you're in, then I'm in!" he declared. Then he shifted in search of a more comfortable position. Running his hand through his dark hair, he scratched his head. "Mary is going to kill me. She won't like this." Mary was Birch's girlfriend, an attractive translator at the commander's office.

"We'll take breaks…go home to recuperate, so to speak." Danny's mouth stretched into a grin. "I love Xiao Mei's dishes. She's a great chef." He licked his lips.

"Good point. I miss her cooking too. *Yi yan ji chu—once the word has come out of your mouth*," Birch cited the first part of a phrase.

"*Si ma nan zhui*," Danny finished. "*Even a chariot drawn by four horses cannot pursue it.*"

They exchanged an understanding smile. Without knowing if they would live another day, the two brothers had just planned a thrilling future.

Chapter 7

‒ ‒ ‒ ‒ ‒ ‒ ‒

August 7, 1945 started the same as every other day in prison. The summer had been uncharacteristically warm, and the sun grew stronger as the morning passed. Without a breeze coming through the window, the room was breathlessly hot.

"*Romance of the Three Kingdoms* is a terrible translation for... *San Guo Yan Yi*," Danny said. He was breathless after his regular exercise. His hair matted in sticky clumps to his forehead. "It doesn't say anything about *Yi*."

"I'm with you," said Birch, sitting next to him on the floor. "But there is no easy way. *Yi* means so much—morality, duty, loyalty, decency, comradery—"

"Brotherhood."

"Right. How in the world do you include so much in a title?"

"It'll be this long." Danny spread his arms wide. Flashing his charming smile, he ventured an idea. "How about *The Virtuous War Between The Three Kingdoms?*"

"Not bad. Beats the official translation."

"*Yi* is a virtue everyone should follow." Lowering himself to the floor, Mr. Ding joined them. "It's an unwritten but accepted rule."

Danny nodded. "So, what happened to the three brothers?" he asked, referring to the characters in the historical novel. "I mean in history. Did they die on the same day?"

Everyone in China knew the unforgettable oath taken by the three close friends in the classic book. Their vow—"though not born on the same day of the same month in the same year, we merely hope to die on the same day of the same month in the same year"—was often alluded to as the ultimate fraternal loyalty, the definitive example of *Yi*. Danny and Birch had used the phrase when they swore to be brothers.

"No," replied Mr. Ding. With a pride of a devoted teacher, he was ready to elaborate. "Unlike their vow, they died on different dates in real life. They—"

Metallic sound and creaking wood cut short their conversation. The cell door swung open, and Jackal, the prison chief, barged in with four guards. They seized the two pilots by the arms and hauled them to their feet.

"Get your paws off us," the airmen shouted in unison and tried to wrench their arms free. "We'll go with you," added Birch, taking Danny's arm.

Side by side, the two friends walked out of the room. With a clang of the door, they were separated from their fellow prisoners who watched helplessly as they were taken away.

———————

The Japanese led them to a small room at the far corner of the compound. They tied the two pilots back to back around a wooden pole. Thin leather straps bit deeply into their wrists and ankles.

The windowless room was hot and muggy. Birch almost felt relieved that they'd stripped off his uniform—before fear registered. The air stank of body odor, urine, and blood, too thick to inhale, so hot it seemed like a furnace.

Holding an iron ruler, Jackal paced back and forth between the two men. He was more agitated than normal. "How many atomic bombs do you have?" he barked in Chinese. "I mean the U.S." His voice shook with fear and anger.

Atomic bomb? Birch knew nothing about that and doubted Danny knew anything either. He'd never heard the American mention a weapon by this name. *How powerful is it?* From the way Jackal talked, he guessed it wasn't a conventional explosive device.

"Never heard of such a thing," answered Danny.

"Tell me the truth."

"That is the truth."

"You are trying my patience," shouted Jackal. "I do not have time to play games with you." His eyes narrowed to the thinnest of slits. He was short. The top of his head didn't even reach the airmen's shoulders. "You could be shot, you know. We've only kept you alive for information we need." He swept the ruler from left to right. The features of his face turned hard, as if the skin had suddenly been stretched over the bones. "You see what we have here?"

A naked bulb coated with grime dangled from the ceiling and dimly lit the room. Spots of congealed blood stained the mud-brick floor. Rusted shackles, whips of different sizes, heavy tongs and blades, and other devices were bolted to the walls. A clay stove with branding irons was tucked in a corner; fire crackled and hissed from time to time, giving out a sickly orange glow, making the room more oppressive. A wooden bench with leather straps stood by its side.

Jackal curled his lips, making a low chuckle. His yellow teeth were crooked and grotesque. "You will talk after I use them one by one." He slapped the ruler against the palm of his other hand. "I will wring the words out of you. You might as well tell me now. Save us time and save yourselves pain." He waited, purposefully letting the silence stretch out. His gaze bounced between the two men, studying them in a mute query.

Birch cringed in spite of his determination not to show fear. He'd seen Captain Zhang's fingers and heard Mr. Ding's hoarse voice. He knew Jackal was a sadist—not long ago, the midget had shot an officer in the face and beaten another to death.

How can I watch Danny go through hell like this? Birch's features reflected the turmoil within as he wrestled with the horrid possibility. Danny was not only his best friend but also an American who had traveled halfway around the world to fight the war for China, for *his* country. But how could he protect Danny when his own life wasn't even under his control? To hide his emotions, he rolled his lips inward, bunched his jaw, and wiggled his fingers, touching Danny behind him. He detected a slight movement from Danny's hands on his back, the only connection between them.

Jackal advanced on Birch, apparently noticing his grimace. Tilting his head, he subjected his captive to an unhurried once-over. Then his beady eyes fixed on Birch's bare chest.

After being imprisoned for six weeks, Birch was no longer muscular. A sleek sheen covered his upper body. A jagged diagonal scar crossed the length of his torso.

Using the tip of the ruler, Jackal traced the pencil-thin scar he'd inflicted over a month ago. His gaze lingered there as if admiring his previous work. Then he tilted his head back. His gaze zeroed in the Chinese pilot's face. Without breaking eye contact, he took a step back, swung the ruler in his hand, and slashed it across Birch's chest.

Birch snapped his head to the side to avoid the impact. His head bumped hard against the wooden pole. The tail end of the ruler caught the bottom of his chin before slitting his chest. Blood spilled from the open wound. The burning pain stole his breath.

"So, how many?"

Birch screwed his eyes shut. His hands squeezed into fists so tight that all the blood was wrung out of them. Taking gulps of air, he clenched his jaw. His whole body tensed as he braced himself for the next attack. Even with his eyes closed, he knew Jackal was getting closer to him, examining him. He could smell alcohol on the little man's breath.

After a beat, Jackal slashed again, putting all his strength behind it.

Birch forced steel to his backbone as the iron ruler went up and down. His eyes rolled back under the lids. Sweat poured down his face. It took every bit of strength to endure the pain. Soon his chest was crisscrossed with bloody marks, but he didn't allow himself to utter a sound.

"You said the U.S. dropped the bomb," Danny yelled, waging a futile struggle against his bonds. "How would he know anything?"

"He is with you."

"Why don't you ask me then?"

Jackal moved to the American. "I see your leg is healed nicely." He paused for effect, twisting the ruler in his hands. Then, in a calm malicious voice he said, "Let me check it."

The smack made Birch's heart sink. "You sick bastard!" He twisted his body, struggled like a tiger trying to free himself from the restraints. His deep-set eyes blazed with pure hatred. Tied back to back, he couldn't see clearly, but he heard Danny's painful groan and felt his shudder.

"Tell me. Otherwise, your leg will be broken again."

The blunt claim filled Birch with desperation.

A moment later, another lash came down. This time, Danny screamed and cursed.

"Stop!" Birch felt sick to his stomach when he imagined the knife-like edge ripping Danny's unhealed wounds. He bowed his head as if the haunting thoughts weighed him down.

Wild with terror, he had to bite his lip to keep himself from begging the enemy. He knew nothing about the atomic bomb. And even if he had known, he wouldn't give up such a secret. Giving a confession, even a false one, had a bad connotation; it showed weakness. As a proud airman, how could he bend to the enemy under torture? As Birch wrestled with the predicament, he tasted blood in his mouth, as bitter and dark as his thoughts.

"How many?" Jackal demanded. Beneath his low brow, his eyes turned even more hostile. He raised the ruler. Blood, Birch's and Danny's, dripped from the tip. He let several seconds lapse and, hearing nothing, he stroked again.

Still no answer...

Silence meant defeat. Anger infused Jackal's face with color. His madness escalated. "I will burn your leg." His voice filled with venom, cutting through the stillness like a dagger.

"Soon your leg will be useless. After that I will burn your other leg. When I am done, you will never walk again." He raced toward the clay stove.

The viciousness of his statement unhinged Birch. His downcast head snapped up. "Stop!" Blood drained from his face. His eyes were wild with fright. "Wait." The exclamation caused his voice to crack. "I'll…I'll tell—"

"Birch, don't—"

"I can't let him—"

"Tell me. Now!" Jackal faced Danny, the iron ruler high in the air.

"One thousand," Birch blurted out.

"One…" The ruler dropped to the floor with a thud. The little man looked like he'd seen a ghost. Staggering back a few steps, he changed into a different person: pathetic and crushed. The madness vanished. So did his spirit. He leaned against the wall, his head hung low, upper body hunched forward. His mouth twitched, seemingly on the verge of a sob. Then he murmured something in Japanese as if he was praying.

Before long, his evil spirit crept back. In a whoosh of anger, he took several huge steps and picked up the ruler. "Is that the right number?" Facing Danny, he lifted it over his head.

"Why ask"—Danny's voice was no more than a whisper—"if you don't believe us?"

"*Baka,*" Jackal barked. A muscle flicked at his jaw, his eyes bulged. "Goddamned Americans."

Neither Danny nor Birch understood the sudden feebleness and outburst of rage. They had no idea how devastating this false information might seem to the enemy. The day before, August 6, the U.S. Army Air Force had detonated the first atomic bomb over Hiroshima, causing widespread destruction and hundreds of thousands of deaths. If one nuclear bomb had destroyed a city, one thousand would wipe Japan from the face of the earth forever.

Ignoring Birch's wail of protest, Jackal sent the iron ruler down onto Danny's leg again.

Chapter 8

▬ ▬ ▬ ▬ ▬ ▬ ▬

"They're going to kill us," Mr. Ding exclaimed. "All of us." It was three days after the airmen's interrogation. He was standing before the front window of the cell. Anxiety shadowed his face as he twirled around. His eyes looked shocked behind his broken glasses.

"How do you know?" Captain Zhang lifted his head.

"I just heard it." Mr. Ding hitched his chin toward the outside. Early morning sunlight poured through the cracks of the boarded-up window. "The guards were talking."

"They said, 'Kill all?'" the captain asked again, straightening up. He moved toward Mr. Ding.

"I think so. My Japanese is limited. But I think I understood."

"I'm not surprised," Danny said. He was sitting on the floor, his face tense. "This won't be the first or the last time."

Zhou Ming joined the conversation, standing with his feet planted slightly apart and hands in his pants pockets. "After they invaded Nanking, the Japs killed thousands of people, including surrendered soldiers."

"Three hundred thousand," Birch confirmed. He sat slouching on the floor next to Danny. His uniform concealed most of his wounds, but cuts were visible at the bottom of his chin and under his left eye.

"Both my father and brother were killed during the massacre. They were—" Zhou Ming swallowed a few times, trying to talk, yet the words died on his lips.

Danny had heard the story before, and he nodded in sympathy. Like Zhou Ming, his father and brother had worked for the Nationalist Army. Their regiment had been ordered to defend Nanking and later to surrender. Nearly everyone in the battalion had died, some during the fight, but most after laying down their arms. Zhou Ming learned that they'd been tied up in lines, chased into the Yangtze River, and machine-gunned by the Japanese. Thousands of bodies floated downstream, turning the water red for days.

"Not long before we were…" Loath to use the word "captured," Danny faltered, then cleared his throat and continued. "I read a report. One hundred and fifty American POWs in the Philippines were killed." *Burned alive,* he added grudgingly in his mind.

As the likelihood of defeat loomed closer, the Japanese had sunk into madness. They'd turned to frantic acts of rage and bloodshed in parts of China and other Asian countries. *A massacre could come about as an outburst of the vengeance-seeking Japs like Jackal,* Danny thought. *Or it could unfold as a matter of higher order.* That disturbing prospect deepened the furrow between his brows.

"I don't want to die before…" Mr. Ding's face turned pale. He stood rigidly, his hands clasped in front of him. Six months earlier he'd been arrested as a communist resistant when the Japanese traced some anti-Japanese pamphlets to his classroom. To this day, he refused to admit responsibility. "My wife was pregnant when…" His voice cracked. He leaned back to the window frame as if pushed by an invisible hand. "I don't even know whether I have a son or a daughter…"

"We can't sit around and wait to be slaughtered like lambs," Captain Zhang said. His uplifted eyebrows and darkened long scar emphasized his fiery spirit. He shook the sturdy boards that bolted their window. "Either we break for it or wait to die."

"What can we do?"

The question hung in the air. No one had an answer. They'd never been allowed outside the compound except for a few times when the Japanese forced them to repair roads or dig trenches. Heavily armed forces surrounded them. There was no way to escape.

Back and forth the captain paced as everyone watched. Minutes ticked by. Except for his steps, there was no sound. The silence in the room was nerve-racking.

Abruptly Captain Zhang stopped pacing and turned to the American. "Dan Ni, you're wounded the worst. Tonight, call out. Act as if you're getting worse. Obviously, we'll play along. Tell the guard you know more about the atomic bomb, whatever the hell that is, and that you're willing to give them more information in exchange for treatment. Hopefully, in the middle of the night, the stupid guard won't think before he opens the door."

Trying hard to judge the feasibility of the plan, no one said anything.

After a pause, Mr. Ding aired his opinion: "It's not much, but it's worth a try. Let's do it. Tonight." His pale face was suddenly infused with color. "Worse to worse, the guard won't care. But with any luck, he might be curious enough to open the door."

"On second thought," Captain Zhang lifted his right index finger, "hold off until tomorrow night. Let's pray they won't start killing today."

"Why wait?"

"Haven't you noticed? It'll be School Boy's turn tomorrow. He's good to Danny. We'll have a better chance."

"Good call." Mr. Ding patted the captain on his back.

Murmurs filled the cell, hope brightening the bleak mood.

"But right off the bat," Danny spoke up, "you have to promise not to kill him. All of you." Sitting on the floor and leaning against the mud-brick wall, he looked haggard and worn. His right hand went to his pants pocket, touching the medical bottle given to him by the guard. There were still a few pills left. In the past six weeks, a strange connection had formed between him and School Boy. The young guard had stopped to talk from time to time and offered fruits and candies in secret. His ability to communicate in English had improved dramatically.

All eyes turned to Danny.

The captain muttered a foul curse. "Why?" His thick eyebrows furrowed. Everyone in the room mirrored his baffled expression.

"We can't use his kindness then abuse it. I won't do it unless you all agree."

"You're joking, right?"

"I'm dead serious. Don't have time—"

"You've got that right. We've got no time to play priests or monks. He's our enemy." Captain Zhang dismissed Danny's request with an impatient wave. "He will kill you if he's ordered to. He won't hesitate—"

"And I won't think twice to fight back. But that's not a man's way."

"Not a man's way…" growled the captain in frustration. "When have they acted like men? I can't believe what you're suggesting after what Jackal did to you and Birch." He folded his arms across his chest. "Why do we have to follow useless rules and morals when they don't?" Shifting his weight from one leg to the other, he glared at Danny.

Mr. Ding sided with Captain Zhang and quoted a proverb. "'Deal with a man as he deals with you.' An eye for an eye. That's fair."

"No. We're not animals," Danny said without averting his eyes from the captain's glare. "If we do what they do, then we're no different than them. Killing School Boy—"

"Danny is right," interrupted Birch. "Killing the boy would be ruthless. He's just a kid. Let's tie him up."

"A bullet from a kid is as deadly as any other bullet." Captain Zhang shrugged, showing his distaste.

Zhou Ming turned his death stare on the captain and moved closer to the two pilots. "Who gives you the right to call the shots? The Nationalist is the leader of this war."

All at once, several men in Nationalist Army uniforms followed suit and stood next to Zhou Ming. A line split the room—the Nationalists versus the Communists.

"Communism is the future of China," retorted Captain Zhang. "We'll fight all capitalists, and we'll win. Mark my words."

Zhou Ming took a long stride toward the captain, closing the gap between them. His fists clenched at his side.

Birch waved his arm, struggling to sit up. "We're in this prison cell together." He pulled the hem of Zhou Ming's uniform, forcing him to back away, and then shifted his focus to the captain. "School Boy is kind to Danny."

"The war is near its end. He's trying to find a better way out."

"Still, not all of them are like him." Birch's eyes were weary, but his chin lifted with resolve. "My father has never tortured or mistreated the soldiers he's captured, even after the deaths of my mom, my sister, my cousin, my aunt, and my uncle."

Most of the prisoners in the room nodded.

"All agreed?" Danny wanted to make sure.

"Yes," they chorused.

Reluctantly the captain went along. "I hope you're not making a mistake. You may end up like the stupid Mr. Dong Guo. Sympathy toward an enemy can be deadly."

Danny looked puzzled. Born in a missionary family, he'd lived in China for several years when he was a boy. His Chinese was excellent, especially after being friends with Birch for three years. Nevertheless, he had no clue what the captain was talking about. "Who is Mr. Dong Guo?"

"Wait." Birch lifted his index finger and turned to Captain Zhang. "That's not a fair comparison. The wolf was never friendly to Mr. Dong Guo, but School Boy has been kind to Danny."

He turned back to the American. "As you know, we have a lot of sayings in Chinese. Some are based on historical events, others come from fables. You have to learn the stories behind them in order to understand the phrases. In this idiom, Mr. Dong Guo was a gentle scholar. He saved an injured wolf from hunters. But—"

"But as soon as the hunters left, the wolf turned to eat the poor man." Mr. Ding finished the story.

"The lesson is to never show sympathy or mercy to an enemy. He'll strike back."

"I'm not Mr. Dong Guo." Danny burst into a hearty laugh. "But if we kill School Boy, he'd be the poor man, and I'd be the deceitful wolf. That's my point."

Another awkward silence descended on them.

Zhou Ming cleared his throat. "But how can we get out of the compound? Even if we get out of the cell, the place is surrounded by barbed-wire. And don't forget the watchtower and the machine guns…"

Outside a dog barked. The sound of its howling sent a chill into the gloomy room.

"Not to mention the German shepherds," Zhou Ming added.

"It won't be easy. Many will end up dead. But at least we die trying." Captain Zhang pointed to the left of their cell. "Here, I noticed the wires are in poor shape."

Danny raised an eyebrow. He was amazed that the captain had paid close attention to the environment and contemplated a prison break.

"Start around midnight." Captain Zhang ordered. "The darkness is our friend. The bastards might be too sleepy to walk straight or shoot anyone." One corner of his lips tilted upward in a half smile.

"Where will we go? Just run?" asked Zhou Ming.

"Run like hell. The rest is up to God."

"We're northeast of Dashan," said Birch, pointing to the direction of the town. "Just so you know, we may want to avoid—"

"The town is still under the enemy's boot," Danny cut in. "At least that was the case six weeks ago."

Captain Zhang nodded. "Let the others know. They must be prepared." He motioned to the other five cells in the small prison. "Whoever takes out the waste bucket today, pass the word around. No sleep tomorrow night. Now, let's talk details. The more we're prepared, the better."

The guerilla leader had that an air of authority. Even here, he liked to be in charge.

Chapter 9

▬ ▬ ▬ ▬ ▬ ▬ ▬

The odds of success were slim. They might all die. But they knew that they must risk everything instead of waiting to be slaughtered.

Most of the prisoners were fighters—Nationalist soldiers, Communist guerrillas, spies, political prisoners, and an American pilot.

Danny knew that his chance of success was compromised by his wounds. They had healed enough to enable him to limp before the beating, but now his wound was covered with congealed blood and pus. He knew he couldn't run fast enough to get away from the Japanese soldiers that would surely be following hot on their heels, and he was afraid that his infirmity would slow Birch's progress. He wanted to tell his wingman to go ahead without him, but he knew that Birch would never leave him behind.

As usual, Danny didn't show his concern. At dinnertime, he nearly gagged on the watery rice. "With every mouthful of this disgusting swill, I crave Xiao Mei's porridge."

Birch drank the soupy rice from a canteen cup without looking at it. "She uses chopped pork, chopped chicken, mushrooms, ginger, green onions, and century egg—your favorite!"

"But the first thing I'm going to do when we get out of here is order a big juicy steak!" Hunger had become an unrelenting condition, like a shadow that followed them, and food was their consistent topic. The tall American had lost over thirty pounds during six weeks of captivity.

"How about Nanking Salted Duck?" Birch's angular face was more defined than ever. His uniform looked baggy over his once-athletic frame.

"Awesome! But my favorite is Roasted Duck." Danny licked his lips as if savoring the taste. Three years earlier, he'd had this dish for the first time at his birthday party, and Xiao Mei, the housemaid, had prepared the dish whenever the two brothers returned home.

"She told Dad we were like *E hu xia shan—Hungry Tigers coming down the mountain.*"

"Isn't that the truth? I bet the nickname will stay with her forever."

"She was so happy when you raved about her cooking. She—"

"Hey, forget about Mary. You should marry Xiao Mei instead. In this way, we'll have delicious food for the rest of our lives," Danny teased. A smug grin turned his mouth up in amusement. Then he looked serious, his eyes focused on Birch. "You know she's crazy about you, don't you?"

Although Danny had met the maid only a few times, he liked her. Xiao Mei might not be the most gorgeous girl in the world, but she was sweet and kind. And he'd noticed the way she gazed at Birch. He knew that look—he'd seen the same look from both Jasmine and Daisy when they stared at him.

"Marry Xiao Mei? You're joking, right? She probably thinks of me as a Big Brother. We've known each other almost ten years. She's like a sister. Even her name says so." Xiao Mei meant Little Sister. "You of all people," Birch added, setting the canteen cup down on the floor, "should understand."

Danny nodded. His mind fogged with the memory of Daisy. Her sweet smile, the admiration in her shiny eyes, the pink scarf gathered around her slender neck. And the sheer terror that appeared on her angelic face as the Japanese soldiers surrounded her. He knew that Daisy had loved him. But to Danny, she was a little girl, and his heart was already taken. Still, she had given her life for him, just like Jasmine. Whenever he thought of the sweet young woman, he felt sad and guilty that he couldn't love her the same way he'd loved

Jasmine. "May I stay in Daisy's room next time we go home?"

Birch was caught off guard.

"I could smell Jasmine's scent each time I stayed in her room. I'm afraid I'll forget..." Complicated emotions squeezed his throat shut.

"Daisy would be honored." Tears welled in Birch's eyes.

After dinner, a loud commotion outside the room brought everyone except Danny to the window. Through the space between the boards, Birch watched in horror at the scene unfolding in the courtyard. The sun had already slipped behind the mountains, and the red streaks in the sky looked like blood. In the fading light, a prisoner knelt on the ground, his hands tied behind his back. In front of him, Jackal shouted as he raised a Samurai sword with both hands. "Who is the ringleader? Tell me! I will count to three. One..."

Horrible screams came from the prisoner's mouth. The blood-curdling sound cut through the twilight like a knife. He was in his late teens. Fear glazed his wild eyes as he pleaded for his life.

"Two..."

Jackal moved behind the prisoner and steadied himself, his legs spread apart. The sword swished as he took a couple of practice swings.

"I've told you everything I know. Please!" The prisoner shrieked at the top of his lungs. Panic twisted his face into a mask of terror.

"Three!" Jackal barked. After pausing for a beat, he raised the sword in a long arc, brought the blade down, and cut off the boy's head.

The screeching stopped. The head fell onto the ground and rolled a few turns. The body lingered for a moment, suspended in an upright position, and then toppled over.

The courtyard grew quiet. Eerily quiet.

Wincing at the viciousness, Birch felt sorry for the boy and sad for the loss of a young life.

"Goddamned traitor!" Captain Zhang growled as he punched the wall with his fist. Bits of dirt fell off the wall. "Now our plan is down the drain."

The loathing in the captain's voice caused Birch to glance at the headless body, and at the ground now damp with fresh blood. Then he turned to the captain. "He was just a kid. He didn't deserve to die—not this way."

"But he was a man, a Chinese. At least he was until he lost his balls. Coward!"

Birch understood why the captain hated traitors with such intensity. The Japanese had long ago put a price on his head. For seven years, with the help of ordinary people, the guerilla leader had managed to escape capture. Only a year ago, a traitor, a man in his group, had given him up under torture. Ambushed during his last mission, the Japanese had beaten him relentlessly. To the Japanese, Captain Zhang was a hated and feared man.

Although Birch respected the man's bravery and his invaluable contribution, he couldn't agree with his attitude toward the young prisoner. With leaden steps, he walked back from the window, unwilling to argue or look upon the poignant scene again.

Sitting on the floor against the wall, Danny tilted his head and asked, "Someone was killed?"

Birch nodded, still absorbed in his anguish and thought.

"What happened? Captain Zhang looks angry."

"The Japs learned of our plan. Not sure how it happened. The poor kid is dead."

"What will they do to us?" asked Danny.

With a sense of premonition, Birch sank to the floor next to Danny. From the way they'd treated the young prisoner, he could not pretend optimism about their future. "We'll find out soon," he said solemnly.

Chapter 10

▬ ▬ ▬ ▬ ▬ ▬ ▬

Along with a few of his men, Jackal stormed into the cell. His saber, still dripping blood, was in his right hand. The front of his uniform was stained with red spots. "I know your plan. I know one of you organized it, though I am not sure which one. Too bad I do not have time to find out." A muscle twitched in his jaw as his flat face twisted with fury. Then his mouth curved in a vicious sneer, as if he'd stumbled upon something amusing. "No problem. I have a better way. To punish your bad behavior, half of you will be executed tomorrow." Lifting a flattened hand to his throat, he made a slashing gesture.

He counted. Fourteen men. "If fewer than seven step out of the room tomorrow morning when I open the door"—his slanted eyes circled the cell—"everyone will be killed. No questions asked. So fight. Or bet. Do whatever you like. One out of every two in this room will be dead tomorrow. Compete for your chance."

He burst into a malicious laugh. "The war is about to end: too bad for you." His laugh tore through the foul air. "Half of you will not see the end of it!"

His smirk vanished as fast as it had appeared. "A pity... You could all have lived had you not planned to escape." With that, he stalked out. His men followed him. The door banged shut behind them.

"Go to hell!" Captain Zhang yelled, waving his right arm after the Japanese. He spat on the ground, trampling the dirt. "Kill us all, you sick bastard; we'll die together!"

"No," said Danny, propped against the wall on the floor, his left leg stretched forward, his right one bent at the knee. "He means business. He *will* kill us all if we don't comply."

"Who's afraid of death? From the moment we started fighting, we expected it. I'm ready." Captain Zhang's eagle eyes panned the room. "No cowards here like that bloody traitor outside. If I find one, I'll kill him with my bare hands."

"'None can escape from death since ancient times,'" Mr. Ding quoted a famous saying. His attitude revealed a steadfast fortitude. "It's an honor to die for our country."

Zhou Ming butted in, "Remember the song?" He stood up straight and began to sing. Everyone followed him:

Use our flesh and blood.
Lay down our life.
Protect the country from the enemies.
Safeguard the freedom of our people.
We are a team made of iron.
We have brave hearts.

"Are you ready?" rumbled Captain Zhang after they finished singing. He punched his fist high into the air, revealing sweat-stained cloth beneath his armpits.

"Hell, yeah!" everyone shouted, except Danny. A collective determination to laugh in the face of death seized the group.

"Have you heard the Chinese saying, 'Beheading leaves only a scar as large as a bowl'?" The captain turned his gaze upon the American. His left hand circled his neck, indicating the size. "I'll be reborn as another warrior in twenty years." His stern face offered a rare smirk; the long scar on his cheek pulsated and darkened. "And I can't wait to be born again…as a fighter."

"No," Danny spoke up again. Leaning against the mud-brick wall, he tilted his head to face the group. His voice was calm and strong. "This life is important. No one knows for sure about the next one… if there is a next one…We can't waste an opportunity. Never give up a chance to live. The war is closer and closer to its end. Each day we live is one day closer to surviving this damned war. To be free again. To live a better life!"

He took a breath: "Germany has already surrendered. The Allies are winning. Even Jackal said so. You've seen his face. The atomic bomb, whatever that is, scares him. We're not far from freedom. Don't give up hope. Don't talk of death so easily. Half of us may have the chance to live."

Everyone stared at the American. His different viewpoint took them by surprise. The room grew quiet, and for a few moments not a sound was heard except thunder in the distance. The air was sultry and stale; a storm was sure to come.

Birch was the first one to break the silence. He was sitting next to his brother. "Danny is right." His voice was as steady as his companion's had been. "The next life is uncertain, but this life is in our hands. We shouldn't give up so easily."

He turned to Captain Zhang who towered over him. "Remember, once you told me, 'No heroes here, only survivors.' Well, this is not the time for being a hero or a martyr. We—"

"What right do we have to live at the sacrifice of others? We can't send our comrades to death," the guerilla leader retorted, a frown pulling at his lips. He waved his arm, dismissed the argument as if he were shooing away a fly. "No! We can't sacrifice others to save ourselves."

"We will not be sending our comrades to death. The Japs are to blame, not us. Don't let them win so easily." Birch looked long and hard at the captain before shifting his gaze to the other prisoners. "If half of us live—that's half a victory."

"The Japs will think of us as cowards if we let half—"

Using two fingers on each hand as quotation marks, Danny interrupted the captain. "'He who laughs last, laughs best.'"

"That's right," Birch said. "Half of us might laugh at them one day after the war."

Captain Zhang dropped his head and mulled over the idea for a moment. "So?" He lifted his head, swiveled around, and asked the group.

No one answered. But the slight nods from some showed the consensus.

"We don't even know if Jackal will keep his word," the captain grumbled, making his last attempt. "He may kill us all tomorrow, anyway."

"We'll find out soon enough, won't we?" Danny raised his broad shoulders in a devil-may-care shrug. "What do we have to lose by preparing for it?"

"Danny is right," Birch said. "Besides, I think Jackal will keep his plan. It'll be more fun for him to taunt us than to kill us."

More heads nodded in agreement.

Captain Zhang marched straight over to Zhou Ming, the Nationalist Army officer. "Let's fight for that chance." He assumed a combative stance.

Before the Japanese invasion of China, the Communists and the Nationalists were opponents and had fought each other vigorously since 1927. It was only the Japanese attack in 1937 that had brought the two sides together. They were temporary allies facing the same foreign enemy. Now the war against Japan was about to end. What would the two parties do? Who was going to rule the country? A civil war was a real concern in many people's minds. More than likely, the two sides would become adversaries again.

The other prisoners began to choose their opponents, using more civilized means to determine their fates.

Chapter 11

Danny turned to his wingman, but before he opened his mouth Birch held up his hand to forestall him. "Don't! Don't argue with me, Danny."

"Listen—"

"No, you listen. I'm the Big Brother. *Da Ge* has the final say. You call me *Da Ge*. Follow my order!"

"No, Birch. Hear me out—"

"Danny, don't argue. It's not negotiable. You're an American; this is not your war. You've done enough. The war is about to end. You can go home soon. So let me do my duty. Allow me to serve my country!"

"You're my sworn brother. It doesn't matter whose war or whose duty. What matters is who can survive, who has a better chance to get out of here." Danny took a deep breath. "Let's face it," he pointed to his left leg, "you know I don't have much chance of walking out of here."

"I can't. I can't let you..." Birch couldn't finish. No Big Brother would let his younger brother...or younger sister die in his place. He knew that he would not be able to endure more of the kind of guilt he'd suffered over Daisy's death. "I can't. I'm not strong enough."

"Yes, you are. Daisy had faith in you. So do I. You are a Tiger. We are both Tigers. But I have a broken limb."

Birch knew Danny was right. But he wouldn't admit it.

"Don't forget the plan," Danny said. "Look for Jasmine. Search for Jack, and all the others…"

Birch plowed his fingers through his overgrown crew-cut in exasperation. "It's *our* plan, not *my* plan. I can't do it alone."

"Don't do it alone. That would be too hard, too dangerous. Find someone to go with you." Seeing that Birch was about to protest, Danny hurried to add, "What about Linzi? He's a good boy. He's brave. He'll help you." Wang Linzi was one of the two survivors of the massacre in the small village.

"Linzi is a great, but he's not you. I can't do it without you."

"Of course you can." Danny paused. Then one corner of his mouth pulled into an impish grin. "If not, I'll haunt you in your dreams." He lifted his arms; his elbow bumped into Mr. Ding sitting next to him. "Oops, sorry," he said in Chinese before he turned back to Birch and wriggled his fingers like animal claws.

"It's not funny, Danny. Stop joking!"

"Sure as hell, you'll miss my jokes."

A whole lot more than your jokes! Birch couldn't imagine life without his friend. They were sworn brothers. And their friendship was cemented by their love for the two girls and the life-and-death experiences they'd shared. The young women had given their lives to save Danny. In a way, the American was a symbolic extension of the girls. As long as Danny was alive, Daisy and Jasmine were alive. Such Brotherhood filled the void in Birch's soul. How could he survive without this unique bond? Danny meant too much to him.

"Please! Don't do this," begged Birch, swallowing the dryness in his mouth. He felt a sharp pain in his chest, and it wasn't because of the wounds.

"Think about Mary. You're going to marry her once the war is over. You promised her to have half a dozen Little Tigers. Remember?" Danny waited a beat. In a matter of seconds, his expression changed. A mischievous sparkle came into his lustrous eyes. "Or perhaps, you'll take my advice," he teased with a wry chuckle, "and you'll marry Xiao Mei instead. Who knows? After all, her dishes are to *die* for."

"Be serious, Danny. What about your sister? What about your mom and dad? They haven't seen you for three years. They're waiting for you to come home. How can you let them down? Susan will hate me forever if—"

"If I had a better chance, I'd use it. But—"

"Then let's die together. We've vowed to die on the same day." Birch quoted the pledge. "'Though not born on the same day of the same month in the same year, we merely hope to die on the same day of the same month in the same year.' Remember?" A frisson of excitement brightened his eyes. "This opportunity is a godsend. Let's give the chance for life to someone else."

Sworn brotherhood was an ancient Chinese tradition. Highly influenced by *Romance of the Three Kingdoms*, a classic novel, many young men dreamed of having such ultimate fraternal loyalty. After Danny had been rescued by Jasmine and Daisy, and safeguarded him with their lives, the two men had become sworn brothers. Together they fought the unbearable pain that neither could endure alone.

"Remember the twist I added?" Danny put his hand on Birch's shoulder. "If one survives, he will live for both."

A lump formed in the back of Birch's throat. He aimed a withering look at Danny. A morose mask covered his features. To hide his emotions, he leaned forward, planted his elbows on his knees, and shielded his face with his hands.

Danny cracked a light-hearted smile. "See, I'm letting you do the hard work. After all, you're the Big Brother, as you remind me every day, so you will have to deal with it." His gold-flecked, brown eyes gleamed with wicked wit from the watchtower's light that sneaked through the cracks of the bolted window shutter.

Birch dragged his hands over his face and lifted his head. The gesture did nothing to rub the anguish from his features. "Goddammit, Danny!" he grunted, reeling with frustration.

"Okay," Danny conceded. "Let's simply toss a coin in the morning. That'll be fair and square."

Birch nodded. But in his mind he was already plotting: *I'll block his way. No matter what happens, I'll step out first. I'm faster.*

Da Ge, Big Brother, was a title bestowing a father-like authority and the responsibility that came with it. A Big Brother was expected to take care of younger siblings. Birch had already failed his younger sister and cousin. *I won't make another horrible mistake,* he vowed. He would give his life to protect his brother. That was the promise he'd made to himself.

"Then it's settled…" Danny seemed content. Holding onto the wall, he stood up slowly and limped to the waste bucket.

Chapter 12

━ ━ ━ ━ ━ ━ ━

"I live in the town of Dashan," Mr. Ding said as he propped himself against the wall. Apparently he'd lost the bet. "If anybody survives this ordeal, please send a message to my family. It's easy to find them. Ask anyone at the high school; they'll tell you. I'm the only history teacher there. Let my wife know…." His voice trailed off.

Then he cleared the hoarseness from his throat. "I hid some money at the bottom of her favorite flower pot. It doesn't belong to our family. It…" He hesitated for a moment and then cracked an awkward smile. "Well, at this point, it doesn't matter who finds out, does it? I'm a member of the Communist Party." He pushed up his slipping eyeglasses, his youthful face stern and proud. "The fund belongs to our party. Tell my wife to give it back. And tell her…" He swallowed hard before continuing, "If we have a son, let him fight the Japs when he grows up. If it's a girl, train her as a nurse so that she can save our soldiers' lives."

Everyone listened in silence. At that moment, it didn't matter who was Communist or Nationalist.

Storm clouds loomed above, turning the sky an ominous black, robbing any light the moon might have offered. Now and then the searchlight shone through the gaps of the barred window. An air of melancholy settled upon them.

Danny returned with two canteen cups. "Too bad we don't have any rice wine." He handed one cup to his wingman and raised his. "To the best Big Brother!"

Birch clinked his cup against Danny's. "Happy…happy birthday to you, *Hao Xiong Di—good brother!*" he said, forcing a lighter tone into his voice.

Danny's thirty-first birthday would be in three days. Now they knew they wouldn't celebrate it together. Birch wanted to express his best wishes while he still had the opportunity. He mustered a faint smile, but his soulful eyes betrayed his inner turmoil. He had so much to say to his younger brother. But tears filled his throat. *I'm honored to be your brother. It's been such a privilege to fly with you, to fight together. I pray to God that we'll meet again in Heaven or in another world, like you said.*

Tilting his head, Birch emptied the cup in one long gulp. "If…I'm just saying—" His Adam's apple bobbed a couple of times to accommodate a painful swallow. "If I saw Jasmine, what would you like me to tell her…other than you love her?"

"Tell her to wait for me. I'll see her soon." Danny gave a firm nod.

Their eyes locked and held for a long time.

Even in the dim light, Birch detected an odd flicker in Danny's eyes. *An unspoken message? Profound love too keen to name?* He stared at those gold-brown eyes, wishing to God he could deliver the heartfelt message to Jasmine.

Danny turned to the others in the room. "Hey, why don't we all introduce ourselves in more detail? Like Mr. Ding said, if anyone survives, he should try to get in touch with the families. Let our loved ones know what we want to tell them."

Flattening his back against the wall, Zhou Ming stood up. Evidently, he'd lost his fight. "I'm from Chungking. My mother is the only one left in our family." His voice trembled. The lanky officer looked frail in the eerie light. Within seconds, he yanked himself back into control and gave the hem of his uniform a tug. "She lives…"

Birch bowed out of the conversation, knowing he couldn't deliver the messages. He sat there thinking about his father. *What can I say to ease his pain?*

He wanted to thank his dad for raising him as a strong man. He'd followed his father's footsteps in his career as a military professional. His decision to become a fighter pilot had surprised everyone. Although he'd always been athletic and competitive, his demeanor was more that of a scholar. It was his admiration for his father that had drawn him to this path. Yet such a notion would only cost his father more grief.

What will happen to Dad? Daisy is dead. Mom is gone. Jasmine's whole family was killed. His father would be all alone with no family member. Birch knew Xiao Mei would take good care of his dad. The housemaid was like a family member. But one day she'd grow up and get married. She'd have her own family to look after. *Then who will be with Dad?*

Birch wiped his forehead and his fingers came away wet. He felt sad for his father. Try as he might, he couldn't find the right words. In the end, a simple "I miss you, and I hope you'll be proud of me" was all he decided to say.

Before his turn came, though, he felt drowsy. The voices in the room turned fuzzy, and sounded far away from him. *What the hell is wrong with me?* Was it because of the rumble of thunder drowning out the conversation? He rubbed his eyes with the heels of his palms, trying to stay awake.

This was their last night. Every moment was precious. Birch wanted to stay up all night to talk to Danny. He had no intention of wasting even a second. *I've never told Danny he's the best brother, as he keeps telling me.*

Nevertheless, his eyelids grew heavy. His mind became cluttered. He slumped onto the floor. Soon he was fast asleep.

Chapter 13

— — — — — — — —

Birch awoke from a deep sleep. He struggled to open his eyes. It took him a few blinks to bring the world into focus. When he spotted half a dozen people in the room, he asked abruptly, "Where's Danny?"

He tried to stand up, but his head started spinning and he took a moment to let the dizziness pass. Flattening his hand on the wall to stabilize himself, he asked again. Anxiety gnawed at him. *Are they interrogating Danny again? Torturing him?*

"Gone," said one of the men. The darkness of the day shaded his face.

"Where?" Birch rushed to the window. *His leg isn't healed. Where are they taking him?* Peering through the slats, he searched for any sign of Danny outside. His nerves tingled in anticipation of seeing the American's tall frame.

Nothing except the dark sky, muddy ground, and thunder echoing off the distant mountains. He dashed to the rear window. All he could see were the heartbreaking forget-me-nots and the dense forests. Wind tossed fallen leaves and twigs.

"What happened?" Birch demanded.

"Seven stepped out, including the American," Captain Zhang hissed through his teeth, shooting Birch a dirty look.

"No!"

The captain didn't say it out loud but his accusing look spoke volumes. His eyes brimmed with reproach.

"This morning?" Birch remembered everything now. Looking outside, he tried to see what time it was, but the bruised sky obliterated the sunlight. "What time is it?" he asked as though he might catch up with his brother if it was early enough.

"Late afternoon."

"What?" Birch's heart wrenched. He hadn't kept his word. He hadn't given his younger brother the opportunity to live. *I didn't even say goodbye.* "Danny!" he screamed through the window.

The only reply was a clap of thunder, the imminent storm moving closer and closer. Silver streaks of lightning carved the gloomy sky. The windows and the door rattled with each strong gust of wind.

Unshed tears burned his throat. Soon his voice cracked, drowned by the growls of the merciless storm. Birch felt paralyzed by the misery as the world squeezed the life out of him.

What did I do? How could I oversleep? He was responsible and punctual to a fault. He'd never been late for anything. *How could this have happened?* These questions made him grip the planks even harder. Splinters of the rough wood stuck into his palms and fingers. When he turned around, his face was contorted into a haunting expression of agony.

He rushed back to the place they had slept, searching for anything that Danny might have left behind. On top of the straw bed lay the white scarf. The blood-stained scarf was folded, apparently left on purpose. He grabbed the scarf as if he were hugging his dear friend. Once he lifted it, he saw a small bottle. It was the pain reliever. Birch picked it up and felt the emptiness of the bottle. The answer came to him in a sudden moment of clarity—Danny had drugged him with the potent medicine. His brother had planned to make him oversleep and safeguard him from the start.

He gave the opportunity of living to me!

Now Birch understood the longing in Danny's eyes.

He was saying goodbye to me!

The profound love was for him, not for Jasmine as he'd assumed.

"Damn you, Danny!" He buried his face into the silk scarf to stifle his cries. "How could you do this? You're the younger brother!"

Image after image rolled through his head. Danny's carefree smile, his gold-flecked brown eyes gleaming with wicked wit, his confident strides toward his P-40, his tall frame sitting proudly in the cockpit while giving Birch the thumbs-up sign. A thousand memories dragged Birch into the past.

Closing his eyes, he could hear Danny calling him *Da Ge* and telling him that he was the best Big Brother.

What kind of Big Brother am I?

Grief and guilt joined force to create an emotional tornado that crashed his spirit to the ground.

Chapter 14

▬ ▬ ▬ ▬ ▬ ▬ ▬

"Dig. Dig!" Jackal shouted, spewing saliva. The rainstorm two days earlier had finally cooled the sweltering heat, but a sheen of perspiration clung to his forehead despite the comfortable temperature. He swung his Samurai sword and yelled again, "Dig, faster! This is for the final fight."

Surrounded by armed Japanese soldiers, the prisoners were forced to dig a trench not far from the compound. The starved, emaciated men worked as fast as their worn bodies were able. When the trench was large enough, without warning, Jackal thrust his sword into a young man's back. Before anyone could react, the soldiers opened fire on the prisoners.

Birch sucked in a harsh breath while bullets hammered into him. The pain was more excruciating than he could describe. He fell hard, and all the air rushed out of his lungs as he hit the ground.

Screams, mingled with animal-like whimpers, ripped at the morning's chilly air. He realized that some of the sounds came from his own throat. His head was bleeding. His right leg didn't seem to belong to himself. His body hurt in more places than he could count. Blood covered him and soaked through the white scarf around his neck. He lay breathless in the trench. Someone collapsed on top of him. Captain Zhang? The guerilla leader had been standing next to him when the shooting began. In time, his body turned numb.

Screams, cries, and more gunshots surrounded him. Dirt scattered on the part of his body that wasn't covered by Captain Zhang. He heard Jackal shouting and exhorting his men to finish off the wounded. His sword slashed up and down, its bloodstained blade thrusting into the dying bodies. Captain Zhang jerked on top of Birch when more bullets hit him.

Through half-opened eyes he watched his fellow inmates sprawled upon the dirt. The sickening odor of blood and gunpowder assaulted his nostrils. Expecting to be shot again, he braced himself for death.

Yet in chaos he felt an unusual peace. Soon he would follow Danny. Before long, he would discover if there was a Heaven. He wished to see Daisy there. He hoped to see Jasmine. His mom would greet him. Birch missed his loved ones and now longed for death. The pain and guilt he'd suffered in the past was killing him anyway. Not a second had passed that he wasn't plagued by turbulent emotions. Instead of dying slowly, now his life would end in an instant. And dying on Danny's birthday was altogether appropriate.

A great weight was lifted off his shoulders and chest. No more pain of missing his loved ones. No more guilt for killing his sister. No more regret about his brother's death. Soon he would be free.

Lying on the blood-saturated ground, Birch closed his eyes, letting his body go and his mind drift. Beneath the captain's dead weight, he sensed himself floating upward into the warmth of sunlight, as if he were flying.

The best time of his life had been spent flying with Danny by his side. They'd soared countless times on beautiful days like today.

Danny?

Then Birch remembered his promise: he would find his best friend. The odds for Danny's survival were next to zero. But what if he had somehow survived Jackal's brutality? No one had seen his body yet. And even if Danny were dead, Birch had vowed to find his remains and bring his body back to America. The idea of finding Danny, alive or dead, had kept him going the past two days. He had to search for Jasmine, too, and for Jack, and for the other dead airmen, just as he and Danny had planned.

Daisy had said that I never made a promise that I wouldn't fulfill. Look at me. I let Daisy down. I let Danny take my place. This is my last chance. Fight! Survive! Fulfill those promises. Don't let Danny down again. He'd want me to survive. To find Jasmine. To bring him and Jack home. Do it. For Danny. For his parents. For Susan.

And for Mary...

Birch planned to marry her as soon as the war was over. He thought about the ring in his pocket. It had belonged to his mother; his father had given it to him after her death. Birch had sewn it into the breast pocket of his uniform where it would be safe and always be with him. He was ready to marry the only girl he'd ever loved.

He had to survive until the day he could take Mary's hands in his, to hold her in his arms. Her striking figure in a carmine red dress appeared in his mind. He remembered he'd burned with desire when she leaned against his chest. *We haven't even made love yet. I promised her to have half a dozen Little Tigers.* He couldn't let her down. He was her Perfect Tiger.

By now the screams and the cries had subsided. The area was eerily quiet. Only occasionally did a breeze rattle the birch leaves and sigh in the high branches of the pines.

Then, a swarm of flies came, making a repulsive buzzing sound. Gathering the last strength he could muster, willing his courage to sustain him, Birch stretched out his arms. He tried to free himself from Captain Zhang's lifeless form, hoping to crawl out of the grave. His right hand moved only a few inches before the movement awakened his numbed body. A sharp pain radiated from the wound below his right collarbone and sent shivers through his body. He moaned in agony.

As darkness whirled at the edge of his mind, he heard footsteps approaching. He fought for consciousness. Were the Japanese returning to bury them? *No!*

But Birch didn't get the chance to find out. He fainted.

Chapter 15

▬ ▬ ▬ ▬ ▬ ▬ ▬

Mary was brimming with joy—Birch was coming home. It had been over two months without a word from him. The last time they were together was a few days before his most recent assignment. Both his and Danny's planes had gone down during the mission. No one knew what had happened to them. Injured? Captured? Killed? She'd been out of her mind with worry. Now, she was elated that he was coming home alive.

Mary put on the carmine red dress that Birch had given her on her twenty-third birthday. The elegant outfit accentuated the curves of her feminine frame. She marveled at his good taste when she studied her striking figure in the mirror. Leaning closer to the glass, she reapplied a fresh coat of lipstick, touched up her makeup, sprayed more perfume, and fluffed her hair. *Got to be at my best in front of the Perfect Tiger.*

Her name was Ma Li, a translator at the commander's office, but she preferred to be called Mary since she communicated with the Americans regularly. A small beauty mark on her right cheek created a permanent dimple and the illusion of a constant smile. For that, Birch had called her Sweet Mary.

With enthusiasm, she dashed out of her apartment. Her permed black hair bounced in loose waves, swaying behind her back.

The streets of Chungking were jammed with a sea of people. It was September 2, 1945. Earlier that day, Japan had signed a surrender document, officially ending the Second World War. Throughout the city, and probably the entire country, people shouted and waved, jumping up and down with unfettered joy. Firecrackers sizzled and popped; the booms rumbled like thunder. The smell of smoke permeated the air as if the area were on fire. It went on for hours. The entire city joined the spontaneous festivity with red banners, flags, gongs, and drums.

A girl with home-made flags of various colors handed a pink one to Mary. Attached to a thin bamboo stick, the flag's slogan read, "We won. The Japanese bandits lost."

Tumultuous cheers erupted when a bright yellow dragon paraded through the town center. Several dozen dancers moved this mythical creature in a wavy pattern. Mary beamed. Still holding the paper flag, she covered her ears and elbowed her way through the crowd.

Besides the victory, Mary had another reason to celebrate: she would be Mrs. Bai in no time. Birch had promised he would marry her as soon as the war was over. Before long, she would be the envy of the Air Force.

A Western wedding will be better than a traditional one. Her grin broadened when she imagined how fabulous she would look in a white bridal dress. *I should think about it in more detail.* The thought brought another frisson of excitement. When the crowd thinned, she twirled a few times as if she were waltzing. *Birch is an excellent dancer.* The memory of the New Year's Eve party they'd attended flooded her mind.

A few people nearby smiled at her. Some clapped. A young man with a big bundle of paper flowers walked over and offered her a red one. Mary blushed and took it.

The hospital was jammed with patients. It was as if she had stepped into a different world. The hallway was filled with temporary beds holding injured men. She heard moans, screams, and rapid orders from the nurses. An acrid smell of antiseptics and body odors permeated the air. Flies buzzed everywhere.

Mary caught a glimpse of a man on a stretcher as it passed.

His face was swathed in bandages except for his eyes, nose, and mouth. He was in a muddy, tattered Nationalist Army uniform. A young woman in a primrose yellow dress ran alongside, holding his hand, crying.

Mary stumbled sideways and shrieked when someone snatched her arm.

"Help me," a soldier in a bloody uniform begged. With the right hand clutching her forearm, he stretched his left arm to his thigh. "They told me I don't have my legs anymore. Why do I still feel them?" He groped with his hand as he stared at her with a vacant expression. "Are they there?"

Mary shook her head in disbelief. Both his legs were gone, and as she had just realized, he was blind. "I'm sorry." She jerked her arm free and fled.

Is Birch hurt like these men? Her pace slowed; her steps were not as steady. *No, not Birch,* she answered her own question. He'd been wounded before, and each time he'd bounced back in a few days. She chided herself for her insecurity, *He's my Perfect Tiger.* Birch's father, General Bai, had told her Birch had come home alive. *He hadn't said anything else.* Her smile returned by the time she opened the door to his private room.

But one glance at his face with black and blue bruises and the bandage around his cranium, and Mary lost her composure. The pink flag and the red flower dropped to the floor when her hands in white gloves flew to cover her mouth.

His eyes were closed, and he looked lifeless.

"Is he...all right?" she asked in a weak voice. The paper flower crumbled under her feet. "Can I talk to him? When will he wake?" The romantic images she'd dreamed of only moments earlier vanished like a puff of smoke. Worry replaced elation.

"Perhaps in a day or two... Maybe longer," said Dr. Deng, a silver-haired man. He glanced at the chart. The patient had been transferred from a military hospital in Yunnan. "It's also possible he'll never come out of the coma."

"Never?"

"The best window for a comatose patient to wake up is within seven days. It's been more than two weeks." The doctor turned his attention to the patient.

Mary rushed to Birch's side and snatched his hand. "Wake up, Birch!" she cried as she shook it. "You promised you would marry me. The war is over. You can't stay here. Wake up!"

The doctor lifted his arm. "If you can't contain yourself, you will have to leave the room."

Mary nodded, tears gathering in her eyes. She backed away a few steps. When the doctor removed the blanket, she gasped. Her cheeks turned paper white. His once muscular body was thin and covered with various bandages. Ugly, puckering scars crisscrossed the rest of his otherwise smooth chest. His right leg was gone.

Mary hurried to his side again. Lowering herself to one knee, she leaned over the bed. Her delicate features collapsed with grief. "Birch," she called in a tortured whisper. Sadness settled like a blanket over her as she caressed his cheek with her soft palm. Tears streamed from her eyes.

Staring at the still form of the man she loved, Mary had the urge to wrap her arms around his battered body. She wished her touch could magically return her Perfect Tiger to her.

The window was closed, but a pane of glass rattled as the noise tried to sneak inside. The festive atmosphere outside lay in a stark contrast to the gloominess she felt.

You've helped to win the war, Birch. Today is supposed to be joyous. You should be out there celebrating. Everyone is happy. Everyone except you and me…

The doctor sighed and thrust his hands into the pockets of his white lab coat as he waited impatiently. Unwilling to be scolded again, Mary straightened, put her hands over her face and fled. Leaning against the wall in the hallway, she bent forward as if someone had punched her in the stomach. *Birch!* A gut-wrenching sob broke from her as she silently called out his name. Her mind tumbled back to the day she'd first met Birch Bai.

Chapter 16

▬ ▬ ▬ ▬ ▬ ▬ ▬

Mary had heard of Birch before she met him. He was well-known—
the son of a high commander, one of the best fighter pilots in the
Air Force, and the wingman of the legendary Flying Tiger Danny
Hardy. The two airmen had undertaken many death-defying missions together, including flying over "the Hump," the eastern end of
Himalayan Mountains. Transporting military supplies from India
to China over "the Hump" was dangerous. They had to fly through
the world's worst weather over the world's highest mountains. There
was widespread acknowledgment: the only thing tougher than "the
Hump" was the men who flew over it. Both Birch and Danny were
the bravest of the brave pilots.

But the first time she'd met him, she saw a different side of this
courageous airman.

It was July 4, 1944. Mary was invited to sing at a celebration for
the American soldiers on their Independence Day. She'd graduated
from Stanford University a couple months earlier and then returned
home to become a translator at the headquarters of the Chinese Air
Force. With her soulful voice, she sang "Jasmine Flower," a popular
Chinese folk song. The audience cheered wildly, so she sang an
encore, an American song she'd learned in the U.S. The crowd was
ecstatic. Mary was sure she'd charmed half the men in the audience.

The other half had already been captivated by her beauty—she wore a lavender silk evening gown, with long white gloves, and a pair of black fabric high heels. She curtsied several times. With a satisfied smile, she turned, moving backstage with grace. Her curvy black hair danced around her shoulders.

And there he was: a broad-shouldered man with a straight nose and intense dark eyes standing tall and erect. He looked dashing in his Air Force uniform, a maroon leather gun belt bearing the Nationalist emblem cinched at his narrow waist, and a Chinese violin in his hand.

Mary caught a flicker of surprise on his face. Then he offered a sheepish smile. It was sweet and innocent, utterly different from the unabashed and lustful looks she was accustomed to seeing. He tipped his head before he marched onto the stage.

"Who is that handsome fellow?" asked Mary.

"You don't know? He's Major Bai Hua, a fighter pilot," answered a stagehand. "He's a real Tiger," he added, as if the zodiac sign actually summarized the man's traits. The tiger, the King of Beasts, was respected for its power and valor.

No wonder he carries himself with such confidence. Mary stood and listened to the music he was playing. Chinese violin was a tricky instrument. If done wrong, the sound was awful, like ducks quacking. But in a skillful hand, the music was so touching that it could bring tears to the listener's eyes. He received a thunderous reception.

Backstage she greeted him in English with a cheery lilt. "Hi, I'm Mary, a newly-hired translator at the HQ." She extended her hand.

"Birch Bai. Very pleased to meet you, Mary," he replied in English. Taking her gloved hand, he bowed and lightly touched the knuckles with his lips.

She was impressed, unable to hide her delight. Birch was the first Chinese young man who had done it properly. She looked up. His luminous eyes held her gaze like magnets.

And that had been the beginning of their romance.

When they were together, people turned their heads with envy and admiration. A tall, handsome man and a beautiful slender woman—they were an eye-catching couple and a perfect match.

They had the same interests in art, music, and literature. They spoke half in Chinese, half in English. Birch had spent a year training in the States, and Mary had lived in California for four years.

She loved to clasp his large hand—strong and always warm. She enjoyed being wrapped in his muscular arms, resting her cheek against the broad expanse of his chest. Most couples didn't dare to hold hands or hug. Chinese were wary of showing affection, even in private. But their western educations had encouraged them to be more expressive, and she'd always prided herself on being a modern woman.

Mary was crazy about Birch and called him the Perfect Tiger. *One moment he can fly a fighter plane as a fearless warrior. Another minute he can play an instrument in a way that moves his audience. What a fantastic combination! Where could I find a better man than Birch?*

Her parents warned her about the risk of his job. Mary dismissed them. Her Perfect Tiger was invincible. She'd seen his medals, read the reports, and witnessed the glory that surrounded him.

Besides, Chinese parents interfered with their children's lives too much. They were old-fashioned, too controlling. She wasn't about to allow it to happen to her. At age twenty-three, she was a grown-up.

The attractive pilot had swept Mary off her feet, so much so that a few days before his last mission, she hinted she wanted to make love with him. It was his thirty-first birthday.

"This is the best gift," he'd said, "but I can't…I can't…" He cradled her rosy face in his palms, eyes blazing. "We have to wait…until we're married." He swallowed hard. "There are certain rules we can't break, lines we can't cross."

Sensing her dismay, he added, "It won't take long. I'll be your Tiger, and yours only. Be patient; we'll have a lifetime together."

His dark, sensuous eyes turned to the pair of Tiger-head shoes for babies that she'd given him. "We'll make as many babies as you want," he said in a soul-filled voice as he placed a prolonged kiss on her forehead.

Mary turned her face to one side and laid her cheek against his shoulder. She flattened her right palm over his heart. He took a quick breath before scooping her into his arms. His nose brushed against her vanilla-scented hair. His hands caressed her back, moving up and down. She felt the heat of his touch. Judging from the rapid rise and fall of his chest and the fever in his eyes, she could tell how much he wanted her.

Mary lifted his left hand to her lips. One by one, she kissed his fingertips. Then she turned her head, picking up his right hand. This time, she kissed his knuckles. "Half a dozen," she murmured while she slipped her arms around his waist.

"Huh?" He seemed puzzled, preoccupied.

"I want half a dozen baby tigers, just like you."

"You have my word!"

Mary felt his hardened body as she pressed tightly along the length of his tall frame. When they separated, she heard his low growl of self-denial. Gazing up, she watched him holding his powerful body rigid with incredible self-control. A ghost of a smile flickered across his face.

Suddenly, Mary was embarrassed for putting Birch through this predicament. It dawned on her that her passion was only part of the motive. The other part was due to her insecurity—she wanted to "seal the deal." Her anxiety had disappeared once he'd promised to marry her.

Chapter 17

━ ━ ━ ━ ━ ━ ━

Wrenched sobs racked Mary's picture-perfect physique as she recalled their romantic encounters. The privileged young woman had never felt so helpless. They had dated for almost a year, although in truth they'd barely had time to meet once a month. And even when they were able to meet, their time together was often too short.

"Ma Li!" Through a mist of tears, she watched her parents rush toward her.

"Mom!" Mary cried out and flung herself into her mother's arms.

Mrs. Ma wore a tailor-made, turquoise cheongsam draped to her ankles. She patted Mary's back, concern etched upon her delicate face.

Nearby her father stood tall and rigid. Even in a dark blue suit and a silver tie, Ma Ning's upright posture bespoke the authority of a military commander. "General Bai told me—"

"What happened?"

Ma Ning's eyebrows furrowed, carving a deep vertical line. "Some farmers found Birch in an open mass grave. There were dozens of bodies. He's lucky. The Japs usually bury them after shooting them."

Mrs. Ma added, "Since the war was so close to the end, they left without—"

"He was unconscious but still breathing, so the farmers carried him to a military base."

"Dear God!" Mary swayed. The thought of Birch lying in a mass grave set off another round of shivers. Moments later, she asked, "Where is Danny? Is he okay?"

Ma Ning shook his head.

"Is he dead?" she pressed.

"Nobody knows for sure. Most likely, yes."

Mary sucked in a harsh breath. She knew how much the Flying Tiger meant to Birch.

"I warned you," said Mrs. Ma, wiping the tears from Mary's cheeks. "A man who goes off to war isn't the same when he comes back. Injuries, psychological trauma—"

"Survivor's guilt," her father added. Shadows fell upon his face.

"What should I do? I don't know how to take care—"

"Listen," her mother cut her off, "I'm sorry to say this, and I know it sounds cruel, but you must leave him."

"What? No! I can't. I love him. He's—"

"I understand." Mrs. Ma tucked a wayward strand of hair behind Mary's ear.

"Don't be a fool," her father grumbled, less patient.

"Listen to me, my child," said her mother, gripping Mary's shoulders. "I know you love him. Birch is an extraordinary young man. He's a rare find. If he weren't wounded so severely…" She faltered for a beat. "The reality is cold and hard. You have seen his injuries."

Her mother's words reminded her of his amputated leg. The Perfect Tiger was no longer picture-perfect. In fact, without a leg, he looked pitiful. *Even if he wakes, he'll be a cripple.* In the best-case scenario, she would live with his handicap for the rest of her life. And in the worst, he would remain in the coma. *He may never again talk to me, look me in the eye, or touch me…* A sense of doom threatened to overtake her as the enormity of his injuries hit her.

"Watch out," someone yelled as a stretcher went by. A white sheet with dark stains covered the body. A young woman walked alongside like a zombie, her hand still holding the dead man's limp hand.

Mary's jaw dropped. She recognized the primrose yellow dress. She lowered her head and chewed her bottom lip, trying to quell her anxiety.

Her silence invited her father to continue: "How do you plan to take care of him? Are you prepared to face a life-long hardship?"

"We're not talking about a day or two," her mother said. "We're talking about a lifetime."

"What about Birch?" Mary protested in a feeble voice. "He needs me."

"Life isn't always fair, Ma Li. You have to think of yourself, your life." Mrs. Ma paused to let the message sink in. "*Fu qi ben shi tong lin niao. Da nan lin tou ge zi fei.*"

"I don't usually like that saying," her father admitted, "but in this case, it makes sense. *Couples are birds in a forest; they fly away in separate ways when a disaster strikes.* You're not even his wife. Don't waste your life. Walk away before it's too late."

"No, I can't!" The thought of losing Birch forever released another downpour of tears.

The father expelled his frustration in a gust of breath, and Mrs. Ma parted her lips to speak. The couple traded helpless glances.

Just then, conversation in the next room broke the silence. "It's such a tragedy," said one voice. "I heard he's unable to have any children...even if he comes out of the coma. He may have trouble being with...a woman, you know?"

"Really?" came another voice. "That's so sad. Hopefully Dr. Deng will come up with a different diagnosis. Major Bai is a real hero. Too bad. Who's going to be with him...?"

Mary couldn't bear it any longer. *I'm so sorry, Birch.* She let out a desperate wail as her parents led her away. With her hands curled over her face, she didn't notice General Bai passing in the hallway.

Chapter 18

▬ ▬ ▬ ▬ ▬ ▬ ▬

General Bai sat at a redwood desk in his study. Bookshelves lined two sides of the room, filled with Chinese, English, and Japanese titles. A large map of China covered the wall behind him. Two scrolls of Chinese paintings of plum blossoms flanked the window on the left side. Morning sunlight poured in and shone on top of the cluttered desk where his elbows rested, his fingers squeezing his temples. The experience he'd had in the past few days had given him a headache.

It had been two weeks. Although Birch was receiving excellent care in the hospital, there was no sign he'd wake up any time soon. "I'm sorry," the chief administrator apologized. "There is not much we can do for Major Bai, other than wait. As you can see, we need more beds than we have." The man paused, readjusting his steel-rimmed glasses. "Is it possible to take your son home? We'll provide everything he needs." The administrator waited, and the father's silent consent prompted him to continue. "Forgive me, General, I'm afraid we can't offer a full-time nurse. But if you hire a caregiver, I promise we'll train her until we're sure she can take good care of him."

General Bai understood. With the end of the war, the hospital was flooded with people from smaller cities and towns. He'd already noticed the congested condition. Even the hallway was jammed with temporary beds. He was sympathetic to those less privileged patients—soldiers and civilians. Eight years of war had left the nation in shambles, wounded in more ways than he could count. Injury, disease, and starvation ravaged the country. "Give me a couple of days to arrange things," he complied.

But he'd had no idea that it would be so difficult to find help.

It wasn't normal for a man to be a live-in caregiver. All the women he'd interviewed had declined, once they understood Birch's condition. As a general, he could easily order his subordinates to do the job. But he refused the temptation.

He despised those individuals—government officials, military commanders—who wielded their powers for personal benefit. Sadly, such misconduct was widespread. And corruption was a major complaint that the Nationalist's government received from the ordinary people, who gravitated to the Communist's policy and promises. *How can I do what I look down on?* Besides, no soldier would be patient enough to care for a person in a coma.

To fend off the frustration, he pushed himself away from the desk, clasped his hands behind his back, and walked in circles around the room. Pressure was growing on the back of his skull. Worries made the lines on his forehead pronounced. As he paced, pounded by a headache, he spotted a small figure stepping into his study.

"Let me do it, General," said Xiao Mei.

"You?" General Bai drew up short. Glancing at the servant girl in a toffee brown apron and a leaf-green shirt, he shook his head. "You're just a girl. How can you take care of him?"

For centuries, physical contact between a man and a woman had been forbidden unless they belonged to the same family, although the custom had been relaxed in recent years when women joined the workforce.

"Nurses are girls."

"They're professionals. They're just doing their jobs."

"It is my job to take care of *Shao Ye*." Xiao Mei always called Birch *Shao Ye—Young Master*.

General Bai was startled. He stood with feet planted apart and arms folded across his chest. Turning his gaze to the maid, he saw a four-foot, ten inch woman in her early twenties. Neatly trimmed bangs nearly covered her eyebrows. Two waist-length pigtails fell on each side of her heart-shaped face. Her limbs seemed too thin to hold her own weight. But he knew that beneath her deceptively weak appearance, she was tough.

"You were very young when you started to work for my brother, weren't you?" General Bai ran a hand around his jaw while he reminisced. Xiao Mei had been a live-in servant in his brother's household. Both his brother and sister-in-law, Jasmine's parents, had been professors in Nanking before the war. The young housemaid had survived the Nanking Massacre and the death of her entire family.

"Fourteen."

"I remember the day you showed up here." The middle-aged man shook his head. A mental snapshot of a skinny, ghost-like girl burned in his mind.

"I was lucky," she answered in a quiet voice. No sadness. No self-pity. Only her left thumb rubbed a small scar on the back of her right hand.

General Bai lowered himself back onto the chair. His hands rested on the edge of the desk, fingers laced. His eyes searched hers in a silent query and found nothing but calm determination. "Okay," he agreed. "I'll let you try. But I'll keep looking," he added.

"I can handle it, General." Her voice was soft, but with an undertone of something much stronger.

Birch was carried home the next day on a stretcher. When Xiao Mei spotted his face, she stood frozen, staring at him with incredulity. The last time she'd seen him was eight months earlier. Both Birch and Danny had come home to celebrate Chinese New Year. In her mind, the Young Master was the most handsome man she'd ever seen, and he'd always carried a gentle smile, but now, lying motionless in the bed, he looked nearly dead. His eyes were closed, his face discolored by bruises, a slashing scar underneath his left eye and a cut at the bottom of his chin. His thick dark hair was gone. Instead, a bandage was wrapped around his shaved head.

"*Shao Ye*," she called out, moving closer to him. Her voice was shaky.

A nurse was sent to train her. She wasted no time. "Let me show you how to take care of Major Bai." She removed the blanket that covered Birch.

Xiao Mei let out a horrified gasp as her hands flew to cover her mouth. Shaking her head, she backed away a few steps. She hugged her arms around her middle as if she suddenly felt cold.

Standing by the door, General Bai emitted a sigh. "I understand," he said, disappointment obvious in his voice. Fatigue bent his shoulders as he moved toward the two women. "I'll interview another caregiver this afternoon. I hope she'll—"

"No, no, no!" Frantically, Xiao Mei waved her hands. She closed the gap between herself and the bed in two strides. "No interview; I can do it!" she proclaimed.

Chapter 19

Wang Hong, the nurse, stayed at the general's house for a few days. She had to make sure that Xiao Mei was well trained. The servant girl needed to handle everything—from attending to his wounds, to changing medicine bottles on the IV, to cleaning and turning his body.

"You like him, don't you?" Wang Hong commented as she watched the girl change his bandage on the third day.

"Yes," Xiao Mei answered without thinking. Realizing that she'd made a slip of the tongue, she then hurriedly denied her admission: "Oh, no, no, no—"

"It's okay. I understand. Major Bai is a great man. I met him a few times. He was…head-turning handsome. My husband is also a pilot. They—"

"No, you don't understand. He's my young master. I'm his *Ya Tou*. That's it. And that's all. I'm just grateful. Without *Shao Ye* and General, I'd be homeless. I would have nowhere to stay, no place to live."

Wang Hong liked Xiao Mei. This petite girl had impressed her. It was hard to take care of a comatose patient. "You know, he may never wake. It's a shame. He's such a courageous man."

"Never?" This prognosis stunned her. "General Bai never mentioned… I thought he would wake once his wounds were healed. How…"

"Even if he wakes,"—Wang Hong lowered her voice as if

vouchsafing a secret—"he won't be able to have children."

Xiao Mei was shocked by the news.

"It's sad." The nurse went to the door to make sure she was out of earshot. "He's probably incapable of being intimate with a woman. You know what I mean?"

Wang Hong wasn't naïve. The young major belonged to an elite group, whereas the servant girl was a member of the lowest class. The social barrier between the two was insurmountable.

In fact, Communists had used this injustice as a weapon against Nationalists; they promised equality for all. The idea was so enticing to the poor majority in the poverty-stricken country that the Communist's followers believed the principle blindly, never questioning how it could be achieved.

In Chinese society, a relationship between master and servant was not possible. Yet Wang Hong was compelled to caution the housemaid. She'd seen the desire in her eyes and hated to see the innocent girl hurt by falling for the wrong man.

Xiao Mei grabbed the nurse's arm. "What can I do to help? How can I wake him? He must come out of the coma. Please!" she begged.

Wang Hong sighed. Evidently her warning had fallen on deaf ears. "You must keep his body clean to avoid bedsores. That's a big problem for comatose patients."

"Anything else?"

"Besides turning him, you can give him massages." Wang Hong put her hands on Birch's arm, stroking softly. "You can also move his arms and legs." She bent his arm a few times. "A person in a coma for a long time will lose muscle strength. By massaging and moving, you'll help him flex his muscles." As a nurse in a busy hospital, she had no time to do either for her patients.

Xiao Mei nodded.

"And exercise his amputated stump, too. That helps to reduce swelling…or the risk of developing muscle tightness around the joint. If either happens, it can be bad for the remaining limb."

"What else?"

Wang Hong pondered a few seconds. "The other thing I can think of is to talk to him or read to him." She'd learned the theory. But again, it wasn't a standard practice.

"But he can't hear or feel…"

"Well, it's like massaging—he can't move, but you can help him exercise. He may not understand, but hearing stimulates his brain." So she'd heard, and assumed. The kind nurse was eager to offer help to this desperate young woman. "And when he does wake," she added, "dietary supplements will be helpful for his long-term recovery."

"You mean ginseng?"

"Yes. But in his case, deer antler will be very helpful."

"Deer antler?"

Wang Hong hesitated a moment before continuing in a confidential tone: "In herbal medicine, deer antler is a potent ingredient to enhance blood flow. It's been used to restore…male sexual vigor and performance for thousands of years. It's a Yang tonic. It'll help him to restore his natural ability…" She couldn't specify further. Anything related to sex or sexuality was taboo.

Hopefully, Wang Hong thought, *the young woman understands.*

———

Xiao Mei followed Wang Hong's instructions faithfully. Since the day Birch was brought home, she'd thrown herself into work. She bathed him and turned his body regularly, massaged and moved his arms and legs as often as possible, talked to him or read to him almost non-stop, and spoon-fed him ginseng tea. When she was exhausted, she just sat in the chair, folded her arms on the edge of his bed, put her head down, and allowed herself to rest for a while. Within days, her thin body became slimmer. Dark circles formed underneath her eyes.

"You can't keep doing this," General Bai warned her. He ordered a cot and set it up next to Birch's bed. "You must rest. If you fall apart, you won't do good for anyone."

Xiao Mei didn't mind hard work. She was thrilled to help the Young Master. On one hnad she hoped he would wake soon.

Everything she did was aimed toward that goal. On the other hand, she also relished the time she had with him. Although she wouldn't admit it, even to herself, she was taken with this gentle and kind Young Master.

As a servant, she had no excuse to be close to him. They'd chatted once in a while when he was home. But that was all. She'd never touched him, not even a handshake. They belonged to two different classes, two separate worlds.

Now she was close to him. Free to stare. Free to touch. Xiao Mei was afraid that she wouldn't be able to go near Birch once he woke. *This is selfish*, she scolded herself. But she couldn't help it. She wished that he was hers and hers only.

Chapter 20

▬ ▬ ▬ ▬ ▬ ▬ ▬ ▬

Xiao Mei had grown up on the outskirts of Nanking, the capital city of the Republic of China. Her parents made firecrackers for a living. The family wasn't wealthy, but they got by without much trouble. Neither Xiao Mei nor her brother had had the opportunity to go to school, though. Even at a young age, they'd had to help the family run the business.

In May, 1934, an accident occurred. Her sixteen-year-old brother was severely burned by an explosion. The hospital refused to treat him without payment first, but the medical expense was beyond their means. So the parents made a decision that no parent should ever have to make: to sell one child in order to save the other.

The night before she was sent away, her brother begged their mother and father, "Don't sell Xiao Mei. Please!" Lying in his bed, he was too weak to speak up clearly. "It's my fault. Let me die. Don't give Little Sister away."

But the parents had no choice. That night, the entire family wept together. When the sun came up, her father dragged her away. He had to pry her fingers from her brother's. Their hands were interlocked. Fresh tears streamed down her cheeks when she thought she'd already cried them dry.

At age thirteen, Xiao Mei became a *Ya Tou*—a slave girl sold for life.

A family of three bought her. In their mid-fifties, Mr. and Mrs. Gao had enough money to play Mahjong with their friends all day. They weren't gentle souls, but they were tolerable. As long as Xiao Mei finished her job of cleaning, cooking, and gardening, they left her alone.

Gao Da, their grown son, was a different breed. Short and thin, he was exactly opposite of his name. *Gao Da* meant tall and big. But even as his stature fell short, his hot temper lived up to his name.

At age thirty, Gao Da had gambled away half his inheritance, but he wasn't always in a foul mood. When he won, he wasn't unbearable to be around. Occasionally, he even offered a smile, revealing ugly yellow teeth. But when he lost, he took out his frustration on Xiao Mei—yelling, pinching, hitting—whatever he chose to release his anger.

Once he asked for hot tea. With one hand holding a cigarette, he picked up the cup with the other. After taking one sip, he slammed the cup onto the table. "Are you trying to kill me?" he shouted. The fine porcelain cup cracked, and hot water spilled over the tabletop. He squealed when a few drops splashed on his hand. As Xiao Mei hurried to clean up, he rammed the burning cigarette butt into the back of her right hand.

That was only one of his many bad days. A year later, Gao Da got himself into deep debt. Without telling his parents, he sold Xiao Mei to a brothel. She was fourteen.

Although she was shy and terrified, she fought him tooth and nail when he dragged her to the bawdyhouse. The overheard word "brothel" prompted her to fight for her life. Her kicking and screaming enraged him. He slapped her across the face, knocking her to the ground in the middle of the street. "You little whore," he yelled. "The brothel is the right place for you to learn how to treat a man." He lifted his foot, ready to kick.

A tall man dressed in a well-tailored suit stepped in. "Stop!" That one firm word spoke volumes. Bookish and genteel, Bai Wen was a professor, chairman of the Department of Art at Nanking University. Like most educated men, he seldom interfered in others' lives, but the bully's viciousness had shocked him, and he felt he had no choice but to intervene.

"Mind your own business," growled Gao Da, lifting his fist, ready to hit again.

A fine-looking lady had already pulled Xiao Mei off the street. Mrs. Bai was also a professor. She shielded the girl with her own body.

Even their daughter stepped up. She touched Xiao Mei's arm, reassuring her. Jasmine Bai was only a couple of years older than Xiao Mei. With silky skin, delicate features, and shiny hair cascading like a cloak of satin down to her waist, she was as gorgeous as the soft lilac georgette she was wearing. "Don't worry," she said in a honey-smooth tone, "my uncle is a commander in the Air Force. He won't allow anyone to treat a girl like this."

Gao Da faltered. The young woman's comment, innocent or deliberate, worried him. No one dared to challenge a military commander. He deduced from their expensive clothing that the girl wasn't bluffing. They belonged to an even higher class. His arm slackened.

It still took a lengthy negotiation before he agreed to sell Xiao Mei to them instead of the brothel. Xiao Mei stood wild-eyed as the event unfolded before her.

"Where do you live?" Mrs. Bai asked after Gao Da left. "We'll send you home." They already had a live-in maid.

With one hand to her cheek where the smack had left a red imprint, Xiao Mei shook her head. No matter how much she wanted to go home, she couldn't. *I have to pay back their kindness.* Even at fourteen, she understood an ancient philosophy—a drop of water shall be returned with a burst of spring. *They didn't give me just a few drops of water, they gave me my life. A life without shame and pain.*

At her insistence, they agreed to keep her as a live-in servant. So she went home with them. The next afternoon, still in a bewildered state, she saw Jasmine step into the courtyard with a young man. For a moment, she thought she was watching a scene in a movie, although she'd seen a movie only once in her life.

Jasmine wore a slate-gray skirt and a rose-pink shirt that hugged her slender frame. Her tall young man, in his early twenties, had a white T-shirt and sporty black shorts that showed off his muscled arms and well-toned legs. They walked and talked, laughing along the way, each holding a tennis racket. Warm sunlight shone on their youthful faces.

"Xiao Mei is our new helper." Jasmine introduced the girl to the young man. "Xiao Mei,"—she turned to the stunned servant girl—"this is Cousin Birch. He lives next door. His father and my dad are twins."

When he smiled and nodded a greeting, her pulse quickened, her nearly translucent cheeks blushing pink. She was mesmerized by his eyes—deep-set, lustrous, and almost holy in their intensity. She bowed her head to hide the telltale rosy stains on her face.

From that day onward, Xiao Mei often stood at a distance watching Birch talk and play with Jasmine and Daisy, his younger sister. She wished she could be with them. But when they asked her to join them, she shook her head and smiled shyly. As a servant she knew her place in society; she wasn't in their class.

A year later, Birch's family moved to Chungking, a city nine hundred miles to the west. Soon Jasmine followed to attend college while her family stayed in Nanking. And then, in July, 1937, after a series of localized conflicts between China and Japan, a full-fledged war broke out. Five months later, the Imperial Japanese Army invaded the capital of the Republic of China—and immediately began the notorious Nanking Massacre, and the ancient city turned into a living hell on earth.

Professor Bai could have left the city before the invasion—most of his colleagues and students had already fled—but he didn't. A graduate of the University of Tokyo, he was determined to act as liaison to negotiate with the Japanese so that his university would not end up in ruins.

On December thirteenth, several Japanese soldiers burst into his comfortable home. They rounded up Xiao Mei, the other housemaid and Mrs. Bai, and dragged them out of the house. Professor Bai stepped in with open arms, trying to reason with them, however he never had the chance. Without warning, one soldier stuck a knife into the scholar's chest. Screams and cries filled the room.

Mrs. Bai yelled in flawless Japanese, "I'll go with you. Just let me close his eyes. Please!" As the startled soldiers released her arms, she leaned over her husband's body. Instead of closing his eyes, though, she yanked the knife out of his chest and thrust the dagger into her own heart.

Xiao Mei watched in horror as blood soaked through Mrs. Bai's white cheongsam and dripped down the handle, across her fingers and onto the hardwood floor. The kind and genteel woman collapsed on top of her husband, her eyes wide open, staring into emptiness.

The shocked soldiers gaped at the two bodies in the living room. The fact that this beautiful woman could speak their language fault-lessly seemed to trouble them. Had they killed one of their own? Filled with doubts, they staggered out of the house, leaving the two shaken housemaids.

The two girls spent a terror-filled night inside the house. The next morning, as they were leaving, Jasmine returned from Chungking, hoping to convince her parents to leave the city.

While one maid tried to go home to her family, Xiao Mei and Jasmine sought shelter in the International Safety Zone estab-lished by a small band of Westerners. With nothing but courage and compassion, the foreigners risked their own lives to resist the Japanese troops. They sheltered hundreds of thousands of people from the massacre.

The Safety Zone wasn't danger-free, though. The Japanese came into the refugee camps at will, searching for disarmed Chinese sol-diers to kill and pretty girls to rape. Xiao Mei and Jasmine witnessed the slaughter of surrendered Nationalist soldiers. They lived with the constant threat of being kidnapped from the camp. But they sur-vived. And with the help of an American priest, Xiao Mei reunited with her parents and brother.

Her family joined her maternal grandparents and three uncles and their families. They boarded a small boat to flee to Chungking. Nine hundred miles away, the wartime capital was supposed to be safe. But before they reached their destination, they ran into an air raid. The Japanese bombed their tiny fishing boat.

To avoid being blasted to death, all leaped overboard. But none of her immediate family knew how to swim. While she held on to a piece of wood for dear life, everyone else either drowned or was killed by the bomb or swept away by the raging water of the Yangtze River.

Xiao Mei crawled to safety on the muddy shore. "Why?" she wailed. Why did her brother have to die at such a young age? Why did her parents and grandparents have to leave her? Why was she left alone? *Why didn't I die with them?* She cried and cried.

As the sun slanted toward the western horizon, she realized that if she didn't get up soon, she too would perish. She wiped away her tears. Twisting her braided pigtails around her head, she buried them underneath her brother's hat. Turning her colorful jacket inside out to cover her flat-chested body, she disguised herself as a boy and soldiered onward. Grief was a luxury she could not afford.

Xiao Mei walked the rest of the way to Chungking. She had no money so she begged for food. She had no choice.

Once she walked in the rain with a high fever before collapsing at the steps of a Buddhist temple. She was rescued by the monks. But soon they chased her out after discovering that she was a girl. Monks were forbidden to be in the company of females.

Another time three teenage boys surrounded her. Dirty and thin as scarecrows, they were also beggars. She'd accidentally entered their "territory." While they wrestled a bun from her, her long braids fell out of the hat. The boys staggered back. After a stunned silence, the one holding the bun handed it back to her. As the other two protested, he held up a restraining hand. *"Hao nan bu he nu dou."* Lifting his scrawny chest, he reiterated, *"A real man doesn't fight with a woman."* He pulled his reluctant companions away, leaving Xiao Mei dumbfounded but grateful.

It took her three months to reach Chungking. She had no idea how she'd survived except she'd clung tenaciously to hope—a tiny spark gleaming like a beacon in the darkness.

When she arrived at the Bai residence, she was as bony as a ghost. Her tattered clothes hung loosely on her starved body. She wore scruffy shoes two sizes larger than her feet; her own shoes were long gone, and she'd found this pair in a trash can.

The security guards wouldn't let her inside. She waited several hours before Birch and his father showed up at the gate. Neither of them recognized her.

Xiao Mei threw herself on her knees, blocking their way. "I'll do anything. I'm a good servant," she begged.

Birch pulled her up by the arms.

She'd meant to remain on her knees until they allowed her to stay, but he lifted her to her feet. He bent down, studying her thin and dirty face. Incredulously, he called to his father, "I think this is Xiao Mei." He turned to her and asked, "You *are* Xiao Mei, aren't you?"

The gentleness in his voice and the concern on his face brought tears to her eyes. She wasn't sad. She was just touched. No one else in the world knew her name, no one cared, and no one had called her Little Sister for months.

Her tears seemed to frighten Birch. "Don't cry, Xiao Mei." He added hastily, "You're home now. You're safe here. No need to be afraid anymore."

From then on, his home became her home—it wasn't just a home; it was her refuge, her sanctuary.

Chapter 21

Birch's condition didn't change; for months the scene inside the house remained the same. But the outside world was very different. After eight years, the war against Japan was finally over. As the celebration subsided, the threat of civil war between the Nationalists and the Communists preyed upon everyone's mind. Since 1927, the two parties had fought for control. The Japanese attack had brought them together to form a united front to counter the foreign invasion, but now that the common enemy was defeated, it was uncertain who would control the country. A peaceful solution didn't seem within easy reach, and war became more and more inevitable.

General Bai was tired of fighting. He'd tried his best to mediate the conflict, but failed. He was one of the minorities that had worked hard for a peaceful resolution. Yet he wasn't powerful enough to influence the decision made from above. The middle-aged man had no interest in another battle. Years of combat and too many deaths in the family had affected his health. He sent a resignation letter and retired from the Air Force, where he'd worked for many years.

His plan was to move to Tao Hua Cun—Village of Peach Blossoms in the mountainous region in Yunnan Province. Japanese troops had slaughtered most of the villagers after they refused to give up Danny Hardy. Jasmine became a heroine who had died for the American pilot. Daisy had perished not far away from the village.

Both General Bai and Birch had vowed to rebuild the once-charming community. It was time to honor that vow.

What about Birch?

During the past six months, the general had met with countless doctors. Their answers to his questions were not encouraging. One prominent doctor, without seeing the patient, had claimed that Birch would not recover. "Even on the off chance that he does wake, it'll be difficult for him to carry out daily functions. It's a miracle he didn't get any worse. Complications like infections and bedsores are more likely to happen as time passes. It's been six months. That's a long time."

The possibility of Birch being bedridden for the rest of his life deeply saddened the general. After many sleepless nights, he made a painful decision.

He dragged his feet to his son's room.

Dressed in a pale blue cotton blouse and gray slacks, Xiao Mei sat beside the bed as usual. She was reading. Her left hand held the book while her right hand massaged Birch's arm.

The bedroom faced the backyard. Through a large window, a cold sun was setting. Long shadows stretched over the wilted lawn. In the corner of the room, a clay charcoal stove with a kettle on top took the chill off the air. The room smelled of fresh ginseng that rose from a porcelain bowl on the nightstand.

General Bai choked. If making the decision was difficult, telling the young woman wouldn't be any easier. He eased into a chair at the other side of the bed. His eyes were sunken and weary. His cheeks were hollow. A perceptible slouch in his posture betrayed the composure he tried to maintain.

Xiao Mei offered a polite smile. She turned the book face down on her lap, but her fingers on Birch's arm kept their firm circular motion.

"What are you reading?" he asked.

"*San Guo Yan Yi.*" She showed him the cover. It was a picture book, a simplified version of the classic novel *Romance of the Three Kingdoms.*

Everyone in China knew the famous pledge made by the three

men in the historical fiction. Their statement was often used as a symbol of ultimate fraternal loyalty. Birch and Danny had made that pledge when they vowed to be brothers.

"*Shao Ye* loves this book. Too bad I can't read the original version." Xiao Mei had never attended school. When she was a maid at Professor Bai's household, Jasmine's mother had taught her how to read and write before the Nanking Massacre. She wasn't fluent. So picture books helped her. When she had trouble with the words, she made up the story according to the images.

A lump formed in General Bai's throat. He couldn't wait any longer for fear he would change his mind. "Xiao Mei," he began, "you know we can't keep him like this forever." He cleared his throat. "I've decided we must let him go."

"Where are you going to send him?" Her tone grew apprehensive. "Which hospital? May I go with—?"

"No, Xiao Mei, I'm not sending Birch to a hospital. He's *not* going to wake up. I've decided to…remove the life support." The muscles of his jaw quivered.

She looked puzzled, unable or unwilling to believe what she'd heard. "Then how…"

"Without nutrients or medicines, he'll be gone in a few days. He won't feel pain. He'll…go…naturally."

Momentarily knocked off balance, she didn't make a sound. Then she waved her arms hysterically. "No, no, no. Oh, God," she shrieked. "Please don't. Don't!" She looked panic-stricken.

Typically a man of unshakable calm, General Bai screwed up his eyes. He'd known it wouldn't be easy, but the immediacy of her grief tore him apart.

"Please," she pleaded. Hearing no answer, she stood up in a hurry. The picture book fell to the floor. She ignored it. Rushing to the other side of the bed, she dropped to her knees in front of him. "I beg you. Please don't let *Shao Ye* go!"

She grabbed his hand, something she would never have done in a normal situation. As kind as General Bai was to her, she wasn't his equal in the rigid class-ridden society. "He's so young. Don't let him die!" Tears spilled onto her cheeks.

The middle-aged man was stunned by this timid girl's strong reaction. Seeing her grief, he had trouble reigning in his emotions. His back was slightly stooped as though the weight of her hands were pulling him down. He tasted bile rising in his throat. With teary eyes, he gave a resolute shake of his head, refusing to change his mind.

"He *will* wake up," she said. "I'm sure. Please give him time. Give him a chance."

General Bai saw the torment on her face and felt a pang of sympathy—for her, for his son, and for himself. "Even if he wakes up, his life is ruined. Look at him." He turned his gaze on Birch.

The young man's hair had grown back and now obscured the scar on his cranium. But his eyes were closed, and his face was white as the sheet. His shrunken figure beneath the blanket lay motionless.

The father's frown deepened as he stared at the pallor of his son's face. "Even if he wakes, he'll be confined to bed for the rest of his life."

"I'll help him." Xiao Mei lifted her right hand, palm forward as if to pledge. "I promise. I'll help him. I'll always be there for him… supporting him. I'll…be his leg. I'll do anything. Everything! I swear to God; I'll never leave him. Don't…" Sobs racked her body as rivers of tears poured down her face.

The general exhaled a ragged breath, but he didn't budge. He couldn't see an alternative. It wasn't a decision made lightly. He'd contemplated it at length. Euthanasia was the only way to allow Birch to die with dignity. This was the last thing a grieving father could do for his helpless son.

"Think about Mrs. Bai," Xiao Mei said, becoming even more hysterical. Her voice climbed to an uncomfortable high pitch. "Think about Miss Daisy. Think about Miss Jasmine. And Major Hardy. If they were here, what would they say? What would they do?" She gasped for air, choking on sobs. "I know I'm just a servant, but I beg you, for Miss Daisy, for Miss Jasmine."

Her words tore out his heart. These were his family members. They were his loved ones. But they were all gone now. Birch was the only family he had left. How could he let his son go? Maybe Xiao Mei was right. What would they say about his decision? Without a doubt, he knew they wouldn't agree with him.

His wife would scold him. She'd yell, "Don't you dare!" Most likely Daisy and Jasmine would beg him just as Xiao Mei now begged him. Danny would tell him that Birch was a strong man and that he would survive. "Never give up a chance to stay alive" had been Danny's philosophy.

General Bai's heart ached with a sharp pain as he remembered his loved ones. *You can't let him go. He's your son, the only family you have.* The voice inside him screamed so loudly that he dropped his head into his hands. When he finally looked up, he nodded at the girl still kneeling in front of him.

Through foggy vision, Xiao Mei detected an almost imperceptible nod. "General?" she asked cautiously, as though he would change his mind if she weren't careful enough.

"Okay, we'll keep him"—he lifted his hand—"until the war starts... whenever that will be." Even though small clashes had occurred here and there between the Nationalists and the Communists, an official war wasn't yet declared. Keeping someone in a coma alive during a full-fledged civil war wasn't realistic.

Xiao Mei exhaled as if her own life had been spared.

Chapter 22

— — — — — — — —

"*Shao Ye*, wake up!" Xiao Mei said, as soon as General Bai left the room. "You've got to live. Please!" Her hands went to his arm, shaking him. "Miss Daisy would be so sad if she could see you now. Miss Jasmine would be devastated. You don't want them to feel bad for you, do you?"

While standing, she put more pressure on his arm. "Your mother had high hopes for you. General Bai is so proud of you. You can't disappoint them."

Frustrated, she pushed at a strand of hair that had fallen from her braids. Without wasting a second, she put her hand back to his arm. "Where is Major Hardy? General said no one knows. You swore you would protect one another. He's your brother. Those vows are sacred. You must keep them!"

Sensing no response from Birch, she raised her voice as if in this way he could hear her. "Do you remember what you told Miss Jasmine? You said, 'If you die, you just let the Japs kill one more innocent person without even using their guns or knives.' Remember?"

Xiao Mei paused to catch her breath. The room seemed too warm. Little droplets of sweat beaded her upper lip. She wiped them off with her arm before rolling the sleeves back to her elbows. "The war is over. Don't let the Japs kill you now."

Tears clogged her throat and made her voice crack. "You told

Miss Jasmine that life is hard. It can be painful. Being alive can be harder than dying." She had memorized their conversation word for word. "You encouraged her to be strong. Now it's your turn. Be a Tiger. Be a hero!"

The typically timid servant was no longer timorous. "*Shao Ye*, I know you can hear me. If you don't wake up, I'll keep yelling at you."

Xiao Mei kept her word.

The only time she stopped was when she prepared ginseng tea. Hailed as the king of herbs, ginseng had a reputation for saving people from death. Xiao Mei had been feeding Birch twice a day, according to an herbalist whom General Bai had counseled. So far the magic herb hadn't shown its power.

Xiao Mei dropped the wild ginseng slices into a fine china bowl. Then she stopped. After a moment of consideration, she scooped up a few more pieces, paused, and added more.

"Don't use too much," the herbalist had said. "Side effects include agitation, nervousness, sleeplessness, and nose bleed."

She almost laughed when she thought about the comment of insomnia. *What difference will it make if he can't even wake up?* She took more. In the end she made the tea almost ten times more concentrated than the recommended dose.

Her hands trembled as she spoon-fed him. She prayed as she watched him swallow the overdose of ginseng tea, his Adam's apple rising and falling. *Dear Guanyin, Goddess of Mercy, help me. Let this be the right thing to do. Don't harm him further.*

Dawn came and went, and dusk appeared and faded away. To Xiao Mei, time lapsed into a frozen state with one purpose and one purpose only. She kept on talking to Birch, sometimes begging, other times shouting, then more pleading. Followed by her prayers. She did it for two days and two nights.

By the middle of the third night, she had worn herself to a frazzle. Without thinking, she folded her arms on top of his bed. The moment her head hit her arms, she fell into an exhausted sleep and soon started to dream.

In the dream, Birch sat in the middle of a large meadow. His right leg was bleeding; crimson blood covered his pant leg. He struggled to get up, but failed. His leg was too damaged to support him. A grenade in his right hand was the only weapon he had. Dozens of Japanese soldiers surrounded him. When they reached him, in one heart-stopping motion, Birch yanked the ring with his left hand.

"No, *Shao Ye*. Don't!" Xiao Mei bolted upright, gasping. Her hands snatched his. Fear glazed her eyes. Even after she realized it was a nightmare, she sucked in one breath after another in an attempt to quell the panic.

Her dream had some truth to it. She knew Daisy was killed by hand grenades, and Birch had never forgiven himself for killing his younger sister.

The dream also jogged her memory of a conversation she'd heard when the two brothers came home the last time. Birch stated that he would rather die than let the Japanese capture him. "I'm going to die anyway. They won't allow us to live. Might as well take a few of them with me."

Danny disagreed, "Never give up a chance so easily." Then he cracked an impish smile. His lustrous eyes twinkled. "Perhaps the Japs don't give a damn about being dead or alive," he said, winking at everyone at the table. "Let me tell you, I do."

Xiao Mei recalled that she'd been floored by this Flying Tiger's lightheartedness. They were discussing a subject as serious as life and death.

While she tried to pull herself out of the nightmare, she felt a small movement from Birch. His fingers twitched a few times in her grip. Her eyes snapped open. The first glint of dawn peeked through the window, streaking the walls with dappled light. However, shadows still claimed most of the room. In the early morning sunlight, she stared at their interlocked hands.

Birch had done this before. It was an involuntary movement. Still, Xiao Mei couldn't suppress a glimmer of hope. "*Shao Ye?*" She waited, gaping at his large hand. Her nerves tingled in anticipation of another movement.

Nothing. His hand remained lifeless. She chewed her bottom lip to stave off a mounting tide of hopelessness.

After a few more callings with no response, she shook his hand in a fit of frustration. Her voice rose, sliding out of control. "Don't forget about what Major Hardy said. A real Tiger will never give up. You are a real Tiger, aren't you? Then prove it to us. Prove it to yourself!"

She sensed his movement again. Xiao Mei lifted her head. Her gaze swept across his face. In the past few months, she'd stared at him so much that she could detect any tiny change. She was familiar with the thickness of his eyelashes, the angle of his nose, the curve of his lips. Now, warm sunlight defined the outline of Birch's face, bringing color to his pale cheeks.

Oh dear Guanyin, Goddess of Mercy. Let him wake up. Her eyes remained fixed upon him as her mind spun back and forth between hope and despair. *Let him live!*

His eyelids flickered.

"*Shao Ye!*" she called out, encouraging him. "Keep trying. You can do it." Never dropping her gaze and barely blinking, she held her breath. Her small hands squeezed his fingers.

Little by little, after several tries, Birch opened his eyes. For the first time in six months, he was awake. His gaze appeared empty. Nevertheless, he was straining to see.

"Dear God!" Xiao Mei exclaimed. Her jaw dropped for a moment before an irrepressible smile spread over her face. A cry of exultation burst from her. Joyful tears sprang to her eyes, blurring her vision. *Thank you, God or the Goddess of Mercy.* She released an enormous breath, as if she'd held it for months.

Birch opened his mouth to talk, but the words died stillborn on his tongue.

"No need to hurry, *Shao Ye.*" She lifted her right hand, attempting to caress his cheek. It was a reflex, a habit she'd developed during the past few months.

In midcourse, she stopped. Even her left hand let go of his. Now that he was awake, he was her young master, and she was his servant. She shouldn't touch him anymore. Tears rolled down her face.

With his awakening, her fear of losing him became real. He was no longer her patient, and she couldn't be his sole caregiver anymore. She could never again sleep on the cot in the same room. With his rebirth, her closeness to him ended.

Heartbroken, Xiao Mei longed to touch his face. She had an overwhelming urge to comfort him with her arms. Birch was only inches away from her, yet he was no longer reachable. In the opening of an eye, they had retreated to their own worlds—unbridgeable worlds.

Her hands balled into fists; each fingernail digging deeply into her palms. She wept, trembling from the collision of two equally strong, yet opposite emotions.

General Bai entered the room. "Don't cry, child. This is a happy occasion."

"I know. I was…" Xiao Mei stuttered, blinking hard to fight back her tears. "I'm…I'm going to fix something for *Shao Ye*." She stood, head bowed, averting eye contact.

Once again, she was an obedient and quiet servant.

Part Two

Rocky Paths

Chapter 23

▬ ▬ ▬ ▬ ▬ ▬ ▬ ▬

"Dad?" It took great effort for Birch to speak; his mouth felt rubbery and tasted of copper.

General Bai sat next to the bed and gripped Birch's hand. His own hands were shaky. "Finally, you're awake," he croaked. The father could not help but think about the decision he'd made. What if Xiao Mei hadn't stopped him? What if he hadn't changed his mind? The mere thought struck terror in his heart. Looking at the young man, he could hardly suppress his gratitude—his son was going to live.

"How…long?" Birch rasped. He strained to remember. In his oblivion, he'd heard noises. Distant voices. Loud yelling. Even screams. Someone had squeezed his hands and shaken his arms. But he couldn't make sense of it. Where was he? What time was it? Memories churned through his mind. There was a ditch. They were digging, and suddenly gunshots erupted around them. He lay among the bodies of fellow prisoners, waiting to die, struggling to stay alive. Now it was all coming back to him. Pain: unbearable, mind-numbing pain. The sounds of dying men. The smell of gunpowder. And death. He closed his eyes to calm himself.

But how long ago was that? He squinted against the early morning sunlight and was just able to make out an olive green model airplane hanging from the ceiling. It took him a few moments to regain his bearings. *What?* He was in his own room—in Chungking! How could that be? How did he end up here…with his father? *Chungking is hundreds of miles from Yunnan. Is this a dream?* He tried in vain to piece together the disconnected stimuli.

"A…while." General Bai didn't have the heart to tell his son the truth. Not yet. Not until the young man felt better.

"I'm home…"

"It's a long story. Don't talk. Take it slow. I'll tell you everything in time."

Birch shook his head. He had to know. He had to find out. No time to waste. He must go back to Yunnan to find his sworn brother. He arched his neck against the pillow. "I have to find…" He was out of breath.

"Find whom?" Seeing his son's anguish, General Bai was alarmed.

"I have to find Danny. He's—"

"Take a deep breath. Speak slowly. Where is Danny?"

"I don't know. But he's out there. I have to—" With shaky hands, Birch tried to push himself up. Exhaustion thrust him back onto the pillow. Even with Xiao Mei's constant assistance, his muscle strength was almost non-existent.

General Bai said, "Be patient. It'll take a while before you can—"

"No! We don't have time. It's been…two days." He tried to get up again.

General Bai's heart sank. Right away, even without knowing the story behind it, he knew this would be another heartbreaking outcome. "You can't. You—"

Before his father could finish, Birch used his elbows to push up to a sitting position. He panted. General Bai had no choice. He had to lend a helping hand. As soon as he was sitting upright, and before his father could stop him, Birch flung back the blanket. Apparently, he was going to get out of the bed. But then he stopped. His eyes opened wide in astonishment when he caught sight of his nearly naked body. Chills ran up his spine as he looked at his once muscular frame. It was thin, frail, and covered with scars. His left arm was still hooked to an IV drip.

In a hurry, he stripped the rest of the blanket off. A look of terror appeared on his face. He raised his head. His mouth dropped open, but nothing came out. Without a leg, how could he walk? How would he ever fly again? How could he find Danny?

Gently General Bai pressed his hand against the young man's shoulder, pinning him to the bed.

"Let me get up." Birch was so drained he had to pause. Only the love for his brother kept him going. "Dad, take me to the hospital." He gripped his father's arm with the desperate expression of a drowning man in search of a lifeline. "The doctors will give me a leg. The doctors…"

His father helped him to sit up again. "We'll go to the hospital. But it'll take time, Birch. You won't—"

"Danny doesn't have time. We have to look for him. It'll be too late if we don't—"

"It's already too late, Son. Too late."

"What do you mean?" An involuntary shudder shot through Birch. "Danny is dead, isn't he?"

"We haven't found him. We don't know."

"Then there is hope."

"Birch, it won't make any difference if you wait a few more days. It's been…six months."

"Six months?"

"Yes. You've been in a coma for half a year. We've tried to look for Danny. But…"

His grip on his father's arm loosened. Leaning back, he closed his eyes. *Too late. Too late!* He kept on screaming in his mind. *Danny is gone. Long gone!*

Birch was undone by all of it—the fatigue of being confined to bed for months, the shock of realizing his disability, the pain of losing his sworn brother, the helplessness… Another surge of dizziness and rockets of heartache hit him. The last thing he heard before passing out was a high-pitched cry of "*Shao Ye*" accompanied by the sound of breaking glass.

Chapter 24

—————————

For three weeks Birch didn't speak or do much of anything. Since the day he awoke and found out six months had already passed, he knew he wouldn't find Danny alive. Even finding his brother's remains seemed impossible, now that he'd lost a leg.

No one knew where the Flying Tiger was.

His father had already contacted the military hospital in Yunnan where Birch had been treated first. All they could say was that several farmers had pulled him out of a mass grave. There was no other survivor. Nobody had mentioned seeing an American among the dead bodies. And worse yet, they had no idea where the farmers came from. The civilians had carried him for a couple of hours before they'd found the army base and dropped him off.

Birch knew where their planes had crashed. It wasn't far from the town of Dashan. The Air Force had already located the wreckage. He had a vague idea about where they'd been imprisoned. He and Danny had estimated that they were about fifteen to twenty-five miles north or east of Dashan. Yet that was a vast area covered by dense forest and rugged terrain. How could he go through the mountainous area searching for Danny without a leg?

At least I should write a letter to Danny's parents and sister. I must tell them what happened. He looked at the yellow notepad on the ebony nightstand. He'd asked for it, but so far he hadn't written a single word. Where would he start?

How can I ease their pain when they have to face the unbearable truth? No words seemed adequate to express his profound love and equally deep regret.

Birch could almost hear them scolding him. "What kind of Big Brother are you?" He imagined Susan pointing fingers at him, yelling, "You and Danny are sworn brothers. Why is he dead but you are still alive? Give back my brother!"

He deserved blame. *How could I cast caution to the wind?* He should have known better. He should have known that Danny would try anything to save him. The Flying Tiger would not give up so easily.

Propped against a stack of pillows in bed, he looked up. The olive green airplane hanging from the ceiling had been a gift from Danny. The Flying Tiger had handed him the radio-controlled plane when they returned home to celebrate Chinese New Year with his father last year. His memory returned to that happy day.

"When we're too old to fly fighters," Birch had said, assessing the well-designed model aircraft in his hand, "we can still fly these."

With a wide grin on his face, Danny suggested, "Let's start a club then." Making quotation marks with his hands, he continued, "How about calling it Old Bold Flying Tigers?"

His father joined in. "There are bold Flying Tigers. There will be old Flying Tigers. But there won't be too many old and bold Flying Tigers."

They all laughed.

His father rarely joked. But now his words came true. Danny would never grow old. He would forever be thirty, two days shy of his thirty-first birthday. The bold Flying Tiger had left the chance to grow old to him.

Birch turned his gaze to the other nightstand. On it lay the only things Danny had left behind—the white scarf and the empty medicine bottle. The scarf had been washed, although there were still smudges of blood that couldn't be removed. *Who did that for me? A nurse?* He was grateful to whoever had saved those and his ring. Nowadays he had nothing but those two items to remind him of Danny.

He picked up the small bottle, stared at it for a long time, and put it in his pocket. Carefully, he laid the scarf inside the drawer, hiding it along with all his diaries.

Two weeks earlier, a number of former colleagues had visited him. One of them brought back his last diary, which he'd tucked underneath his pillow in their dorm room. He couldn't bear to touch it. The leather-bound journal seemed non-threatening, yet what lay within was too much for his weak heart. In time, he hoped he would be strong enough to read it. But for now, the wound was too raw and his sense of loss too overwhelming.

Birch turned his head toward the window as if seeking escape. He hadn't been outside for months and he missed the sunshine on his face. Fresh air and beautiful nature always cheered him. *Outdoors was another passion I shared with Danny.*

It was a beautiful winter morning. A smattering of white clouds dotted the crystal-blue sky. Beyond the wilted lawn and amongst the bony gray branches, clusters of small pink flowers speckled the edge of the woods. Bright sunlight poured through the large window, illuminating a red paper-cutting of a tiger on the glass.

One look at the tiger and Birch felt a lump form at the back of his throat. After so many years, the color had faded. It wasn't as vibrant as he'd first seen it. "That's a fierce tiger," he'd commented when Daisy handed it to him on his twenty-fifth birthday.

The fifteen-year-old girl had curved her lips up. "How could I create a tiger that is not fierce?" Her smile was so innocent and sweet.

"You mean you made this? You didn't just buy it?"

She laughed. "You don't think I can make something as intricate as a paper-cutting, do you? You think only Jasmine has the artistic ability? Well, you're not too far off."

She lowered her voice and moved closer, as if telling a secret. "I've tried many times and wasted lots of paper." She pointed to the fine lines. "I had a lot of trouble. They broke easily. I almost gave up. But I didn't. It's a gift for you, my Big Tiger Brother." A broad grin had lit her face like summer sunshine. She'd always been so proud of him.

The vivid memory of her smile tore out his heart. The lump in his throat expanded and started to burn. Daisy, his sweet younger sister, was forever a soft spot. Birch screwed up his eyes to calm himself. When he opened them, he shifted his gaze to the inside of the room, avoiding the painful reminder.

But the room wasn't any safer. His eyes settled on a wood-framed oil painting on the wall. It was a stunning landscape of a snow-capped mountain and a meadow filled with wildflowers in full bloom. A lonesome figure sat on the ground. Her face was partly obscured, but her sorrow was more than evident.

Birch knew the image by heart. On the brink of the Japanese invasion, Jasmine had returned to Nanking in an attempt to convince her parents to leave, but had only found their bodies in a pool of blood. Having experienced the horror of the massacre, for a moment she lost her will to live. It was he who had encouraged her to keep going.

He remembered he'd told her to be strong, to pull herself together. "I know it's hard. It's very painful. Being alive can be harder than dying."

Did I say that to her?

Afterward, Jasmine had painted this picture for him as a gift, but more significantly as a promise. She was going to live, no matter how hard life proved to be.

Now it was his turn. And he found that it was harder than he'd imagined. He'd told Jasmine to live a productive life. What kind of worthwhile life would he have? The war against Japan was over. He wasn't needed as a fighter pilot anymore. Even if he were needed, he couldn't do anything. *What can a cripple do?* His career as a pilot was over. In fact, he'd already been honorably discharged from the Air Force.

Birch leaned on the side of the bed, reaching for a pack of Lucky Strikes and a lighter on the nightstand. The doctors had warned him not to smoke. *To hell with the doctors!* With shaky hands, he lit a cigarette, inhaled deeply, and exhaled in a rush.

The doctors had told him that his survival of multiple gunshots was a miracle and his awakening from a long coma was a wonder. They said his recovery was another unexplainable marvel. Although he was nowhere near a healthy state, he wasn't in terrible shape either, as they assumed. The doctors were baffled. "Someone must have helped you," commented one of them with a broad smile. "It's definitely a miracle."

A miracle for what? To test his endurance? To study human capacity to tolerate pain? To see if he was a brave man? *And am I still a man? A man can be intimate with a woman. What kind of man can I be? No wonder Mary left me.*

When he'd asked about Mary, he saw a grim look on his father's face. The mere fact that she hadn't visited him said it all.

Through a swirl of smoke, his gaze turned to a pair of tiger-head shoes on the dresser. The tiny children's footwear was made of scarlet red cloth. The toe-cap was embroidered to look like a tiger's head.

Mary had given them, half as a joke and half as a hint. "You can wear them," she'd teased, "or you can save them…until we have a good-looking baby tiger just like you." Her face flushed when she handed him the shoes. "Oh, my Perfect Tiger, take…" She bowed her head. Biting her lip for a few moments before she whispered again, "You see, I'm your birthday present."

She leaned into him, her hand caressing his chest. A whiff of her intoxicating perfume enveloped him. She was wearing the rich carmine red dress he'd bought for her. The elegant outfit accentuated the curves of her feminine frame. Birch remembered his body had hardened, burning with desire. It took every ounce of restraint he'd possessed not to take up her offer.

He recoiled at the vivid memory. Her seductive words still echoed in his mind, but the girl was nowhere to be seen. How could a woman be so cold after she'd already considered "giving herself to him" and having a child with him?

And have I done the right thing? Birch had mixed feelings about what he'd done, or hadn't done.

On one hand, he was relieved that he'd stopped her. He would be hurt by a guilty conscience if he'd followed his desire. It would be detrimental, for her, if they were intimate. She would suffer the scorn of the society. She might have trouble finding a suitable husband later on. Even though Mary wasn't his anymore, he still cared about her. He wanted her to be happy. He was positive he'd made a right decision on that day.

On the other hand, Birch almost regretted not accepting her offer. *What the hell were you thinking, you fool?* A self-deprecating chuckle followed, bitter and hollow. *You may never know how it feels to be intimate with someone. Dammit! You may never taste the sexual pleasure of being with the one you love. Or with any woman!* From a selfish standpoint, he'd made a huge mistake.

What would he do if he could turn back time? Would he still do the *right* thing? Or would he treasure the once-in-a-lifetime chance to be with the only woman he'd ever loved? It didn't really matter now. No matter how he felt, the past was in the past, and Mary was part of his history.

One cigarette after another, Birch smoked as he thought, haunted by his memories and dark emotions.

Chapter 25

▬ ▬ ▬ ▬ ▬ ▬ ▬ ▬

A little before noon, a soft rap on the door interrupted Birch's thoughts. Seconds later, Xiao Mei came in with a tray in her hands. Although he had no appetite, his father insisted that he eat. The young housemaid always prepared more than he could consume.

"It's lunch time, *Shao Ye.*" Xiao Mei pushed the notepad and the pack of Lucky Strikes aside and set the silver platter on the ebony nightstand. Right away, the fresh aroma of ginseng from the steam of a teacup mingled with the harsh odor of the smoke.

"Here is your favorite rice porridge." She picked up a white porcelain bowl with a gold rim. "I made it the way you like it—chopped pork, chicken, century egg, mushrooms, and ginger. It's hot." She blew air to the dish while she stirred it with a spoon to cool it.

Birch waved a hand. "Not hungry." He took another long draw on the cigarette. Smoking only discouraged his appetite.

"You must eat. Otherwise, how can you get better?" She pushed the bowl in front of him. "I remember Major Hardy was stunned by the century egg's dark color. But when you dared him, he ate the whole thing. He liked it once he tried it. I bet not many Westerners are as brave as the Flying Tiger." She offered a smile as cheerful as her apricot colored shirt.

Birch wrinkled his nose in distaste. He genuinely didn't care about food at the moment. And the thought of Danny and his love for

Xiao Mei's dishes tightened his throat.

Reluctantly she put the bowl back on the tray. "How about some fruit? Perhaps it'll stimulate your appetite." With one hand holding the plate full of various colors, she picked up a large piece of mango using a pair of ivory chopsticks. "Mango is your favorite. You—" She moved the golden wedge before him as she talked.

Birch turned his head away as if the fruit were poison. "Take it away. Take it away from me." His voice was trilling. As he waved his arm, blocking the sight of the fruit, his hand accidently bumped into Xiao Mei's.

It took her by surprise, and the plate dropped from her hand onto the tray. Concurrent with her scream and jump, the silver platter tipped over. Instantly the fine china teacup, plate, and bowl shattered into fragments. Ginseng tea and the rice porridge splashed everywhere; pieces of fruits scattered all over the hardwood floor.

For a moment, they stared at each other, stunned by the incident.

"Birch!" General Bai stepped into the room. "Your mother raised you to be a gentleman." His tone was harsh, a flicker of disappointment in his eyes. "Don't take it out on Xiao Mei."

"No, no, no," protested the young maid, waving her arms. "It's my fault. *Shao Ye* told me he didn't want to eat. I insisted. I shouldn't have. It's all my fault."

The father let out a weighty sigh. He softened his voice. "Birch, I know you don't feel well. You have no appetite. But smoking will only make matters worse. Xiao Mei is trying to help."

Birch knew that the servant girl had tried her best to make his favorite dishes. Even though he was in a foul mood, he wasn't blind. He saw the affection in her eyes. "I'm sorry," he apologized. "It was an accident. I didn't mean—"

"No, no, no. It's okay." She squatted to pick up the larger pieces of china. "I'm going to bring another bowl. I'll clean up later." She stood and left the room in a hurry.

General Bai pulled a chair close to the bed. "Son, what was that all about?"

"Mango…" Birch's voice cracked. A low, mournful sound erupted from the back of his throat. "It's Daisy's favorite. I can't..." His eyes clouded so fast he had to look away. He remembered buying mangos for his little sister whenever he came home. He loved to share them with her. Her smile had been sweeter than the fruit.

The father inhaled heavily. "You can't keep blaming yourself for Daisy's death. She would have died even if you didn't... Her fate was sealed the moment she was captured. She would have died an undignified death. You know what happened to Jasmine. What she went through was painful and degrading. You saved Daisy. Don't torment yourself."

Birch lowered his head and shut his eyes, preventing his father from seeing the depth of his pain. His closed eyes were quivering behind his eyelids. When Danny was alive, he'd been able to transfer his love for his sister and cousin to the newfound brotherhood. Now that Danny was gone, he had nowhere to channel his emotions. As a result, his feelings of melancholy and guilt consumed him.

"I would have done the same—"

"Would you?"

"It took strength to do what you did. You are Daisy's hero. She'd never blame you like you blame yourself. I'm sure that she was grateful to you, Birch!"

His father's words didn't cheer him.

General Bai bent closer. "*Zhang xiong ru fu.*" He repeated the phrase, "An elder brother is like a father. You're the Big Brother. I understand you want to protect your younger brother and sisters. But Son, you couldn't. You couldn't even protect yourself." The general expelled a hard breath. "You have to accept the reality—they are gone. You mustn't dwell on it." He put his hand on Birch's arm. "But you *can* do something about the present and the future."

"What can I do?" Birch's eyes were empty.

"You can try to find Danny."

"How?"

"If you want to find him, then eat and exercise. You'll need a healthy body and a sharp mind. You know the Old Man has already contacted a hospital in California. He promised that you will get a state-of-the-art prosthetic limb. As soon as you're well enough, you'll have a leg."

The Old Man was General Chennault, the U.S. Air Force commander in China. He knew the brothers; he was touched by their story and was willing to provide any assistance to Birch's recovery.

"A prosthesis won't be easy to get used to—it will hurt. But you can handle it. You are a Tiger." General Bai squeezed Birch's forearm. "Get well, Son. Go look for Danny. Search for Jasmine. They're your brother and sister. And look for Jack. You've never met him. But if he's Danny's brother, he's your brother too."

His father's words reminded him of the future that he and Danny had planned: searching for Jasmine, Jack, and other airmen. He remembered the sudden lift of spirit he'd felt when they talked about it in that grim prison cell. Now he was left alone, like the forlorn figure in Jasmine's painting.

Birch considered hiring Linzi to help him, as Danny had suggested. The boy would surely accept the offer, but Linzi wasn't his brother. Danny was not only Birch's brother, he was his equal. How could he find the same support from a boy?

His father interrupted his thoughts with a sigh. "Birch, you're lucky to be alive. So many others didn't make it."

The memory of Mr. Ding's pleas on the night before his death crystallized in Birch's mind. His frown deepened as the cold fact hit him: out of the dozens of people from the prison, he was the only one who had survived. If he didn't deliver Mr. Ding's message, his family would never know what had happened to him. Although Mr. Ding was a communist, they'd fought the same enemy. They'd been comrades and friends. He owed it to Mr. Ding to send his last words to his family.

In fact, each person in the room had introduced himself that night. What had Zhou Ming said? The Nationalist Army officer was from Chungking. His mother was the only one left in their family. But where did she live? Birch now regretted not paying more attention at the time.

I must write the letter. Now! He had to let Danny's parents and sister know what had happened.

Not knowing what was on his son's mind, the father continued, "There is much to be done. Don't waste time. God knows it'll be hard. But you can do it." General Bai coughed into his fist and tightened the collar of his brown twill jacket before citing a proverb, "'Nothing is hard in the world for a strong-minded man.' You are such a man, Birch. Don't wallow in your grief. Take one step at a time. A real Tiger never retreats from challenges."

The general purposely let the silence stretch out, waiting for Birch to respond. When there was no response, he pressed on: "Daisy was always so proud of you. You're her Big Tiger Brother. Jasmine believed in you. You're the one who convinced her to live. And Danny trusted you. Remember your vow?"

"To die on the same day of the same month in the—"

"No," his father cut him off. "I meant the part that Danny added. Remember?"

How could Birch forget? "If one survives," Danny had said, "he'll live to the fullest, for both."

Birch sat up straighter, his chin tilted upward, a muscle in his jaw bunched. Although he was no longer a fighter pilot, he was still a warrior. *It's time to fight again.*

His grief began to dissipate, replaced by a newfound fortitude. By the time Xiao Mei walked into the room with another tray in her hands, Birch had regained his composure. He watched her eyes brighten with an unexpected delight as she apparently noticed the change in his spirit.

Chapter 26

━ ━ ━ ━ ━ ━ ━ ━

Spring slipped away and summer was fast approaching. Xiao Mei had not taken a day off for years, so when she asked permission, General Bai was more than happy to grant her request. "Take as much time as you need. You've worked so hard." Still, Xiao Mei asked for only one day a month, the day after she was paid.

Wearing gray slacks, a forest green cotton blouse, and black cloth shoes, she stepped out of an ornately carved archway. These days, two stone lions were the only guards on duty at the Bai residence.

"Xiao Mei!" A young man stopped her at the door. Dressed in the Nationalist Army uniform, Wu Pan was twenty-five, of medium height, and well-built. His suntanned face bore witness to hours spent outdoors.

"Captain Wu," Xiao Mei greeted him with a polite smile. A home-made purple-and-black patchwork bag crossed her chest. "Is this your day off, too?"

Wu Pan nodded. He'd guarded the Bai residence for two years before the general had retired. Since then, he'd spent all his days off at the residence.

"General is always happy to see you."

"Going shopping?" he asked as he walked alongside, a silly grin on his face.

"Not today." Xiao Mei didn't have to go to the market often. Mrs.

Bai had made arrangements with several peasants to bring fresh vegetables, eggs, and meat. Occasionally, Xiao Mei had to buy unusual ingredients, and even then she never had to go far.

"Where are you going?"

"To the city center."

His gaze shifted from her face to her outfits. "Need new clothes?"

Xiao Mei shook her head. Her clothes were always clean, but most of them were getting old and the colors had faded. She could certainly use new outfits.

"It doesn't matter what you're going to buy. I'll go with you. The city isn't safe. I'll make sure no one—"

"No, you can't." The words tumbled out her mouth a bit too fast. Realizing her harsh tone, Xiao Mei softened her voice. "I'm sorry, you can't come along. I'm going to…to the Buddhist temple. To pray to Guanyin, the Goddess of Mercy, for my family."

"I see." Captain Wu's beaming smile faded, but he kept walking. "But you've never done that before. Your parents and brother passed away many years ago. I don't remember you ever going to a temple."

"I knew the ritual, but I didn't understand how important it was until Auntie Liu told me," Xiao Mei answered, referring to the part-time helper that General Bai had hired when Birch was in the coma. The middle-age woman was a devout Buddhist.

"Auntie Liu?"

"Yes. She said burning incense at a temple for the deceased would help them to shorten the wait for the next life. She does it regularly for her husband," Xiao Mei recited the same excuse she'd used when General Bai asked.

Feeling a pang of guilt, she added a feeble smile to make the lie more palatable. "I want my loved ones to enter the next life as soon as possible."

Accepting her explanation, the young captain flagged down a rickshaw for her. "Make sure she gets to the temple safely," he told the puller as he kicked the wheel. "You hear me? You'll be in big trouble if—"

"Don't worry. Nothing will happen," Xiao Mei interrupted him and stepped onto the rickshaw. But even as she said it, she knew the captain's concern wasn't farfetched. The city center was unsafe.

Two months earlier, she'd run into an anti-civil war demonstration orchestrated by college students. The march turned into a riot when the police and military authorities tried to disperse the crowd. The angry protesters threw rocks, sticks, and whatever else they could find at the policemen. Dozens of young people were beaten and arrested by the Nationalist government. Xiao Mei had retreated to a store in time to avoid being detained.

Another time the road was blocked, and the rickshaw in which she rode had had to take a detour. She'd learned from the puller that a public execution was taking place near the city center. "They're labeled as terrorists," said the coolie in a conspiratorial tone. "Rumor has it they're communists or communist followers." Xiao Mei had heard the gunshots.

"So, Auntie Liu will cook today?" Captain Wu's voice interrupted her thoughts. The young man was walking backward toward the gate, his dark eyes still trained on her.

"Yes."

"I don't know how anyone can put up with her cooking." He placed his hand over his throat and made a face as if throwing up. "Will you come back to cook dinner?"

"Yes, I will."

"Great." A big smile spread across his face. "I'll wait for you."

Xiao Mei leaned back in her seat, breathed a soundless sigh, and waved goodbye.

Clattering over the cobbled streets, the rickshaw took her over the hills of Chungking toward the city center. The day was balmy with sunshine and a light breeze. The young coolie wore nothing but cotton trousers and a conical straw hat. A toffee-brown rag was draped on his bronzed chest and bounced as he ran.

The squeal of the wheels took Xiao Mei back to her past. There had been more people at the Bai residence when she first arrived. Mrs. Bai was alive. Jasmine and Daisy were there. They had two live-in maids and guards. Mrs. Bai used to take the girls to the city center. Even though they had a car, she hired rickshaws. Daisy had loved the smell of gasoline, but Mrs. Bai couldn't stand it.

Then everything changed. June 5, 1941, Japanese airplanes rained incendiary bombs on the city. Mrs. Bai was headmaster of a kindergarten. All the children and teachers in her preschool managed to find protection. The shelters in Chungking were deep caves dug into mountainsides. They were supposed to be safe, but the bombing destroyed their entrances. Along with several thousand residents, Mrs. Bai was buried alive, and suffocated to death.

Soon after the tragedy, General Bai sent Daisy and Jasmine to a small village in Yunnan. The area was too remote to be touched by war. *Or so he thought.* He hadn't minded sending Birch to the front, but he wouldn't permit the ugly conflict to reach his daughter and niece. Delicate young ladies had nothing to do with horrifying warfare. How could he ever imagine that the violence would find them? How could he know that an American pilot would bail out near the village and that both girls would sacrifice their lives for him?

From then on, the Bai residence became very different. Even though the rooms remained unchanged, there was no laughter now. No music. No liveliness. When the live-in maids left to take care of their families, the general didn't bother to replace them. There wasn't much to do, and Xiao Mei was more than capable of handling everything.

The home had become even quieter after General Bai retired. Xiao Mei was glad when Captain Wu paid a visit. What she didn't like was his hidden agenda. She was afraid her cooking wasn't his only interest. She sighed as she recalled the past. *Life is so unpredictable.* Within just a few years, almost everyone in her life had gone. Birch and General Bai were the only ones left.

Half an hour later, she leaned forward and called out, "Stop here, please."

"Not there yet." The puller straightened his back. He mopped his face with the rag around his neck and pointed ahead. "See, it's there." The Buddhist temple was sitting high on Lionhead Hill a few blocks away.

120

"It's okay," said Xiao Mei. "I'd rather walk."

"But the officer said—"

"Don't worry about him." She paid the fare and stepped down.

The city center was filled with block after block of shops. Even on the brink of civil war, the streets were teeming with shoppers and sellers. In high-pitched cries, sidewalk vendors offered everything from cheap household items to expensive jade jewelry. Nearby one man was baking sweet yams on a clay stove. Another man was dry-frying chestnuts with hot pebbles in a large wok. His rhythmic stirring joined forces with the heartbeat of the city. Several kids stood around a Tanghulu stand. Their eyes were glued to the cinnabar hawthorns skewered onto bamboo sticks. The mouth-watering aroma of food permeated the air.

But Xiao Mei paid no attention to any of these sights, sounds or smells. As soon as the rickshaw turned the corner, she crossed the busy street and made a beeline for a large store. Above the door, a few golden characters on a red wooden banner announced the name: Chungking Herbal Dispensary. The distinctive scent of herbs greeted her even before she entered the shop.

Chapter 27

— — — — — — —

Twenty minutes later, a little bell jingled overhead as Xiao Mei exited the drugstore. With one hand protecting her bag, she waved down a rickshaw. "General Bai's residence." She gave the coolie the address.

A block later, two black cars and several military vehicles rolled into view. Small flags on the front bumpers had the Nationalist's Blue Sky, White Sun, and a Wholly Red Earth. The puller towed the rickshaw close to the curb, squeezing past the oncoming convoy on the narrow street.

Xiao Mei crinkled her nose at the fuel exhaust that spewed out of the vehicles. She placed a hand over her face. But a tender smile broke through when she spotted several kids running alongside the cars. They laughed, jumping up and down. The youngster's gap-toothed grins reminded her of Daisy, who'd liked the smell of gasoline.

But her smile was short-lived. Along with Daisy's beaming face, Birch's pained eyes floated into her mind. Her mouth curved into a frown. She felt a tug of sympathy for the girl who would never grow old, and for her war-torn brother. Xiao Mei's hand tightened over the patchwork bag.

Suddenly, an explosion roared like thunder. Shards of metals flew in all directions from a detonated car. Broken glass shot up to the sky and then rained down everywhere. In a matter of seconds, revolting odors of burned flesh filled the air. Screams and cries of injured people rose above the chaos in the crowded street.

A razor-sharp shard caught the coolie. It slammed into his head, turning his skull into a mass of blood and brain. He collapsed, fell face down, twitched once, and then lay still.

The rickshaw lurched to a stop and threw Xiao Mei off balance. She pitched forward, tumbled out of the seat, and fell on top of the young man. Her hands touched the bloody mass oozing from his wounds. She shrieked, reeling from the shock. But she couldn't hear her own voice.

Xiao Mei scrambled off the body and squirmed away. Her own forehead now showed a purple bruise. Blood seeped through her green cotton blouse and gray slacks where her left knee and elbow were scraped. She tried to stand up, but her legs buckled. She crumpled back to the ground, her teeth chattering with fright. As she struggled, a strong hand grabbed her forearm. Whipping her head around, she saw Captain Wu looming over her. In the thick smoke, his face was smudged. A trickle of blood dripped from his right temple.

Her eyes widened in disbelief. She opened her mouth, but Wu Pan lifted his hand to forestall her, and said something she couldn't hear. Without delay, he flung her arm around his shoulders and hauled her to a standing position.

Out of the corner of her eye, she caught a glimpse of a boy's lifeless form. His face was a bloody pulp. His small frame was sprawled on the cobbled ground a few steps away from a burning car. A piece of wreckage covered his lower body.

Xiao Mei cried out, aghast at the sight. Jerking herself free, she stumbled toward the youngster. But two steps later, Captain Wu recaptured her arm. "Too late," he yelled. "We have to leave!" He yanked her away from the body. She fought to free herself, but he held on with a tenacious grip.

As he dragged her along, gunshots erupted around them. Wu Pan wrapped his arm around her head, using his body to protect hers. Ducking low, he ran quickly down the side of the street. Seconds later, high-pitched whistles blew and loud voices yelled, "Stop!" Nationalist military personnel had arrived to detain everyone. With rifle butts they beat anyone who resisted arrest. Rude shouts mingled with painful cries.

"Stop!" A harsh voice barked behind Xiao Mei and Wu Pan. "Move one more step and I'll shoot."

Xiao Mei flinched while Captain Wu knotted his soldier's fists at his sides. They had no choice but to comply.

"Raise your hands. Turn around slowly."

They did as they were told. In front of them was a sharp-faced young man pointing a rifle at them. He was dressed in the Nationalist Army uniform and stood with his feet slightly apart and shoulders braced. His watchful eyes widened as he stared at the captain. "Wu Pan?" He switched his aim to Xiao Mei, but his stern face softened.

With an exclamation of surprise, Wu Pan lowered his arms. "Put the gun down, Tan Ying. What are you doing here?"

"We were ordered to escort the general and a foreign military adviser," said Tan Ying in a rush of words. "They were in the car that blew up." He took a breath. "We got orders to arrest everyone here. The terrorists can't be far away. The communists, I mean." Tan Ying shifted his gaze to Xiao Mei, who looked dumbfounded.

"Let her go." Wu Pan said in a commanding voice. "She has nothing to do with the communists. She works for General Bai."

Tan Ying searched the captain's dark eyes before he glanced over his shoulder. Chaos surrounded them. Fifteen yards away, two soldiers in Nationalist uniforms wrestled a young man to the ground and pinned him by the wrists. One of them rammed his boot at the poor fellow's jaw. A few steps away, another soldier held a young woman at gunpoint. He shoved her so hard that she lurched forward and fell to her knees.

Tan Ying's gaze trained on Wu Pan, then sliced over to Xiao Mei, and finally swung back to his friend. A muscle flickered at his jaw. After a strained silence, he snatched Xiao Mei by her arm. "What are you waiting for?" he shouted at Captain Wu, who immediately took her other arm. Before she understood, the two men carried her away from the bloody scene.

At the next intersection, Tan Ying guided them into a narrow alley. They ran for three blocks. Then he let go of her sleeve and abruptly left them.

"I owe you," Wu Pan called out without stopping.

Up and down the steep hills, through a maze of alleyways, they ran. Fifteen minutes later they reached a deserted street. No more noise or stench. Only their footsteps clattered on the cobble stones.

"Slow down, please." Xiao Mei waved her hand, panting. Her chest rose and fell with labored breathing. Her legs and lungs were burning.

Wu Pan trimmed his gait to a walk. His hand still clasped her right sleeve.

"Those poor kids…" She managed to push the words past the lump in her throat. Her eyes were bright with tears. "The bomb…" Sadness and anger ripped through her. Drawing several ragged breaths, she asked, "Did the communists do it?"

"Most likely."

"Why? Isn't there enough death after eight years of war?"

The young captain had no answer.

Xiao Mei shook her head, disbelief mixed with contempt and horror. She brushed aside loose strands of hair that had fallen from her pigtails. "I'm glad you were there, Captain Wu. Thank you." Her eyes narrowed, her eyebrows furrowed with puzzlement. "But how did you happen to be there?"

Wu Pan shrugged, and then asked, "Did you have a chance to go to the temple?" With head cocked, he watched her, his eyes traveling from her face to the bulging bag in front of her chest.

Finding his gaze a shade too inquisitive and skeptical, she dropped her chin to her chest. The trickle of blood down his temple made her feel guilty.

"Xiao Mei," Captain Wu stuttered, "don't go to the city center alone. It's too dangerous. You could have been killed today. Or arrested as a communist… God knows what they would do to you if—"

He stopped mid-sentence and heaved a deep sigh. With a free hand, he brushed off the debris tangled in her hair. His palm lingered over her head a moment longer than necessary. "Next time, wait for me." His voice was low and rough. "I'll go with you."

Her gaze rose to collide with his, but she couldn't possibly let anyone know what she needed to buy.

Chapter 28

As General Bai had said, physical rehabilitation was a grueling process. But he'd also pointed out that Birch was a tough man. Once the ex-fighter pilot set his mind to it, as a typical Tiger, he exerted all his effort, struggling without complaint.

Before a prosthetic leg was fitted, he had to exercise and build his overall health and muscle strength. At first, he could exercise only while lying in bed, but soon he was hopping around the house on crutches, his right pant leg empty.

The doctors were amazed at the speed of his recovery. Less than three months after he woke from the coma, he was well enough for an artificial limb.

As all amputees, Birch experienced a host of painful sensations. The soreness was worse when he first used the artificial leg. Adjusting to a prosthesis wasn't easy. It took perseverance. He had to relearn basic things such as balance and coordination.

The area where the skin met the socket caused pressure and stabbing pains. The doctors prescribed painkillers, but no matter how bad he felt, Birch refused to take the pills. He clenched his teeth until his jaw hurt. The veins on the back of his hands bulged and his knuckles turned white when he gripped the crutches. Sometimes every muscle in his body screamed at him to stop. Each pain-filled step was a hurdle to overcome.

"Please take the pill!" the nurses at the rehab center begged him. More than a few had tears in their eyes when they witnessed his suffering.

But Birch refused.

Wang Hong, the nurse who had trained Xiao Mei, was so frustrated that she yelled at him, "You just want to show off." She sounded angry, but tears trickled down her cheeks. "Show off that you're a hero. Brag about being a brave man with no fear of pain. We already know you're a hero." Her husband, Meng Hu, was also a fighter pilot. He'd shared the dorm room with Birch and Danny.

The next day Wang Hong handed Birch a carton of Lucky Strikes. "I shouldn't give this to you. It's not healthy. But Meng Hu convinced me. He said smoking might offer you some relief. Why are you so stubborn? Why can't you just take the pills?"

With unwavering determination and the great strength of a warrior, Birch struggled and endured as the days passed. In six months he made more progress than any doctors had expected. Everyone in the hospital was impressed with this ex-fighter pilot. Soon he was nicknamed 'Tough Tiger.'

No one, except his family, knew the other side of this incredible hero. Hidden underneath layers of calm fortitude, painful memories lay buried, often terrorizing him.

On the night of August 11, 1946, a year after Danny was killed, sleep eluded Birch. The horrible events a year earlier played over and over in his mind. He remembered everything as if it had happened only the day before—the torture, the plan to escape, the decapitation of the teenager, the life-and-death choices they'd made, the miserable and forlorn days that had followed, the shooting and the mass grave...

Oddly, out of so many memories, Danny's joke disturbed him the most. Danny's impish smile and wriggling fingers always made Birch teary. Danny's words, "I'll haunt you in your dreams," sadly became true. Rolling the small medicine bottle left by Danny in his hand, Birch tossed and turned. The images of his friend wouldn't go away, no matter how hard he tried to block them.

The night was hot and sticky. Along with Nanking and Wuhan, Chungking was known as one of the Three Furnaces in China. The window was wide open, but it offered no relief. The leaden heat and the humidity hurt the wounds on his body. Outside two cicadas shrilled somewhere in the reeds.

Lying naked to the waist, Birch stared at the ceiling. Moonlight shone through the window. It illuminated the room with a silvery hue and cast ever-changing shadows. On the second night he was in prison he'd watched similar shadows. Aches and pains from various wounds had kept him from sleeping. Earlier that night Danny had offered him the pain reliever given to him by School Boy, a sympathetic guard. But Birch had declined his offer. There weren't many pills in the bottle, and he'd hoped to save them for Danny.

What if I took the pills? Then Danny wouldn't have had them to drug me. He might still be alive! Had his well-intended act cost his brother's life?

Exhausted, he dozed off before dawn. Soon he began to dream. Danny and Mary were on a stage. The American was playing a guitar. There was a white scarf around his neck. Mary stood beside him, singing. She wore a silky pink dress and lily-white gloves. Their youthful faces were lit up under the warm stage lights.

In the front row sat Daisy and Jasmine, each with a halo above her head. They waved to Birch with huge smiles upon their faces. He waved back and grinned from ear to ear, realizing with relief that his sisters had become angels.

Just then a group of Japanese soldiers emerged from the darkness. They opened fire. Danny was shot and fell backward. His head hit the floor as if he had been beheaded, just like the teenage prisoner. His white scarf turned red in a pool of blood.

Birch was flabbergasted, but he had no time to analyze. He had to save Mary. He kicked and thrashed, yet he went nowhere. His legs were like concrete; they weighed him down. Only his outstretched arm could move.

Meanwhile, Mary spun, running and screeching. Her hands fluttered in the air as if she were trying to fly away. One of her white gloves dropped off before she flung herself at him.

"Mary!" Birch cried as he drew her into his embrace. She didn't answer. He looked down and saw blood oozing from her chest, blooming on the silky pink dress like a peony. A pall of black flies hovered over her wound, making a repulsive buzzing sound.

The horrific scene jerked Birch upright with a scream. Fear and sorrow glazed his eyes. A sheen of perspiration clung to his face, neck, and upper body.

Then in a haze, at the first glint of dawn, he spotted a girl bursting into his room. *Mary? Is that you?* He sat up straighter in bed and reached out. Wrapping his arms around her, he didn't let go, even when he felt a little resistance. "No, Mary, don't go. Don't leave me. I miss you. Stay here, please!" He hadn't seen her for fourteen months.

Although Birch had never talked about it, he missed Mary terribly. Her leaving had torn out a piece of his soul. She was his only love.

On July 4, 1944, the Air Force hosted a performance to celebrate their American friends' Independence Day. While Birch waited for his turn, a young woman in a silky, lavender evening gown sang, "*Mo Li Hua.*" The melody and her soulful voice struck him like a thunderbolt. "Jasmine Flower" was the song that Daisy and Jasmine had sung at Danny's birthday party two years earlier. Time after time, Danny had praised the beautiful folk song. A dull ache settled in Birch's chest as his mind fogged over with images of his sister and his cousin.

Still immersed in thought, he heard the girl start another song. Immediately the lyric of "Danny Boy" penetrated deep into his soul. He imagined that it was Jasmine or Daisy singing the song to Danny.

The young woman flashed him an infectious smile as she passed. An intoxicating scent of perfume hovered around him.

And that was it! The brave pilot's heart was stolen. It was love at first sight. Mary was gorgeous. A lot of young men in the Air Force fell for her. But she chose Birch over other admirers. They were a perfect match; even his rivals admitted it.

Mary dazzled Birch. Her beauty took his breath away, her sweet voice tugged at his heart, and her mere presence made it beat faster. He longed to be with her. What else could one ask from a relationship?

"You wear your heart on your sleeve," Danny laughed at him. Then the Flying Tiger warned him, "Take it slow."

Birch couldn't help it; at age thirty he was head over heels in love for the first time.

Now, after a year separation, Mary had finally come back. She was sitting next to him on his bed. Still holding her in his embrace, he planted small lingering kisses on her neck, on the tip of her chin, the sweep of her cheekbones, the corners of her eyes. And on her mouth! Reveling in the feel of her silky skin, he was brimming with joy in his delirium. He hadn't felt this way since he'd awakened from the coma. "Mary! Oh, darling," he murmured under his breath as he tasted the girl.

Abruptly he stopped. Something wasn't right. Mary liked to let her hair fall on her back, not pulled into braided pigtails. And Mary wore an expensive brand of perfume. The lavish scent had become part of her identity. Birch had often smelled it before seeing her. But the woman in his arms wore no perfume. He drew back from her. In the faint light, a look of shock and confusion spread across his face. "I'm so sorry," he stammered, backing away from the girl.

It was Xiao Mei.

His back thudded against the headboard as he snatched the sheet to conceal his bare chest. *How could it be? What happened?* He tried to unfreeze himself, to find logic.

He knew, however, he'd done something wrong, even unintentionally. Of course, things like this happened all the time—after all, *Ya Tou*—servant girls or slave girls—were their masters' personal property, sold for life. But as a gentleman, Birch would've never considered doing anything like this.

"I'm truly sorry," he apologized again. That was all he could do.

Xiao Mei seemed as stunned as he was. His continuous apology made things worse. Seeing his awkwardness, she became uneasy. "I…I…" she mumbled, trying to explain, yet made no sensible sentence.

Chewing her lip, she stood up in a hurry. Her head hung low, but the redness on her cheeks was evident. Nervously, she wound the hem of her shirt around her finger and then unwound it. "I heard…I heard your screams. I…" she whispered, breathless. Then she stole a glance at the Young Master before fleeing the room.

Birch remained in bed for a long time. *What have I done?* He wasn't an insensitive man. The housemaid's fondness for him was more than clear. Nevertheless, his heart was already taken. Even a year after Mary had left him, he couldn't forget her. There was no room in his heart for anyone else.

Birch sagged against the headboard and dropped the sheet. In the daylight, the jagged scars on his bare chest became more pronounced, reminding him of both visible and invisible wounds. The fact remained that he couldn't offer much to any woman.

He scraped a hand over his sweat-soaked hair while trying to organize his thoughts. His eyebrows furrowed with concern. In a tradition that dated back thousands of years, physical contact between males and females was forbidden. A man and a woman couldn't touch each other unless they were in the same family, even though this was now beginning to be questioned by the younger generation.

But I didn't just touch her, I kissed her! His naked body had enfolded her in a tight embrace. He'd kissed Mary only once, on her forehead. Mary had been his girlfriend and he'd had every intention of marrying her, yet it would have been inappropriate to do anything more. What had just happened between him and Xiao Mei was an accident. He hadn't meant for it to happen. He'd been half-asleep.

Birch was mortified by the event long after Xiao Mei had left the room. Reluctantly, he got out of bed. He was in deep thought as he secured his artificial leg.

The first few steps of the day were always very painful. His hands flew to his right thigh. Clutching the muscles around the socket where the limb met the prosthesis, he tried to press out the throb-bing pain.

Drawing a deep breath, he slid the crutches underneath his arms. With a heavy heart, he limped and shuffled toward his father's study. The thump-thumping noise echoed in the empty hallway with each step.

Chapter 29

— — — — — — — —

Xiao Mei waited in the dining room. It was a large area lit by porcelain lamps with white silk lampshades. Scrolls of ink-and-brush paintings of peonies, plum blossoms, and lotus flowers hung on the walls. The table was covered with white embroidered linen and set for three. An enticing aroma permeated the air.

She didn't know why it took the two men so long. Her uneasy feeling wouldn't go away. *Did I do something terribly wrong? I shouldn't go into the Young Master's room.* She'd felt compelled to help when she heard his cry. This wasn't the first time. She knew his nightmares often terrorized him. Every time she heard the screams, her heart ached for him.

It had happened early this morning when she passed his room. In the heat of the moment, she hadn't thought twice before entering. Her eagerness to comfort was instinctive and irrepressible. Now she realized it was wrong to go into his room—she'd embarrassed him. She could still feel the heat of his touch and the burn of his kiss. Chewing her bottom lip, she savored his taste. A giddy mix of joy and anxiety turned her face the color of the peony in the painting. She folded her arms against her body, waiting like a prisoner for her verdict.

When the two men finally appeared, Xiao Mei brought the dishes she'd kept warm in pots and pans. Quietly, she slid onto a chair at the side of General Bai, and across from Birch. Unlike servants in other families who ate their meals separately, she was asked to sit with the family. Even though everyone was very nice to her, she never felt completely relaxed. Often she found excuses to get up, prepare more dishes, or bring more food. Today was particularly awkward.

"Xiao Mei, you know the Civil War has started." General Bai broke the quietness as he picked up the delicate china teacup with a gold rim. "Birch and I have decided to leave Chungking."

Less than a year after the war against Japan had ended, the truce had fallen apart, and a full-scale civil war between the Nationalists and the Communists had broken out. Both the general and Birch were against a battle within the country, and they were tired of fighting.

"We're planning to go to the Village of Peach Blossoms." As an afterthought, General Bai added, "As soon as we sell the house here."

Not knowing where the conversation was headed, Xiao Mei sat erect, placing her hands on her lap underneath the table. Her left thumb rubbed the small scar on the back of her right hand, reminding her to remain calm.

"Xiao Mei, how long have you worked for us?"

She moistened her lips before answering. "Eight years."

"Eight years? If we count the two years you worked for my brother, you've been with us for ten years. That's a long time."

Alarm shone in her eyes. She put more pressure on the scar, trying to calm her nerves.

General Bai cleared his throat. "You're twenty-four this year. Most girls your age have already married. Their kids are probably in school by now. You should get married. We hope you'll be wed before we leave here."

Xiao Mei seemed dazed. *Get married? To whom?* Although she knew the odds, she couldn't suppress a distant hope. *What if?* Her nerves tingled with anticipation of his next words.

"I called a couple of people," General Bai continued after sipping his tea. "A friend of mine recommended an excellent matchmaker. Madame Tu is very successful—"

"Please don't chase me away…" Her tone became apprehensive as she expelled the thread of hope like the air out of a pricked balloon.

"We're not driving you away. We're giving you your freedom. Can't you see? We just want you to be happy, to live a normal life like other women. You deserve a good man as a husband. You should have lots of children."

Xiao Mei closed her eyes and shook her head.

"How about Wu Pan?" General Bai asked, referring to the former security guard. "He's a year older than you. A reliable man. He's never said anything, but I'm sure he has a crush on you. He doesn't hide it very well." The general broke into a smile as he remembered the young captain's sheepish grin. "Even with limited education, he's bright. Not a bad choice. Didn't he save you a couple of months ago? Isn't that something? If you like, I'll talk—"

Xiao Mei stood and rushed to the other side of the table between the two men. Without saying a word, she fell to her knees. A look of desperation twisted her features.

"Oh, for heaven's sake, get up." General Bai reached down, pulling at her arm.

Birch also stretched out his arm, but stopped and let his hand fall.

She resisted the pull and remained kneeling. Her lower lip quivered.

"It doesn't have to be him. Don't worry. There are lots of choices in a big city. This matchmaker will find—"

"Please! You'll need a servant in Yunnan. As long as I can work, please let me stay. I'm a good housemaid. I know what kind of food you…and *Shao Ye* prefer. I know how to prepare it the way you like it. Anything…I'll do anything—"

"My silly child, you're an excellent maid. We won't find anyone better than you. We'll miss you and the delicious dishes you make." General Bai swallowed. "But you shouldn't be a servant for the rest of your life. We just want you to be happy."

"I'm happy here. I don't want to go anywhere."

"You can't remain a servant forever. You should have your own family. I'm sure you'll make a wonderful wife and mother. You're such a loving woman. That's what we hope for you."

She shook her head. "I'd rather be a maid…stay in the family. I don't care about anything else." The last few words ended on a woeful sob. Tears streamed down her distraught face.

"Don't cry." General Bai sighed. "You're still young. In the long run, you'll understand. There are better choices. You can enjoy a normal life. You'll regret it if you don't."

"No, I won't regret it," she answered without the slightest hesitation. "You and *Shao Ye* are the only people I know in this world. Don't make me leave you!"

"Listen to me, Xiao Mei. We'll give you enough *Jia Zhuang* so that the groom's family won't look down upon you. We'll pay you and your family to visit us in Yunnan every so often." With excitement growing in his voice, General Bai said, "I'd love to see your children. I can't wait for them to call me *Ye Ye*." Unable to have his own grandchild, his face lit up with the thought of being called Grandpa.

"I appreciate you and *Shao Ye* looking after my welfare." Her voice trembled. A fresh wave of tears stung her eyes. This time, they were not caused by sadness.

Jia Zhuang, the transfer of parental property to a woman at marriage, was crucial. A woman who brought a large dowry was often considered more virtuous and would be treated accordingly by the groom's family.

"I'm deeply touched that you'd give me…*Jia Zhuang*. I'm flattered. That's very kind of you. I don't know what else to say. Thank you very, very much." Xiao Mei bowed and knocked her forehead on the floor three times, showing her sincerest reverence and gratitude.

Only a daughter would receive a fund like a dowry. General Bai was treating her as if she were part of the family, as if she were his daughter. His statement of being called Grandpa tugged at her heart.

Then she straightened her body, her eyes still downcast. "But no, I don't want it or need it." Through gritted teeth she appealed, "Please, let me stay with you and…*Shao Ye*. That's all I ask. Nothing more. I don't need anything. I won't ask for…anything else."

The older man shook his head. He didn't know how else to convince the young woman, but he wasn't about to change his mind.

"If you are determined to drive me away," she croaked with a sense of foreboding, "I'll…I'll go to a monastery. I'll become a Buddhist nun."

General Bai's jaw dropped, and Birch gaped at her in stunned silence.

Under Buddhist discipline, strict celibacy was a must for an ordained monk or nun. For centuries, short of suicide, becoming a female monk had been the ultimate way for a woman to show her determination to refuse marriage.

The men had known that it would be hard to convince her, but her strong resistance was more than they'd expected. Most girls were too shy or too submissive to object. They might not like the proposal, but they were trained to obey. Few girls would speak their minds about such a sensitive subject.

General Bai exchanged a helpless glance with Birch. Her objection had rendered him speechless. After a long silence, he heaved a tired sigh. "Okay, you can stay." He pulled on her arm again. "But think about it. Consider the alternative, my child. Anytime you're ready, we'll be more than happy to help you find the finest match."

Hope sprang to life in her tear-flooded eyes.

Chapter 30

▬ ▬ ▬ ▬ ▬ ▬ ▬ ▬

In the fall of 1946, the family sold the house and was ready to leave for the village in Yunnan. At their farewell party, a few of Birch's fellow airmen clustered at the end of a table full of treats.

"I don't think you will find these up the mountain." Meng Hu handed Birch two cartons of Lucky Strikes. With an angular face, the fellow fighter pilot oozed confidence. He lived up to his name—*Meng Hu*, Fierce Tiger.

"I told him smoking isn't good for anyone," complained Wang Hong, the nurse who'd trained Xiao Mei. A mint green floral dress draped over her small frame, which was dwarfed by her brawny husband's size. She scooped up a mooncake with lotus seed paste. Shaking her head, she added, "But he insists."

"Yet, the stingy bastard won't even give me one pack." Chen Bin, one of the ground crew, twisted his lips, pretending to be unhappy. He was in his mid-twenties with playful puppy eyes and a boyish face. "Lucky Strikes are hard to come by nowadays." He helped himself to a cigarette from a box on the nearby table. The smoke from his mouth dissipated instantly in the current produced by whirring ceiling fan.

"That's right," Du Ting, a tail gunner, butted in. His jet-black hair was plastered down with grease. He snatched a pan fried dumpling from a plate. Scrunching up his nose, he wiggled it from side to side before he said, "Not to mention they cost a fortune." He tilted his head back, dropping the hot dumpling into his mouth. Immediately, he hissed and fanned his open mouth.

Birch thanked the kind couple. Steadying himself with a cane, he picked up a package he'd asked Xiao Mei to prepare earlier. "I didn't get a chance to give you a gift." He handed it to Wang Hong. The couple had gotten married when he was in the coma.

They opened the package, and a bag of dried red dates came to view.

"*Zao sheng gui zi*," Birch offered his good wishes to Wang Hong first and repeated it to Meng Hu. "May you soon have a lovely son."

"Boy, oh, boy—" Meng Hu started to joke about the sentimental gift, but abruptly stopped himself.

The term *zao zi*, red date, had the same pronunciation as "have a son soon." It was often given to newlyweds as a propitiatory gesture.

Meng Hu must have heard about Birch's condition from his wife. He slapped Birch on the back, and then twirled to face Wang Hong. Rubbing her slightly bulging stomach, he said, eyes blazing, "Hong, why don't we ask Birch to be our child's godfather?"

Wang Hong responded with a head bob. A faint blush stained her cream-colored skin. "It would be an honor."

"The honor will be mine." Birch clapped Meng Hu on the shoulder, nodding in appreciation. His eyes glistened.

"If it's a boy, we'll name him Meng Xiao Hu, just so you know."

"That's a perfect name—Fierce Little Tiger."

"This is so unfair," Chen Bin protested. He took another quick drag off the cigarette. "I want to be a godfather. Why don't you ask me?"

With a mouth full of dumpling, Du Ting nodded in agreement. More people surrounded them, intrigued.

"I'm a hero, too." Shoulders back, smiling proudly, Chen Bin traced a finger over a medal pinned to his uniform. Then he switched his gaze to the six medals bristling on Birch's chest. "I guess I need five more." He ran the palm of his hand over his buzz cut and grimaced. "That's not fair. It's easier to get awarded, being a fighter pilot."

"Easier? Like hell." Meng Hu smacked the back of Chen Bin's head. "You mean easier to be injured or killed?" He regarded his boyish face. His mouth stretched into a wide grin as he pinched Chen Bin's plump cheek. "You don't need more medals. Grow up and be a man first before you think about being a father."

Everyone laughed.

Everyone except Birch.

All the references to fatherhood reminded him of Mary and her comment about having half a dozen "Little Tigers" with him. He glanced around for the hundredth time since the start of the party. The large room was lit by brilliant crystal chandeliers and packed with his and his father's former colleagues and associates.

His gaze swept the crowd, searching. Mary wasn't there. She hadn't shown up. They might never see each other again, and he wanted to say goodbye to the only woman he'd ever loved and still could not forget. His right hand went to his left pinky and twisted the ring. He still carried it with him. *What was I thinking? That she would change her mind when she sees it?* A surge of disappointment tore through him.

Pushing aside unpleasant thoughts, Birch forced a hint of a smile to match those of the others. He raised a glass to his lips to dilute the bitterness. The fragrance jogged his memory to the fruity wine brewed in the village. An idea came to him, and he blurted out, "Hey, why don't you visit me in Yunnan, all of you?"

He scanned the crowd around him, his dark eyes shining with an eagerness he could hardly hide. This time his lips stretched into a genuine smile. Lifting the glass, he added, "I'll show you a piece of heaven on earth."

Soon after the party, the family left for the Village of Peach Blossoms.

The air smelled of bittersweet magnolia as they stepped through the curved archway. Above them two yellow warblers fluttered past, playing tag in the golden leaves and the clusters of white flowers.

Birch turned to take one last look at the house where they'd lived for ten years. With the olive green model airplane from Danny in one hand and the cane in the other, he felt a wave of nostalgia wash over him.

His mother had decorated the interior, choosing colors and fabrics that were subtle and elegant. Everything remained the same as she'd left it. Throughout the house, fine paintings and artifacts of flowers adorned the walls. Peony represented wealth and glory. Lotus symbolized purity for the flower rose untainted by mud. And blooming in the midst of winter, the plum blossom embodied perseverance and hope.

His mother had loved flora. That was why they'd named him Bai Hua—White Birch, and his sister Bai Chuju—White Daisy. She'd also suggested Jasmine's name—Bai Moli.

Birch felt a lump form in his throat at the thought of Daisy and Jasmine. A vivid picture of another time came to his mind—his sister and cousin sitting side by side in front of their grand piano. They'd enjoyed playing together. The cheerful music and their laughter echoed in his mind, but the girls were no longer there.

He longed to hear his mother's cheerful talk, Daisy's blithe giggle, Jasmine's soft voice, and Danny's hearty laugh. He missed them all.

As he reflected, Xiao Mei stepped closer to one of the stone lions. Prowling at the side of the gate, the animals had guarded the house for decades. She put the luggage down and circled her arms around the statue. Her eyes were closed. Her cheek touched the lion's nose.

A sudden stab of pain struck Birch as he watched. Daisy used to rub the lion's nose whenever she walked past. He could still hear her say, "Good boy, keep us safe."

The lion hadn't kept her safe. And neither had he.

He turned and limped toward the car before Xiao Mei let go of the statue, before she could see the mist in his eyes.

Ahead of him, his father walked with leaden steps. His shoulders slightly drooped and his hands balled into fists at his sides. Yet he pushed onward without a backward glance.

It dawned on Birch that he'd never seen his father shed tears. *Not when he heard about Uncle's and Auntie's deaths. Not when he held Mom's body. Not when he received the tragic news of Daisy and Jasmine.*

Was his father born strong? Or had lifelong discipline enabled him to maintain a stoic appearance? Filled with admiration, Birch straightened his spine and pressed onward.

Chapter 31

━ ━ ━ ━ ━ ━ ━

The small village was a thousand miles from Chungking. They flew first to Kunming, capital of Yunnan Province.

Xiao Mei had never flown, for flying was a privilege for rich people. She was afraid of heights and very anxious. Yet she said nothing. Riveted to her seat, she clutched her hands and pressed her left thumb into the small scar on the back of her right hand.

Sitting next to her, Birch sensed her nervousness. He was compelled to reach over and comfort her. They'd known each other for more than ten years, and he cared about her. He knew she must be frightened. The young woman seldom displayed her emotions. He'd noticed that pressing the scar seemed to be her way to suppress anxiety or fear.

They were so close that their elbows touched. The scent of jasmine pinned to her milky blue sweater teased his nostrils. Even so, his fingers tightened around the model airplane in his lap to keep them from reaching out to her. He was worried about sending the wrong message or giving false hope. He couldn't offer something he didn't have. The incident several months earlier in his bedroom was still fresh in his mind, not to mention embarrassing, although no one had ever mentioned it.

"Xiao Mei, take a deep breath," he urged. He allowed a teasing note to enter his voice. "Relax and enjoy the scenery. Not every day you'll see something like this."

His calmness and concern put her a little more at ease. Closing her eyes, she leaned back and drew a cleansing breath. When she opened them again, the plane was already in the air. One look out of the window and her eyes brightened.

Xiao Mei was born and raised in Nanking. She'd traveled only once in her life, when she fled the killing field of Nanking to the war-time capital, Chungking. But that was a journey of survival. She'd not had the opportunity to enjoy the scenery.

It was a crisp autumn afternoon with a few white clouds floating in the blue sky. Far below, different crops turned the earth into a multicolored patchwork—green, gold, red, and purple. Over the verdant highlands, lakes shone like cerulean jewels. The elevated view obscured the ugly remains of war—charred buildings, blackened ground, and scarred forests. For the rest of the trip, Xiao Mei pressed her forehead against the window and fastened her gaze to the scene outside.

Before landing, she turned to Birch. The sun was setting. The last rays burned the sky a fiery orange, casting a glorious glow on her face. She was brimming with joy as she said, "Now I understand why you love to fly."

He nodded. Appreciating the beauty of nature had been his way to balance the ugliness of war and to combat the stress of being a fighter pilot. "Danny used to say he wouldn't trade his job for anything in the world. He loved it." He fingered the olive green airplane. A wistful look came over his face. "He said he'd be a pilot in his next life. And I agree with him."

"In my next life," she blurted out, eyes shining, "I'd love to be a pilot, too."

Her bold comment took Birch by surprise. "A couple of hours ago I was afraid you were going to pass out. Now you want to be a pilot?" He grinned. Her high spirits amused him. For the first time, he caught a glimpse of a hidden side of this quiet girl.

Their gaze came together, and her eyes were so dark that the irises were indistinguishable from the pupils. As she stared at him, he could see her longing, and his breathing suddenly became uneven. Hastily he broke the connection.

145

Chapter 32

From Kunming they took an overnight train to Anning. Wang Linzi and a couple of young villagers were waiting for them at the train station with half a dozen hired donkeys. The path they took up the mountain was so narrow and steep that it wasn't passable even for oxen-carts. Donkeys or bamboo-pole sedan chairs were the only means of transportation. Given their heavy luggage containing hundreds of books, donkeys were a more practical choice. The ride was bumpy but uneventful, except for Xiao Mei's occasional exclamations of fright or delight. Hours later they arrived in the Village of Peach Blossoms.

Only two people had survived the massacre by Japanese troops, who were furious that the villagers wouldn't give up Danny Hardy. Ding Xiang, a teenage girl, had been set free by a remorseful translator after the Japanese soldiers gang-raped her. She was the one who told Birch what had happened to Jasmine and the villagers. The entire experience was so painful that General Bai helped her find a factory job in Chungking, far from where the traumatic events had happened. She was very grateful for her new life, but in the last four years, she'd met up with the general and Birch only once and apologized for not staying in touch. She had tried everything to forget about the unspeakable past. They understood and left her alone as she wished.

The other survivor, Wang Linzi, had been an eighteen-year-old boy at the time of the massacre. He was one of the herbalist's grandsons. His younger brother had helped to rescue Danny. Linzi was away from the village when the killing occurred. His grandfather had sent him down the mountain to tell General Bai and Birch about the Japanese invasion of the town.

General Bai and Birch had recruited people from the nearby communities to clean up the village, farm the fields, and renovate the houses. By the time they arrived in the village, more than half of it was occupied again.

The remote area lacked modern conveniences. No electricity. No telephone. Not even tap water. Xiao Mei had to learn to fetch water from a well in the yard. She had to gather and chop branches to fuel the wood stove. Her job was hard, and living conditions were austere. Yet she had no complaints. She stayed in Jasmine's room. Birch chose the one Danny had used; it was in the middle of the house. General Bai took Daisy's room.

The first two nights were miserable for Birch. The familiar place evoked a flood of memories and emotions. Being so close, yet a lifetime away from his loved ones, took a toll on him. Staying in the same room where Danny had lived, and lying in the same bed his brother had used, he had worse nightmares than before. His screams caused Xiao Mei to cringe and weep in the dark. His cries woke his father, who wondered if he'd made the right decision to move here.

On the third day, Birch left early in the morning without telling anyone where he was going. He didn't even know. He wanted to go to Dead Man's Pass where Daisy had died, but he didn't think he could make it that far. So he focused on getting to a cave where Danny and the two girls had lived. It had taken him and Daisy several hours to get there. This time it seemed to take forever. Hiking up a rugged mountain was very different from walking on the smooth and level ground where he'd exercised.

The leaves had changed color. Different shades of green and yellow painted the dense forest. A last batch of wildflowers dotted the edge of the woods. Tree branches stretched over the trail, offering dappled shade, breaking the sunlight into dozens of golden beams. As far as he could see, the uneven path continued upward.

Birch considered turning back. Instead, he pushed onward. The cave was like a magnet, luring him forward.

He rolled his sleeves back to the elbows. His white shirt turned soggy from perspiration, dried in the cool mountain breeze, and soon dampened again. From time to time he wiped a clammy palm on his pants to get a better grip on his cane. Every step became a test of will.

All the while, Birch appreciated what Danny had done four years earlier—the Flying Tiger had had to hop on one leg up the mountainside. Even with his help, and Daisy's support, the task had been more than challenging. Birch thrust his right hand into his pants pocket, touching the small medicine bottle left by his brother.

Not far from the cave, his prosthetic leg started to give him trouble. It had been hours. He was exhausted. His thigh cramped while he was stepping over two rocks. His leg gave up power, and he stepped into an irregular gap between the rocks. The cane failed to catch him. Birch fell, landing hard on the surface. Pain raced up his leg.

He cursed his luck. Half sitting and half lying on the rock, he folded his arms around the cramped thigh and hugged it to his chest, trying to suppress the pain. Blood leaked through his pant leg where the amputated stump met the socket, and a large piece of skin on his left elbow was scraped.

But the pain was only a small part of his dismay. An athlete all his life, Birch felt defeated by his inadequacy. Hiking and rock climbing were once his preferred pastime. Now he was hindered by his injuries.

A small cluster of forget-me-nots bloomed an arm's length away, reminding him of Danny and Jasmine. He turned his head, keeping his eyes averted, and expelled his frustration in a gust of breath.

Legs stretched before him, Birch remained motionless until his heartbeat calmed and the sweat stopped pouring from his face. He pushed himself to full height and gathered his waning energy.

Shutting his mind to the pain in his leg, he pressed onward, despite the protests of every bone, joint, and muscle.

His shirt was so wet with perspiration that when he tried to dust himself off, he left streaks of mud wherever he touched. Xiao Mei kept his clothes clean and starched. He wondered what she would think when she saw him.

By midafternoon Birch finally reached the bottom of the cave. A steep cliff, about one hundred feet, stood in front of him. A natural rock staircase led straight up. Last time he was here, he hadn't thought twice before he climbed. Even Daisy had done it with just a few cries. But there was no way for him to get up now. He sank onto the first step of the stair to catch his breath.

He longed to see the hideout where Danny and the girls had lived. Four years earlier, he'd met the Flying Tiger for the first time when he came here to pick him up. Danny wouldn't leave without Jasmine, the woman he loved. Birch had to coax the Flying Tiger, and they left in a hurry. Birch remembered the pictures Jasmine had drawn on the rock wall, even though he'd glanced at them only briefly. The scenes were so striking and familiar.

Two hawks drifted high above him in the vivid blue sky. Birch looked enviously at the birds. He wished he could soar as they did. Danny was up there. Jack stood next to him. And the two young women looked at them in admiration. Now he was so close, barely a whisper away, yet a world apart. He couldn't reach the spot where he yearned to be.

A soft wind rustled the birch woods, sending golden leaves whirling around him. The lush hillside was awe-inspiring under warm sunlight. Facing the gorgeous scenery, Birch also thought of Mary. His ex-girlfriend had never been outdoorsy. She preferred museums, concerts, and movies. However, when he told her about the cave, she'd been intrigued. "Promise to take me there, Birch. I'd love to see it. I'll borrow my cousin's camera. Those pictures will have historical significance."

He'd been thrilled that Mary had agreed to hike up the mountain with him. She was different from most young women; she was his equal. Now he was here, but Mary and her camera were nowhere to be found. Only the ring on his left pinky reminded him of her.

Through the trees, the glowing sun slanted little by little toward the horizon. Birch just sat there, thinking, dreaming, and smoking cigarettes one after another.

Finally he stabbed the cigarette out on the sole of his boot, stood up, and faced the bluff. Raising his long arms, he searched the rocky step above to find a good grip. *This is what Danny had done four years ago.* As he groped for the cracks with his fingers, he wondered if these were the same spots his brother had touched. Taking a deep breath, and using the strength of his arms and left leg, he jumped. He was successful, landing on the first step.

The second one was much harder. The foothold was higher and smaller. Danny had failed when he tried. Now Birch understood why. Landing precisely on the small surface was impossible. Danny had been lucky to have people like the herbalist and the teenage boy to catch him when he fell. Falling now without anyone to help him would be dreadful. It could do more damage to his already battered body. And even if he miraculously made it, there was no way he could reach the top. *I'll be back*, he declared.

Climbing the cliff became his goal. He vowed he would exercise more vigorously and grow stronger. He promised himself that he would make it to the top. *Not just to the cave, I'll reach Dead Man's Pass as well. I swear!*

Chapter 33

When Birch didn't return home in the afternoon, General Bai asked Linzi and several young villagers to search for him. He guessed that his son had gone to the mountain. But he had no idea how far. It wasn't a good sign that the young man hadn't shown up for lunch. Had he fallen? Was he hurt?

The father was worried. Birch was tough, but he wasn't in good enough shape to climb the mountain. Again, General Bai questioned his decision to come to Yunnan. The screams he'd heard in the last two nights had already made him wonder. This place was close to their loved ones. Too close. There were so many sad memories. How would Birch cope with them?

"Don't worry, General," said Linzi. In a peasant's smock and straw shoes, he was short but sturdy. "We'll find *Bai Hua Ge*. He's probably too tired to walk." Like all the young villagers, he'd been calling Birch *Bai Hua Ge—Big Brother Birch*. He pointed to the bamboo-pole sedan chair which the villagers had used to carry Danny four years earlier. "We'll bring him home in no time."

As they were leaving, Xiao Mei dashed out of the house. "Wait for me," she called as she waved her arms, her long braids bouncing in front of her chest. A purple-and-black patchwork bag dangled from her right hand. "Water and food. It's getting late. *Shao Ye* hasn't had anything to eat the entire day."

"Good idea," General Bai said as he nodded in appreciation. Then he asked, "Where are you going?"

"I'm going with them."

"No need. It isn't easy to hike up the mountain. Give them the bag." General Bai was in his late fifties and wasn't in good health. Even though it was a warm day, he wore a brown corduroy jacket. He didn't think he could keep up with the villagers. Xiao Mei was young, but she wasn't an outdoorsy girl.

"I might be able to help," she begged, "Please!"

General Bai knew how hard it would be to convince her, once she made up her mind. "All right. Be careful. No need to run." He turned to the young villagers. "Take good care of Xiao Mei."

The sun's last rays burned the sky a fiery orange when they met up with Birch on the path close to the cave. He was limping badly, his white shirt wrinkled, stained, and clinging to his skin. Droplets of sweat shimmered on his forehead and dripped down his cheeks. Only he knew whether the perspiration was due to exhaustion or pain.

"Are you hurt?" Xiao Mei asked.

He shook his head.

"But…" She swallowed her question.

"*Bai Hua Ge*, please get on the carrier." Linzi and the other young man set down the sedan chair. "You must be tired." The villager wiped his face with the back of his left hand as he stretched his right arm, trying to grab the pilot.

"No!" Birch waved him off. Being transported by others was too humiliating. He understood how Danny had felt. He was now in the same shoes. Soldierly pride kept him from accepting the help he needed. Ignoring the needles of pain in his legs, the emptiness in his stomach, and the dryness in his throat, he staggered and inched his way down the hill.

"Wait!" Xiao Mei rushed forward, opening her arms to block the Young Master. "You shouldn't do this. You can't—"

"I'll not—"

"*Shao Ye*, listen to me." The servant girl moved one step closer, standing toe-to-toe with him. A foot shorter, she had to tilt her head back to talk to him. Her petite body seemed so frail before the broad-shouldered man, yet she didn't budge. She nibbled her bottom lip before continuing. "It's getting late. If you hobble like this, you won't get home until midnight or later. The General is worried. You can't keep him wondering if you're okay."

She pointed to the villagers. "We've got four strong men here. They do this all the time. They're more than willing to give you a hand. Why don't you let them help you? It'll make them happy."

She turned to the villagers and saw their nods. Then to the Young Master, she moistened her lips and continued. "Major Hardy was carried like this. Everyone needs help from time to time. No need to feel bad about it."

Birch's eyebrows lifted. He was awestruck by the typically quiet housemaid. She didn't beg. She didn't whine. Her logic was clear. In a few sentences, she presented the problem from different perspectives. What better argument could one give? The tough fighter pilot had no choice but to comply. Dragging his feet, he stepped closer to the chair, and grinding his teeth, he sat.

"Wonderful!" A tender smile graced her lips as she gathered the strap of the patchwork bag and handed it to him. "Nothing too tasty, but at least you won't starve to death." Her face beamed in the golden light filtering through the trees.

Chapter 34

--- --- --- --- --- --- --- ---

It was almost dark when they arrived at the village. General Bai was happy once he caught sight of his son stepping down from the sedan chair in the cat-gray twilight. "Thank you." He shook hands with the young villagers while Birch patted their backs.

After the young men left, the three of them stepped into Birch's bedroom.

"Dad, I've done a lot of thinking today and have come up with some ideas," he said, sitting on the edge of a wooden framed bed.

Meanwhile, Xiao Mei lit an oil lamp and set it on the table. Except for two timeworn hard-backed chairs, there was no other furniture in the room. Cardboard boxes full of books lined the wall. Despite the sparseness, the place was clean.

She dipped a cloth in a teak wood washbowl on the floor. After wringing out the excess water, she handed it to the Young Master. "I'm going to cook something quickly for you." She turned around, getting ready to leave the room.

"Wait." Birch signaled her to stay. "You may want to hear this." He wiped his face absent-mindedly and turned to his father. Birch looked worn-out, but a glimmer of excitement shone in his eyes. "I think we should rebuild the bridge." He was talking about the one at Dead Man's Pass.

The Japanese had destroyed the primitive footbridge four years earlier when they chased Danny and Birch. The only escape route for Daisy had been cut off, and she was stranded on the other side of an impassable gorge, separated from the two men she loved. Birch had no choice but to kill his adored sister after the Japanese had captured her. He knew that they would not let her live, and that she would die a painful death.

Sitting next to the table, General Bai opened his mouth. After an awkward pause, he pointed out warily, "It won't be easy." He was referring to something more than the physical effort of constructing a bridge. The wooden chair squeaked as he shifted his weight.

"I know," replied Birch. "But if people could build a bridge hundreds of years ago, we should be able to accomplish it now. There are towns on the other side of the pass where villagers used to go." His eyes shone with unbreakable fortitude. "Dad, remember you said you wanted to rebuild the village? Right now, the only way out is the path down the mountain. You told me that years ago an earthquake blocked this village from the outside world for months. What if a quake hits again? Yunnan is prone to earthquakes. We have to think long term."

Birch took a deep breath, holding his chin high. "Also, Dashan is on the other side of this mountain range. Using the current route, it'll take days to travel around the mountains. If we can go through the pass, it will take only a day, which will help when I begin the search for…Danny."

The general shook his head in disbelief, and then nodded in approval.

"We can use the trees around the gorge," continued Birch. "Why don't we build something everyone can use, hopefully for generations? This time, we'll make something stronger and safer, so that someone like…Daisy won't be afraid to cross."

His father tipped his head again. Tears glossed his eyes.

"And we'll place two statues, one on each side of the gorge—"

"Statues?"

"Yes, a sculpture of an angel on this side," said Birch, eyes glinting. "Daisy died there, and Jasmine wasn't far away. Both were Danny's guardian angels. And hopefully, as Danny liked to say, they are angels now."

The general reached out, grabbing his son's hands. "What a marvelous idea!"

"We'll set another statue on the other side. A statue of a Flying Tiger. Both Danny and Jack died in Yunnan." Birch paused. The knot of his Adam's apple rose and fell. "They died for China, for us. We owe them this much."

Still holding Birch's hand, General Bai replied with another nod.

"Not just for Danny and Jack. Other American airmen have sacrificed their lives for our country. We must honor them, remember their kindness and their bravery. We should use white marble." Birch elaborated, "And we shouldn't call it Dead Man's Pass anymore. Daisy hated that name. We should call it—"

"Angel's Pass!" Xiao Mei blurted out. Standing by the door, she'd been listening to every word. Even in the faint light, her face and eyes glowed.

"Yes, Angel's Pass," Birch affirmed. His eyes locked onto Xiao Mei's as her smile filled the room with warmth and vitality.

Chapter 35

During the next eighteen months the normally quiet pass teemed with activity. Weather permitting, Birch and his helpers spent time at the gorge. He lived with a dozen young villagers in a large canvas tent, worked with them closely, and shared the delicious food Xiao Mei cooked for everyone.

Lying between two mountain ranges, the gorge was one of the deepest canyons in the world. To build a suspension bridge over such wild terrain would have been challenging even with modern engineering and machinery, but the villagers had only primitive tools. They cut down trees with old-fashioned axes, interlocked the boards with homemade ropes, and carried whatever they needed on their backs.

"If our forefathers could build the Great Wall," Birch encouraged the young men whenever they encountered a problem, "then we can build this bridge."

With determination, they made progress one step at a time.

In the evenings, Birch told stories to the illiterate villagers. Sitting around a warm campfire, the villagers hung on his words. Their thirst for knowledge became his incentive.

Romance of the Three Kingdoms was their favorite. It took Birch months to get through this classic novel. Along the way, the concept of *Yi*—morality, duty, loyalty, decency, and brotherhood—was revealed. He hoped that it would have a lasting impact on their lives.

But Birch never mentioned the war against Japan. Nothing about the six medals he'd received; nothing about the rescue of Danny or their friendship; nothing about their flights over the Hump or any of the dangerous missions they'd accomplished. No reference to the life-and-death experiences they'd shared, or those that he'd endured alone.

"*Bai Hua Ge*, why don't you tell us your own stories?" asked one of the young men. "You were a fighter pilot. I'm sure you have lots of stories."

Right away his eyebrows furrowed. Xiao Mei sucked in a quick breath. Her gaze darted toward her young master.

"Please, *Bai Hua Ge*," the young man persisted. But Linzi stopped him. Birch's face darkened and sadness lurked in the depths of his eyes. From then on, despite their curiosity, no one asked again.

Later, some nosy villagers tried to pry the information out of Xiao Mei. Naturally, they didn't succeed. She didn't know everything, and the things she knew, as a good servant and someone who cared about the Young Master, she wouldn't tell anyone.

For Birch, the personal accounts were too painful to share. He was terrified that he would crumble if he did. He'd read his diary once. And once was enough. Afterward, he'd buried those memories deep inside the steel walls of his heart, just as he'd locked his journals in a box.

Even a courageous Tiger had limits.

There was another limitation—Birch had never undressed like the villagers. All the young men enjoyed stripping off their shirts on hot days. Their upper bodies were as bronzed as their faces. They loved to jump naked into the stream or pour cold water from the well over their heads. But Birch always kept his shirt on. He never took those "communal" baths or showers. The villagers asked him to join, but he politely refused. So they assumed that, like most educated city folks, he was reserved. No one saw or knew about his scar-covered body.

These drawbacks didn't prevent Birch from being their leader.

He was their *Bai Hua Ge—Big Brother Birch*. His fighting spirit and his knowledge had earned their respect, even if they didn't fully understand him.

––––––––––

The villagers spent a year and a half of backbreaking work to finish the suspension bridge. At one end stood a life-size statue of an angel, and at the other was a sculpture of a Flying Tiger.

Placed on pedestals, the figures seemed larger than life. The angel displayed an ethereal serenity, and the white marble accentuated her wholesomeness. She faced the gorge, overlooking the perpendicular cliff. Her arms stretched out and wings spread upward, ready to fly over the chasm to be with the one she loved.

Across the gorge, a young Westerner stood facing her. He held a model airplane above his head in his right hand. Tall and muscular, he wore a flight suit, and a long scarf wrapped around his neck. A pair of goggles rested on his forehead.

"Holy smokes!" exclaimed Meng Hu when he and his wife came to visit. It was now the summer of 1948. "He looks just like Danny."

Birch had urged the couple to spend time in Yunnan after they suffered a miscarriage. It took them over a year to finally make the trip. Wang Hong still worked as a nurse at the hospital in Chungking. Meng Hu was no longer a fighter pilot. Tired of war, he'd retired from the Air Force and become a flight instructor.

"This place is unbelievable," said Meng Hu.

Wang Hong simply stared at the gorge.

Hanging between sheer rocky cliffs, the suspension bridge was three feet wide and sixty feet long. It was made of sturdy planks interwoven with heavy rope. Handrails and safety nets protected the walkway on both sides. It swayed when they stepped onto it. Once they reached the middle, Meng Hu turned sideways, leaned over the mesh, and looked down. With a yelp of surprise, he gaped at the bottomless chasm.

A hawk drifted in the sky beneath them. With several beats of its powerful wings, it swooped and plunged. A shrill cry broke out as it disappeared into the fog hovering above the river.

Meng Hu asked, "How did you do it? Danny told me that the old bridge was rotten with holes and broken planks."

Wang Hong stood behind them with hands clutching the rails, unwilling to look down. Her skin rippled with goose bumps as a cold mountain draft blew up from the abyss. The breeze stirred the pines at the rims, making the branches sway and sigh. "You're tall, but Major Hardy was taller and heavier. How did you manage to carry him on your back?" Her voice wavered. "With this new bridge, I know I won't fall, but it still gives me the creeps."

Every time Birch came here, the images of that day played like a movie in his mind. He had trouble picturing how he'd done it. It was the summer of 1942. He'd met Danny several hours earlier. They hadn't even become friends yet. Was it a sense of responsibility? A sense of *Yi*—duty, loyalty, decency—as a Chinese to an American who was so willing to help China?

"Don't stay here," urged Wang Hong. "Keep going, please." The cold had fought its way through her long pants and climbed up her spine underneath her sweater like a sly little mouse. She shivered and tightened her grip. The warm sunlight lost its power to stop her tremors.

Once they reached the other side of the gorge, Wang Hong bent down and took several deep breaths to steady herself.

Meng Hu circled the statue, checking it from different angles. Up close, the American gave an even taller and stronger impression. Although he wasn't smiling, there was a touch of lightheartedness in his expression.

Moving back a few steps, Meng Hu clicked his heels together and threw a crisp salute.

Birch followed suit, holding the cane in his left hand.

A full minute of reflective silence elapsed before Meng Hu looked at the angel on the other side of the gulch. She seemed so eager to soar over the gorge. "Lucky son of a gun," he murmured under his breath. "He gets to see a gorgeous girl—"

"This is wonderful, Birch," Wang Hong cut her husband off mid-stream. "We should never forget about the Flying Tigers. Major Hardy would appreciate this. Your sister and cousin would be so proud of you."

"Have you heard from his family?" asked Meng Hu.

Birch shook his head, sadness darkening his eyes. Weeks after he awakened from the coma, he'd written a thirty-page letter to Danny's family. He told them of Danny's sacrifice, apologized for not being able to protect his brother, and vowed to find their son's remains and send them home. It had been two years. He hadn't heard anything from the family. He assumed that they were angry with him and decided not to bother them until he found Danny.

Meng Hu put a hand on Birch's shoulder. A flicker of sympathy and understanding appeared on his face before his easygoing manner returned. "Seriously, you've done a hell of a job here. This is more than a beautiful place. It's like—" He snapped his fingers, searching for the right words.

"*Shi wai tao yuan.*" Wang Hong finished for him.

"Yeah! Out of this world. This is Shangri-La."

They basked in the gorgeous sunlight. The sky was a brilliant cobalt blue. Over the rocky rims, lush forests stretched as far as they could see. Yellow, white, and magenta flowers dotted the edge of the woods, and a vast array of ferns spread out like a thick green carpet. The smell of wildflowers and pine trees hung in the air.

Birch's voice stuck in his throat, so he just nodded. Danny had loved this remote place and called it *shi wai tao yuan* before the Japanese assault. It had been a haven of peace and happiness.

And that was the reason that Birch and his father had come to rebuild the community—they wouldn't allow their enemy to destroy a piece of heaven on earth.

Chapter 36

▬ ▬ ▬ ▬ ▬ ▬ ▬ ▬

Soon after the bridge was finished, Birch proceeded with his plan to go to Dashan. Many times during the past year, he and his helpers had tried to look for Jasmine near the village, but even after they'd widened their search area, they were not successful.

He prayed he would have better luck finding Danny. Deep down, he feared the result. He didn't know exactly where they'd been imprisoned. Even if they found the prison, where would the graves of Danny and six other prisoners be?

While the pass reduced their travel time, it still took a day to walk up and down the mountain. By then Birch was in good shape, recovering his lean build and supple grace of an athlete. Nevertheless, his artificial leg couldn't withstand such a long strenuous hike. So, as much as he detested it, he had to be carried in the bamboo-pole sedan chair. Linzi and three other young villagers accompanied him on the trip.

His first goal was to look for Mr. Ding's wife and parents. He wanted to deliver the young teacher's last words. Out of the dozen people in the prison cell, Mr. Ding's message was the only one he could recall.

As Mr. Ding had said, it was easy to find the high school; there was only one in the town of Dashan. But it took Birch a couple of hours to find out where the teacher's family lived. Everyone he asked seemed nervous when he mentioned the name. Either they said they knew nothing or simply walked away. In the end, after some sweet-talking and arm-twisting, he got the information from the headmaster, who warned, "Don't be surprised. They live in a poor neighborhood."

Through a maze of narrow back streets they found the house at the edge of town. Even though Birch was prepared, he was still stunned.

The low, one-story dwelling before them looked shabby and neglected. After a recent downpour, water overflowed from the drainage and formed murky puddles along the base of the mud-brick wall. The foul-smelling air from trash assailed his nostrils.

A dull-eyed man opened the door, his hunched figure lurking in the doorway. Unsteady and weak, he appeared to be in his seventies. Hard living had etched deep lines into his leathery face. "Whom are you looking for?"

"Is this Ding Fang's home?" asked Birch, using Mr. Ding's full name.

"Yes," the old man answered. He narrowed his eyes with suspicion. "Who are you?"

"My name is Bai Hua. Ding Fang was my friend."

A look of fear spread across the old man's face. Quickly, he glanced up and down the street. Seizing Birch's arm, he pulled him inside. "Come inside." He signaled the other young men to follow.

The room was primitive and dilapidated. Except for a narrow bed, a timeworn wooden table, and a bamboo stool, there wasn't any furniture. In one corner stood a clay stove, and nearby several pots and pans lay scattered on the floor. The walls were covered with dust, and cobwebs dangled from the low ceiling. A musty smell permeated the air. Only a ray of daylight filtered through a soot-covered window.

The room was so small that there was hardly enough space for all five visitors. Birch took the only stool available, and the young villagers crowded around him. The host apologized as he sat on the edge of the bed next to an old woman.

"Did you say that you are a friend of my son?" she asked.

The word "son" rendered Birch speechless. Mr. Ding had been in his late twenties, and Birch had assumed that his parents would be in their late forties or early fifties. But this woman seemed much older. Everything about her was sunken and shriveled—her hair was thin and white, and her skin had a gray pallor.

"Are you a communist?" asked the old man. His age-spotted hands rested on his lap, fingers laced. "You shouldn't come here. If anyone finds out, we'll all be in trouble."

"No, I'm not a communist. Ding Fang and I were in prison together. We were friends."

"Good heavens!" The man stood up, his thin limbs shaking. "You and my son were in the same prison?"

Birch rose quickly and took the father's hands. "Yes, we were locked up in the same cell." He spent the next half hour telling them the story, but he skipped the beating and the torture Mr. Ding had endured. No one interrupted except to utter spontaneous exclamations of dismay and disbelief.

"Your son was strong," Birch assured them. "He's a hero."

Tears poured down the old man's face. It took several minutes for him to stop weeping, and after wiping away tears with his knuckles, he said, "No one has ever told us anything…after the Japs took him. It's been three years, and he never came home. We guessed that he was gone. But we had no idea how." He pumped Birch's hands. "Thank you for coming to tell us."

"Your son was a great man. He was brave and kind. I'm sorry for your loss." Birch leaned forward to bridge the gap between them. Then he steered the conversation in another direction. "When will his wife return home? I have a personal message—"

"You don't know?" The old man's voice trailed in a fragile moan. "His wife…long gone."

"Thank God he didn't know!" Hugging her arms around her skinny frame, the old woman looked heartbroken, yet she hadn't shed a tear.

Birch was baffled. "What happened?"

"The Japs… We went to the market that morning. When we came back…our neighbor grabbed us and hid us…" His voice was barely audible.

164

"We heard her scream. There was blood everywhere," she said in a strangled sob.

Through their incoherent ramblings, Birch pieced the story together:

The Japanese had captured Mr. Ding's wife before they found him. They didn't bother to take her to the prison because she wasn't a target. Right in their home, they threw her on the table and took turns raping her. After they found out she was four months pregnant, they threatened to kill her baby. When she refused to talk, they sliced her stomach open and cut out the fetus.

Was she a communist like Mr. Ding? Maybe she didn't know anything as she wailed and begged for her life and for her child's life. No one knew the truth.

Several months later Ding Fang's mother lost her eyesight; she'd cried too much. His father had also become ill and couldn't hold a job. He picked trash for a living. Soon both of them looked much older than their age.

Because they were family members of a communist, the government evicted the parents from the school housing. It was a year after the war with Japan ended, and Yunnan was under Nationalist control. The Nationalists and the Communists were fighting a ferocious civil war.

"We had to sell most of our belongings to buy food," the old man said. "If it weren't for the money we found under a flower pot, we wouldn't even have a roof over our heads."

Birch went pale. He knew that money belonged to the Communist Party—Mr. Ding had told them so on the night before his death, and he wanted his wife to return it to the Party. But Birch decided on the spot not to relay that message. The Communists could go on without the money. To the old couple, it was a lifeline.

Sympathy and compassion exploded in Birch's chest. He couldn't stand to watch the old couple suffer another day. Without thinking, he gave them all his money and decided to stay in Dashan for just one night. He would come back later to search for Danny. And he was certain that Danny would agree with him.

As the father accepted the money, he dropped to his wobbly knees.

"Thank you!" he murmured, his lips trembling.

Kneeling showed the highest reverence and gratitude but was almost always done by someone of a younger generation, or at least younger age, and rarely the other way around. But the old man's stick-dry body bowed all the way to the floor.

Birch stood and pulled the old man to his feet.

———————

That night at the inn, sleep eluded Birch for hours. When he finally dozed off, a familiar nightmare returned and tormented him in the early hours of the morning. Mr. Ding pleaded in his croaky voice, "Take my son. Let him fight the Japs." He was holding a bloody baby high above his head. Then Captain Zhang barked, "Nationalists are fucking animals, just like the Japs." His fingers curled into fists and waved wildly in the air. Before Birch could react, a woman's bloodcurdling wail jerked him upright. He had to take large gulps of air to break the fierce grip of his nightmare.

The sky was a dull gray as they started on their way home. The leaden sky mirrored their mood. Birch was still shaken. This wasn't the first time he'd heard of Japanese atrocities, but his heart always ached over such viciousness.

The reality that he couldn't have children heightened his sensitivity to violence against them. Birch was grateful that the teacher had never learned the truth about what had happened to his wife and unborn baby. He understood why the mother had cried out, "Thank God he didn't know!"

"Mr. Ding had wanted his son to fight the Japs when he grew up," said Birch in a despondent tone to the young villagers. He sat upon the bamboo-pole sedan chair and clutched his hands together between his knees. "Both he and his wife died for China. He's a hero. It doesn't matter if he was a Communist or a Nationalist. He fought the Japs. He died for our country."

"But I'm confused," Linzi said as he walked. The bouncy and creaky bamboo poles rested on his shoulders. "Mr. Ding is a hero, but…" Perplexed and still in shock, he lifted his right arm and pressed his fingers against his skull as if to drag an answer from within. "…but look at the life his parents have? What happens to *Yi*? Does the concept apply only to individuals, but not to the country?"

Birch had no answer. He was troubled by the same questions. For the first time in his life, he began to doubt the concept of *Yi*. Morality, duty, loyalty, decency—those were the values he'd grown up with and had taught the villagers. *If an individual is supposed to practice these beliefs, why shouldn't the country do the same? China should treat all soldiers' families with dignity and respect. Not abandon them!*

The visit to Dashan had traumatized Birch in many ways but would not keep him from returning very soon to the city.

Chapter 37

On his third visit to Mr. Ding's family, several men stopped Birch and the villagers on the street. They were young and hard-muscled, dressed in black suits, with guns slung on their hips.

"Who are you?" asked a sharp-faced man. He was about thirty with an air of self-importance. "Why are you here? Don't you know Ding Fang was a communist?" He gave Birch a mean once-over. "I heard you came here several times. You must be one of them."

He pulled a revolver out of his holster and said to one of his gang. "What do you say? He looks like a communist to me. Let's check him out." He sneered, revealing a row of crooked front teeth. His demeanor matched a malicious snake tattoo coiled on the left side of his neck. "What do you think he'll do if we throw him in the torture chamber and test a couple of new devices on him?"

"He'll crack in no time," laughed a moon-faced man. "Remember that hard nut—the one we caught a month ago? All clamped up and tough, but once we used the electric shock, he cracked before he shit."

"It was after," retorted the third one, hair growing out of a mole on his chin. "You pig head, it was after he shit."

The man in charge pointed his gun at Birch. "I bet you'll lead us to other communists."

Birch was livid. His eyes widened in revulsion. He'd guessed who they were—the secret police of the Nationalists. The words "torture chamber" released a flood of memories. His mind sprang back three years to the beating that he and Danny had endured.

Danny fainted after the last lashing in that windowless torture chamber, and Birch rushed to his side as soon as they were released from the wooden pole. As he held Danny in his arms, Jackal splashed cold water on the American's face to jolt him back to consciousness.

"Cold water will do you good on a hot day," Jackal said with a sneer. The savagery of his tone and the sinister look in his beady eyes had rendered Birch speechless. All he felt was hatred, pure hatred.

When he carried Danny back to the cell, Mr. Ding was the first who hurried to their sides, as if they were his responsibility. Yet the young communist had no way to help them.

At dinner that night, and for several days afterward, Mr. Ding, along with Zhou Ming, the Nationalist army officer, skipped his meals and gave his rations to the wounded men. "At least you'll have a full stomach to go to sleep," he'd murmured.

The past rushed forward to Birch in seconds. A relentless assault of sound and vision stirred his soul. All the grief, rage, and frustration he'd experienced since his first visit to Mr. Ding's parents erupted like hot lava.

He let his cane drop, and in one fluid motion, he wrenched the pistol from the policeman's hand. He pointed the gun between the man's eyes and shouted, "Do you know how Ding Fang died? Don't you know the Japs killed him? Haven't you heard the Japs killed his wife and his unborn child?"

"But...but..." the man gasped. He was tall, close to Birch's height, yet his confidence was ebbing fast. Cringing, he raised his hands to his face as if to defend himself from a blow.

His gang took out their guns and aimed at Birch's temples. "Lower the weapon. I'll shoot if you don't," barked one of them.

But Birch stood his ground, tall and strong. His undaunted posture identified him as a proud officer. His penetrating gaze swept the three men in a single glance. "The Japs shot me more than half a dozen times without killing me." A bitter laugh rumbled from deep within his gut. "Let's see how many bullets it'll take you."

He jabbed the muzzle even harder into the man's forehead, and his fingers caressed the trigger's smooth slope. The gun fitted snugly into his palm. "I'm a damn good gunman," he added.

The last time I used a gun was in that meadow. Surrounded by several dozen Japanese soldiers, he'd raced toward Danny's crashed airplane, hoping to reach his brother. His expression darkened as he ratcheted his finger a notch. The trigger passed its first safety, and in the silence, the click was audible. Both men flinched and their hands trembled, but they held onto their guns.

Linzi and other young villagers stepped forward and seized the men's arms and shoulders.

"Take a good look at who you're talking to," said Linzi. "This is Bai Hua, Major Bai Hua of the Air Force. He's a decorated hero. How dare you to point a gun at a hero of our country?"

The moon-faced man leaned over to the leader and whispered something in his ear. He probably recognized Birch from the military reports. It was true, the fighter pilot was well-known.

"You'll be in serious trouble if you dare to harm a hair of *Bai Hua Ge*," persisted Linzi. "His father is a general. Sure as hell, he'll skin you alive."

The leader slowly lifted his arms in surrender and signaled his men to lower their guns. He muttered a curse, and then apologized: "Sorry, I didn't know." In the class-ridden society, he was several ranks below a major, let alone a general.

Birch handed the weapon back to him. "Keep your gun and your ugly face away from me. Get the hell out of my way. I'm ashamed I worked for the same government as you." He had to unclench his teeth to spit out the words, and his face was flush with contempt.

He started to walk away, then twisted back and yanked the man by the collar. "You're alive because someone like Mr. Ding died for you. Remember that. Do something useful with your sorry life." Birch had no idea that the men would listen to him, but he couldn't help himself. "I warn you—all of you—don't hurt anyone like Ding Fang or his family."

Gasping for air, the man nodded and tried to escape Birch's iron grip. Instead of letting go, Birch tightened his grasp. Their faces were so close he could smell garlic and alcohol on the man's breath. "If I ever hear of you bothering Mr. Ding's family, I swear to God, I'll strangle you with my bare hands." He released the man and poked a finger into his chest, making him stumble backward two steps. "Do you understand?"

"Yes, Sir," the man mumbled. He ran his tongue over his lips before fleeing.

The incident did not keep Birch from going back to Dashan. On the contrary, it propelled him forward with more determination than ever. He had to visit Mr. Ding's parents. If the Communist Party was in hiding and couldn't bother to take care of their own, and if the Nationalist government was so cruel that it harassed its opponents, then it was his duty to step forward. He wouldn't let the concept of *Yi*—morality, duty, loyalty, decency, and brotherhood—die so easily. *Yi* was his lifeline. He had to do the right thing.

And he had to search for Danny.

During their numerous visits, he and his helpers had interviewed many townsfolk. Several mentioned a secret prison used by the Japanese near a village about twenty miles northeast of Dashan. Birch planned to go there as soon as the thick blanket of snow melted from the pass.

Chapter 38

━ ━ ━ ━ ━ ━ ━ ━

The spring of 1949 was uncharacteristically wet and cold in the mountains of Yunnan. Rain and snow fell non-stop. The new life and vibrant color that spring usually brought was delayed. To a world already bleak, the dreary weather was a bad omen.

The Civil War was close to an end. Apparently, the Communists were winning. Once they took over, what would they do to the people who had worked for their opponent? While General Bai was a member of the Nationalist Party, Birch had never joined. He was a military professional and not interested in politics. Nevertheless, he'd worked for the Air Force, which was controlled by the Nationalists. Most of the high-ranking officials and military personnel were planning to leave for Taiwan.

"I'm not leaving," Birch insisted, sitting beside the ebony table in his room.

"I don't like the idea either," admitted General Bai. The evening was damp and chilly. He folded his hands around a steaming cup of tea, trying to warm his fingers. "But the communists are ruthless."

Birch reached for a cigarette on the cluttered tabletop and lit it with an air of quiet frustration. *Words like mercy, forgiveness, or compassion didn't seem in Captain Zhang's vocabulary.* He thought about the communists he'd met in prison. *Was he an exception? After all, Mr. Ding was very different from him.*

General Bai continued, "They'll fight to the bitter end for what they believe. That makes them very dangerous. You haven't paid much attention, Birch. There are all kinds of horrible stories." He tapped stacks of newspapers. There was no mail service to their tiny village, so he often sent Linzi or other young villagers down the mountain to buy newspapers. "They—"

"You can't believe everything in the newspapers. They're controlled by the government. We can't trust their reports."

"Point taken. But you can read between the lines and get a good sense of the truth. They can't make up everything. Besides, remember Auntie Liu? You know how she became a Buddhist, right?"

Birch shifted in his chair and narrowed his eyes. A frail, middle-aged woman appeared in his mind, along with the tasteless dishes she'd made for him. Auntie Liu had been hired by his father as a part-time helper when he was in the coma. He'd heard her story after he woke up.

Auntie Liu's husband had been a freelance writer. Disappointed with the Nationalist government, he, along with other scholars, left Chungking for Yanan, the Communist base in northern China. Unfortunately, though, he became a victim during the Communist Rectification Movement of 1943. Aiming to purge any members who opposed or criticized the leadership, the movement initially engaged in study and self-criticism. But it soon developed into a witch hunt of falsely-accused spies and traitors, and ended up with thousands of innocent people being put in jail or to death. Labeled as a Nationalist spy, Mr. Liu was executed.

Auntie Liu had supported her husband and believed in communism. If it weren't for her aging parents, she might have joined him. Mr. Liu's death not only saddened her but also presented an unexpected financial burden. At age fifty-five, she had to work as a servant. Trusting neither Capitalism nor Communism, she devoted herself to Buddhism.

"If they were so cruel to their own comrades," General Bai said, interrupting Birch's thought, "how tolerant do you think they would be of their enemies?"

Birch nodded. He recalled a heated argument with Captain

Zhang in prison. He'd been puzzled and horrified by the Rectification Movement. Now his eyebrows crinkled as he remembered the captain's feverish defense: "It's good for us. We have to kick those goddamned traitors out of our party. Anyone who isn't firm in our belief has no right to stay."

A gust of wind swept through cracks in the house, creating eerie moans and groans. General Bai pulled his coat collar up a little higher around his neck.

"Believe it or not," said Birch, trying to convince himself more than his father, "the Communists weren't too bad to the surrendered soldiers. Meng Hu and Wang Hong told me that."

"In some cases, perhaps. But read this..." Swallowing hard, the general took a folded envelope out of his pocket and handed it to Birch. He'd kept communications with his friends and colleagues in Chungking. "It came yesterday. I was afraid to tell you. I'm sorry. Ma Ning is...dead."

"How is Mary?" At the mention of her father's name, Birch asked, grabbing the letter.

"Don't know. No mention of her."

Leaning closer to the oil lamp, Birch scanned the pages. The color drained from his face. "Why did they kill him? He'd already ordered his regiment to put down their weapons. I thought... Meng Hu was so sure... Poor Mary! I wish..." he rambled on. The news upset him so badly that his speech became slurred and incoherent.

Birch wished he could be with Mary. His heart had already flown toward Chungking. Yet his mind was more realistic. *Even if I were in Chungking, what could I do?* Mary wouldn't accept his comfort or help. He wasn't needed. He was no longer her Perfect Tiger. The cold reality hit him squarely in the stomach.

A ponderous silence descended on them.

Birch read the letter again as General Bai sipped his tea. Outside the wind howled, and the light rain turned torrential.

Birch put down the letter and took a long drag on the half-smoked cigarette. As if talking to himself, he murmured, "Perhaps the Communists won't come here. The village is so small and remote."

"I said the same thing seven years ago." Bitterness and regret laced General Bai's voice. The fragile flame in the lamp flickered. Shadows fell across his gaunt and contrite face. "Remember? I never thought the Japs would come here. Look what happened?" He set the teacup down and coughed into his fist.

"Did you take medicine today?" asked Birch in a worried tone. He stabbed the cigarette out on an overflowing ashtray and picked up a thermos to refill the cup. The mint green aluminum bottle with two red-pink peonies was the only cheerful thing in the dreary room.

General Bai nodded and coughed a bit more. As an afterthought, he added with a rasping voice, "Sooner or later they'll come. It's too risky to stay."

"What would I do if…?" Birch stopped mid-sentence. He rubbed the bridge of his nose and felt the beginning of a headache.

Yunnan Province was his home and his only hope. Here he was surrounded by young men who respected him and helped him. Living with the kindhearted villagers kept his pain under control. And looking for Jasmine and Danny made his life meaningful. How could he live somewhere else without this support system? How could he ever find Danny and Jasmine if he weren't in Yunnan? "I made a promise—"

"A gentleman's word is as good as gold," interjected General Bai. "But what good is it if you end up in jail? Or worse?" His voice rose over the rain pounding on the roof. Then he quoted a Chinese proverb: "'As long as the green mountains are there, no need to worry about a shortage of firewood.' While there's life, there's hope."

Trying to sound nonchalant, he continued, "You'll fulfill the promises one day. Taiwan is a temporary stop. We'll come back when the Army reconquers the Mainland; or if the Communist government is truly forgiving, as the propaganda claims."

Outside the wind moaned like a tortured soul.

Birch felt a chill run through his body. Would he remain on the Mainland or flee to Taiwan? They went back and forth until Xiao Mei walked into the room holding a bamboo tray with two porcelain bowls. Fragrant steam filled the air.

"I made egg drop soup," she said. "It's good for a cold evening like this." She set one dish in front of General Bai and pointed to the ingredients. "I put in dried tangerine peels and black dates. And I replaced the sugar with honey. They're all good for your cough. Let me know if you like it this way."

The general nodded his appreciation.

She offered the other bowl to the Young Master.

"Thank you, Xiao Mei." Birch took a long breath and sighed contentedly. "This is just what I wanted." A smile broke through his dark mood as he took a spoonful of soup.

Biting her lip, she flashed him a bashful grin before she turned and left the room.

"What would we do without her?" murmured the older man as he stirred the soup.

What choice do we have if we leave here, thought Birch? His smile faded.

———

After weeks of debate and counsel with their former colleagues, the two men finally made up their minds—to leave Yunnan for Taiwan. It was a hard decision. But the tougher job was to convince Xiao Mei to stay behind. Birch and his father tried to make it as easy as possible. They transferred the deed of the house to her name and left her enough money to last a lifetime. A servant like her could never accumulate such wealth, even if she worked three lifetimes. But Xiao Mei paid no attention to the fortune in front of her. She repeatedly begged to stay with them. In the end, the two men gave up the fight after she threatened suicide.

"You saved my life," she said. "If I can't be with you, I might as well give it back to you." Her downcast eyes fixed on a pair of scissors on the table.

Knowing how strong-minded she was, they had no choice but to take her with them. It was unheard of for any family to take servants from the Mainland to Taiwan.

Chapter 39

Taiwan was an island in East Asia. On its west side, Taiwan Strait separated it from the Mainland, creating a natural barrier. The family spent the next weeks traveling, first by donkey, then by train and plane, and finally by boat. The distance between the village in Yunnan and Taiwan was over a thousand miles and the move was cumbersome, but luckily uneventful.

They found a big house in a quiet neighborhood on the outskirts of Taipei, the largest city on the island. The house was on the top of a hill, and the back porch overlooked a park the size of a football field, bordered by Taiwan cypress and pine forest.

Despite the great view and modern luxury, life was empty for Birch. He had no real purpose in life. The family fortune, along with his and his father's retirement, allowed them to live comfortably, so he didn't have to worry about earning a living. But being so far from Yunnan, he couldn't do anything to keep his promises.

Birch had been trained as a soldier. Now, unable to take action, he felt like a caged Tiger. What kept him going was a dream to return to Yunnan. He spent a lot of time lifting weights and taking long walks. His body was as well-built as before his injury, but inside he felt hollow.

One crisp autumn day, he sat on the back porch after finishing several hours of exercise. His hair was damp and gleaming from a shower. A book lay on his lap, but he didn't pick it up. Pigeons fluttered overhead. His gaze followed the birds until they disappeared into the western sky, the direction of the Mainland.

Emitting a long sigh, he dropped his head and his gaze turned to a radio-controlled airplane on the wrought-iron table. Gently he caressed its wing. The olive green plane was a replica. The one from Danny was hanging from the ceiling in his bedroom. Birch wished that he could still fly.

Xiao Mei appeared and placed a cup of ginseng tea on the table. "You had the plane for several days. I'd love to—"

Her voice broke his trance-like spell. Birch looked up. "You want to fly it?"

"Yes. I'll be a pilot in my next life. Remember?" She flashed a shy smile. "Well, I'd better practice."

"That's right," he grinned, recalling their conversation when they flew from Chungking to Kunming. "Okay." Finishing his tea in one long gulp, he picked up his cane. "Let's do it."

Xiao Mei followed him down the stone steps toward the meadow. She placed the model airplane on the ground.

"Turn it to face into the wind." Birch pointed to the direction. "It's important. Don't look down. You have to watch the plane. Pay attention to where it goes and how it flies."

Xiao Mei dipped her head. She held the transmitter and applied a small amount of "up elevator." Soon the little plane took off. "Oh, my God!" she cried.

It was a sunny day with white clouds floating in the blue sky. They basked in gorgeous sunlight.

The plane brought back memories to Birch. *The best time of my life was spent flying with Danny.* Tears clouded his eyes, and he blinked to keep from crying. "Don't let it go too far. Remember, don't make sharp turns. Keep the movements small and smooth."

Around and around the model airplane sailed. The plane seemed to take Birch along into the sky. A surge of vitality lifted the burdens that weighed upon his shoulders.

What would Danny think, if he knew Xiao Mei was learning to fly?

It had never occurred to them to include someone like a housemaid in a flying club when they talked about it. *Danny would be amused.* That brought a smile to his lips. "Okay, ready to bring it down?"

Xiao Mei gave a nervous nod. She stared at the green dot in the sky while her hands clutched the transmitter.

"Steady," Birch called out again. He reached out to her shaky hands, but quickly stopped himself. Although it had been three years, the incident in his bedroom still made him uneasy. He'd held Xiao Mei in his arms and kissed her when he awakened from a nightmare and mistook her for Mary. So now, instead, he encouraged, "You can do it!"

When the plane landed, Xiao Mei jumped up and down, forgetting her reserved manners.

"You can definitely be a pilot in your next life," said Birch with an air of amusement.

She blushed to the roots of her hair as she began to stage another flight.

A small group of people gathered around them. They looked at the airplane with curiosity and interest. Birch caught sight of two boys, the younger one in a wheelchair, his left leg missing. The older boy stood behind him. Sunlight lit their smiling faces as they clapped their hands. Something stirred inside Birch. He walked over and greeted them. "My name is Birch Bai. I live up there." He pointed to the house with his chin.

"I'm Yan Ping," replied the older boy. He looked about thirteen. His thin hands gripped the back handle of the wheelchair, which seemed too heavy for him to push.

"My name is Xiao Hu," said his friend in the wheelchair. He wore a mint green long-sleeved shirt and tan slacks. His left pant leg was empty and flapping.

"Little…Tiger?" Birch stumbled over the name. An array of emotions paraded across his face. Mary had wished to have half a dozen Little Tigers with him; Meng Hu had planned to name his son Meng Xiao Hu—Fierce Little Tiger. *I'm supposed to be his kid's godfather. Did he have a son or a daughter?*

"Yes, I'm eleven. I was born in 1938, the Year of the Tiger."

"Guess what?" Xiao Mei pointed to Birch, a proud smile on her face. "He's a Tiger, too. He has several nicknames related to Tiger."

Including Mary's Perfect Tiger, Birch thought and grimaced. Immediately, he caught himself. Clearing his throat, he said, "My best friend was a Flying Tiger. We were fighter pilots."

"Great ones," Xiao Mei added.

"Did you fight in the war?" asked Little Tiger. His eyes were round with excitement.

"Eight years."

The boy leaned forward, his translucent cheeks blushing pink. With reverence and awe, he grabbed Birch's hand. "Did you kill any Japs?" His dark eyes shone with an eagerness he couldn't hide.

"You bet!"

"Lots of them," Xiao Mei couldn't resist elaborating. "He's a hero. So was his best friend."

"Wow! You... I..." The boy was so excited that his voice became incoherent.

Yan Ping finished it for his friend. "His leg was damaged during a Japanese raid. Both his father and grandfather were killed in the same attack."

Birch felt a tug of sympathy for the child he'd just met. He put a hand on Little Tiger's shoulder. "So, I gather you're not brothers. Are you cousins?"

"No. But we're best friends, like brothers."

Birch gave a nod of approval. His eyes brightened as an idea sprang into his head. "Do you live around here?"

"We live in the city," Yan Ping answered. "We took a bus here. In fact, we should go soon."

"When will you come again?" asked Birch quickly. "I mean, if you like, I'd love to show you how to fly this plane." He motioned to the model in Xiao Mei's hands.

"Are you serious?" both boys asked in unison.

"Of course."

"We can be here next weekend," replied Yan Ping. Then Little

Tiger joined him, "Thank you, Uncle Birch." Smiles lit their faces.

"The pleasure is mine," said Birch in a voice thick with emotion. "Uncle Birch"—the form of address touched him deeply. Even though he couldn't be a father, he could still be someone's uncle. He could still share his passion and knowledge with the younger generation. He felt a sudden lift of spirit. For the first time since they left Yunnan, he'd found something meaningful to do.

Chapter 40

━ ━ ━ ━ ━ ━ ━ ━

A year passed. There was no sign they could return to the Mainland anytime soon.

The Nationalist Army shouted about fighting back. Slogans like "Exterminate the communist bandits!" and "Counterattack the Mainland to liberate and rescue our compatriots!" were everywhere. But so far there was no action.

The Communists didn't keep their promises. Although there was no official communication between Taiwan and the Mainland, rumors from various sources painted a bleak picture. Soon after they took over, the new Communist government launched a political movement designed to eradicate the opposition, mainly former Nationalists.

Birch waited. Each passing day dragged.

He was still single. Although several matchmakers had gotten in touch after their arrival in Taipei, he hadn't dated anyone since Mary left him. On the outside, the former fighter pilot appeared to be a perfect gentleman and a fine catch. He was in his mid-thirties, tall, well-built, and handsome. He was highly educated and well mannered. His family belonged to the upper class.

But only Birch knew how broken his body was. In the daytime, long pants shielded his prosthetic leg, but each night when he removed the artificial limb, the amputated stump seemed detestable to him. Whenever he undressed, he saw only ugly scars. His broken body reminded him why Mary had left him.

Worse yet, he suffered constant emotional pain. His abiding grief and guilt would have been hard for anyone in peace time to understand. On top of everything else, he also had to deal with the dreadful reality that he could never be a "real man."

Birch believed the doctors. Several had delivered the same verdict: he could never be a father. "You may or may not…perform. To say the least, you won't have much sexual drive or urge."

And it was true. He didn't have any desire. He had no idea that the combination of the doctor's opinion, his depressed mood, and self-pity hampered his ability. They acted like a self-fulfilling prophecy, successfully killing his sexual need.

As a social being, though, Birch longed to be with someone. He craved for a soft touch, a warm hug, especially when he was overwhelmed by nightmares. Mostly he missed having someone to talk to, someone with whom to have a heart-to-heart conversation about life and death, and to discuss his own sadness and survivor's guilt. Out of politeness, he carried on small talk with his father and Xiao Mei, but his heart wasn't in it.

If Mary had left him because of his broken body, then why would anyone else be interested? He wasn't willing to go through that heartbreak again.

Far away from Yunnan where his loved ones lay dead, Birch retained no hope of fulfilling his promises. He crawled into his grief and cocooned himself against the world. He became, in their society, a reclusive bachelor. The only thing that gave him pleasure was his flying club. Soon after meeting the two boys, he had started a flying club and spent every Sunday with the kids. Their innocent smiles brightened his gloomy days and warmed his wounded heart. Being an "Uncle" was as close as he could come to being a father.

It was near the end of 1950 when several former colleagues invited

Birch to a party to celebrate the New Year. He appeared wearing a dark blue pinstripe suit that fit his broad shoulders to perfection. His gray-blue tie lay neatly against a white shirt. Soon after they were settled at the luxurious clubhouse, several young women sitting at a nearby table noticed him. They cast longing glances at him, and one spoke animatedly, while the others covered their mouths to stifle giggles.

Birch paid little attention to the giddy young women, but one of his colleagues also noticed them. Du Ting walked over to their table. Soon the former tail gunner eased one girl onto his arm, and off they went, waltzing on the polished dance floor. And that was just the beginning. The entire evening was spent dancing and flirting with every girl there.

Birch was staggered by what he saw. "What the hell is wrong with Du Ting?" he said, talking to himself. A cigarette dangled between his long fingers.

Chen Bin, an engineer, raised his shoulder in a shrug. "The truth is, he's scared." His bloodshot eyes looked empty. His once boyish face had aged too fast in recent years.

"About what?"

"His wife."

"She was left behind, I know. But no reason to worry. She's never worked—"

"She's related to a Nationalist. That's enough to get her in trouble."

Birch shook his head, unconvinced or unwilling to believe.

"Oh, hell… You don't know what happened to Meng Hu, do you?"

"I tried to convince him to leave, but Wang Hong was pregnant again. They didn't want to take the chance." The couple had had a miscarriage once. Birch had invited them to visit Yunnan afterward. Three weeks in the serene mountains had helped Wang Hong to heal. "I haven't heard anything since we left. I don't even know whether they have a boy or a girl."

Chen Bin took another sip of his wine. "Wang Hong is no longer a nurse. She was fired," he said in an oddly disconnected voice. "Meng Hu was put in jail."

"No!"

"Yeah, he'd fought the Japs for eight years and lived through their bullets..." Chen Bin choked out a raspy laugh. Tilting his head back, he emptied the rest of the wine down his throat. "...only to end up in jail...and he died in peacetime!" His hand started to shake as though the glass had suddenly become too heavy.

Birch opened his mouth, but nothing came out. He was dumb-struck, as if an iron hand clamped round his neck. "Are you sure?" Feeling suffocated, he reached up to adjust his tie. "Is the information accurate?"

Without looking up, Chen Bin dropped his head. All his attention seemed to be fixed on the bottom of the empty wine glass.

"Why?"

"He'd worked in the Air Force, that's why."

"So many people worked for the old government. They can't kill all of them."

"No, but they have to eliminate ones like Meng Hu." Chen Bin paused to catch his breath. "Haven't you heard their policy?"

"'Lenient treatment to those who confess frankly. Severe punishment to those who remain stubborn.' Right?"

"Yes. Well, he refused to confess or admit he'd done anything wrong. He didn't point the finger at others. So they beat him... for days."

The words landed like another blow. Birch felt a deep sadness for his friend.

Chen Bin slammed the glass down on the table. "How stupid was he?" He uttered a string of profanities, but tears sprang to his eyes. "Many people made false confessions. Why couldn't he just say something they wanted to hear? Why was it so hard to lie?"

Birch understood. Meng Hu was a Tiger. He would rather die than bend under pressure. Certainly he wouldn't hurt someone else to save his own skin.

"I still can't believe he's gone. He was so strong." Looking at Birch, Chen Bin pleaded for an answer.

Birch shook his head. Bile rose in his throat, cutting off his words.

Meng Hu had fought the Japs like a fierce Tiger. He had two medals to prove it. And Wang Hong was such a kind nurse. They were his colleagues and his friends. He was supposed to be their child's godfather. At that thought, he asked in a hurry, "Did they have a boy or a girl?"

"No idea," said Chen Bin.

A great emptiness opened inside Birch. He was so dazed that he forgot about the cigarette in his hand until it burned down to his fingers. From that moment on, nothing cheered him. The music was too loud; the laughter sounded too harsh; the flashing light hurt his eyes. Through a cloud of smoke, he squinted at the women dressed in formal gowns and the men in suits and ties.

Is this what we fought for? He'd been taught from the time he could crawl that the highest duty was to defend his country. *Jing zhong bao guo—Serve the country with the utmost loyalty* had been drilled into his head. Peace was what they'd struggled to gain; freedom was what they'd fought so hard to keep.

Yet, these cheerful partygoers were blurred by the gray smoke and dissolved into all the sad events of his life—Daisy's panicked eyes, Jasmine's bloody cheek, Danny's bullet-riddled body thrown in an unmarked grave, his mother's stiff corpse, his uncle and aunt with knife wounds on their chests, the herbalist's yard piled with twisted bodies, Wang Hong's pain-filled gaze, and Meng Hu's muscular figure covered with bruises. Birch blinked a few times to clear the images from his mind. He dropped his head forward, battling dark thoughts.

What if Dad and I had stayed in Yunnan? The question sent fresh chills down his spine. They might have been imprisoned or killed. Meng Hu's fate would have been their fate as well.

Birch thought about Captain Zhang and Mr. Ding, the two communists he'd lived with in prison for seven weeks. *Is this what they wanted? A country divided by deep hatred? If they'd survived, would they treat me the same way the other communists treated Meng Hu?* The possibility shook him to the core. *We fought the same enemy. We were comrades and friends.*

A headache was building behind his eyes, and Birch used it as an excuse to leave the clubhouse. He was in such a hurry that he bumped into a waiter, splashing red wine on his tailor-made suit and tie. He stumbled outside and gulped fresh air.

Chapter 41

A light rain was falling, and the night sky was as black as death. The street was nearly deserted and vertical neon lights in Chinese characters pulsed in the darkness.

Birch pinched the bridge of his nose to stem the headache that had settled behind his eyes. Leaning heavily on his cane, he patted his pockets, searching for the cigarette, and realized he'd left the pack on the table. *I'm not going back in there. No way.*

The air was chilly. A gust of cold wind set off another round of shivers within him. *Better get going, keep moving. Kill this pain.*

With leaden steps he plodded toward his car several blocks away. Horrible images of his friend being beaten to death invaded his mind. His head bowed between hunched shoulders, and a deep stab of loneliness struck him. In the empty street, his lonely figure looked lost and forlorn.

At an intersection, he heard noises that sounded like a beating and moaning. At first he thought he was imagining it, that he was visualizing Meng Hu's torment. Shaking his head, he tried to clear the sights and sounds, but then he realized it was real.

The noises were coming from a narrow alleyway off to his right. In the dim light, he saw three figures punching and kicking someone that lay upon the ground. Groans of pain and shouts of irritation assaulted his senses. He was so angry that without so much as a blink, he yelled, "Stop! Stop!" and started toward them.

I really shouldn't be doing this. The dark alley looked eerie and forbidding. He had no idea who they were and why they were there. Street punks and gangs fought all the time. Although Birch was strong and well-exercised, he could no longer fight as he had once fought. With a prosthetic leg, the odds of winning a match against three men were slim.

Yet, in the heat of the moment, images of Meng Hu's bloody body propelled him forward. *Meng Hu wouldn't be dead if someone had stood up for him.* Birch couldn't save his friends. Not Meng Hu. Not Danny. But maybe he could help this poor guy.

He ran as quickly as his artificial leg permitted. Rage surged through his usually calm facade as he bore down on the gang. His cane thumped furiously on the ground, and the loud noise reverberated in the narrow pathway. The light from the main street shone behind him, outlining his frame, and casting a long shadow in the alleyway.

"Stop!" he shouted again. His deep roar barged into the darkness, and his warning tone carried effect. In the dim light he could see that they were street urchins, dirty and young. Affronted by his boldness, the teenage boys dashed down the alley.

"Punks!" Birch muttered a curse before moving toward the figure on the ground. "Are you okay? Do you need a doctor?"

The man groaned faintly. He lay curled up for a moment before waving his hand. "I'm all right." He struggled to push himself off the ground, but fell in a heap.

Birch extended a hand and pulled him to his feet.

"Thank you."

His familiar voice startled Birch. "Are you…?"

The man had a hollow, unshaved face, and was as thin as a reed. His collarbones bulged through his filthy, patched clothing. Except for his distinctive northern accent, he bore no resemblance to the young, brawny captain that Birch remembered.

"Wu Pan?" asked Birch. He could hear the doubt in his own voice.

"Birch! I can't believe this."

"It *is* you. What has happened to you?" Birch snatched Captain Wu's skinny hand and arm.

"Long story." Wu Pan's body stiffened. A suffering sigh escaped him.

The wind funneled down the narrow alley, carrying the smell of damp rubbish and wet stones.

"Well…" Birch was ready to send Wu Pan home, but changed his mind. He doubted the former captain had a decent place to live, so he took Wu Pan by the elbow and steered him toward the main street. "My car is over there. Let's go to my home. Dad and Xiao Mei will be thrilled to see you."

"Xiao Mei?" Captain Wu's eyes widened. "She is here in Taiwan?"

Birch nodded. "Oh, Dad will be so happy to see you. He—"

"How is the general?"

"Not doing too well. Heart problems. In fact, a doctor is coming tomorrow. Regular checkup. I'll tell him to take a look at you, too."

"I'm all right," protested the battered man.

"Like hell you are!" Birch opened the car door for his friend, walked around it, and slid in behind the wheel. "Dad has probably gone to bed, but I'm sure you'll see Xiao Mei soon."

Wu Pan lowered his head, dusted off his filthy tunic, and gave the hem a tug.

"I'm so glad to see you again." Birch turned to Wu Pan and threw a fake punch. He smiled, unable to suppress his delight. He couldn't believe that his impulsive decision had saved a family friend. "Tomorrow you'll get to meet my kids. They—"

"Your kids? You're married to—?"

"Oh, no. I'm teaching some kids to fly radio-controlled airplanes. They're great. I call them *my* kids." Birch reached over to the glove compartment and tossed Wu Pan a pack of Lucky Strikes and a lighter. "What the hell happened to you?"

With shaky hands Wu Pan lit a cigarette and took a couple of quick puffs, trying to maintain his composure. His sunken eyes stared out the windshield.

Birch kept his eyes fixed on the road, waiting for his companion to collect his thoughts. They drove in silence for a while. The light rain had become a heavy downpour, and water hammered the metal roof of the car.

Taking a deep breath, Wu Pan began, "You know I grew up in a village in the northeast…"

Chapter 42

━ ━ ━ ━ ━ ━ ━ ━

Wu Pan's family had managed several dozen acres of wheat fields and lived in a self-sustaining way before the Japanese conquered the northeast of China in the early 1930s. Their province became part of the Japanese-controlled puppet state of Manchuria. His father and elder brother were forced to work in a coal mine after the invasion. Soon the older man's health deteriorated under the harsh living conditions and sixteen-hour daily shifts. He died of typhoid a year later.

On April 26, 1942, a gas and coal-dust explosion sent flames bursting out of the shaft entrance. Instead of evacuation and rescue, the Japanese shut off the ventilation and sealed the pit head in an attempt to curtail the fire. More than fifteen hundred Chinese workers were trapped underground. Wu Pan's elder brother was one of the unlucky miners working that day.

"He was right behind me," one of the survivors told Wu Pan and his mother. "I heard him when the Japs sealed the pit head, so I turned back. But a guard smashed my head, and before I went down, I saw...I saw him being shoved backward. His hand stretched out to me, and his face... Oh, God, I've never seen anything so horrible."

Wu Pan hadn't intended to join the army. He was afraid to leave his mother alone. It was she who urged him to join the fight after his brother's death. "You can't protect me. No one is safe as long as the

Japs are here," she said. "Go! Chase the bastards out of our country."

So Wu Pan became a Nationalist soldier. Although he loved his mother, he visited her only once after the war against Japan ended. When his regiment was ordered to retreat to Taiwan, he asked for a two-week vacation to say goodbye to her. From Fuzhou in Fujian Province, where his unit was stationed, he took a train home, leaving his identification paper with a friend in the squadron. It was the summer of 1949. By then the Communists had taken a large part of the country, including his hometown.

Dressed in civilian clothes, Wu Pan sneaked into his village late one evening. His mother was elated. They spent the best two days since his father and brother had left. On the third evening, they were enjoying his favorite dumplings when their dog began to bark. Wu Pan knew something was wrong. He grabbed his mother and pulled her toward the door, but it was too late. The sound of the front gate being knocked down cut through the nighttime silence.

They turned around. His mother pushed and shoved him through their back window. Wu Pan tried to pull her through as well, but she shouted, "Go!" and locked the window. Knowing he was the target, he sprinted toward the woods behind the house. As he disappeared into the dense trees, he heard the sharp explosion of gunfire—three shots.

Instantly, he swiveled round and ran back. A few steps later, he stopped.

It could be a trap. The Communists and their followers wanted him to go back so they could capture him. And if they had shot his mother, it would be too late anyway. He shouldn't waste his life when he knew he couldn't save her. Wu Pan dropped to his knees, his face contorted in pain.

He didn't stay long. He was too close to the house, and he could hear people talking and he could see torches in the darkness. He shot to his feet and ran through a barrier of thick bushes that scraped deep into his arms, legs, and face. For three days he hid in a small cave where he and his brother had played as children. Wild berries and mushrooms were the only food he could find. On the fourth night, he crept back to the house. He had to find out if his mother was alive. The Communists might still be there, but he couldn't wait. His authorized leave would end soon.

The house was dark. He crouched among the trees until long past midnight.

He smelled it as soon as he entered the house. The stench of blood, decay, and death permeated the air. His mother lay sprawled on the floor. Three bullet holes had punctured her chest. The room had been ransacked. Anything of value was gone, and everything else was destroyed.

Wu Pan found a piece of old cloth and wrapped his mother in it. He picked up her frail body and climbed back out the open window. Carrying a rusty shovel, he took her deep into the forest.

The moonlight was eerie as he started to dig. A torrent of emotions struck him: grief, rage, guilt. As he gently placed her in the shallow grave, a dozen men suddenly came out of the darkness and surrounded him while pointing guns and farm tools at him.

"Down with the Nationalist spy," they shouted, kicking and punching him.

"Wait!" he screamed, protecting his head with his hands. "Please let me bury my mother."

They ignored him. He worked for the Nationalists, and his family had just enough fields to be labeled as a "landlord." Landlords were *enemies of the people.*

Wu Pan crawled to the rim of the grave. He shoved dirt with his bare hands, for a good son wouldn't let his mother be exposed to the wilderness.

But the Communists and their followers didn't give him a chance. One man smashed his head with a shovel. A wall of pain hit Wu Pan. A deep black pit opened and swallowed him.

When he awoke, he was alone in the woods. It was dark. He had no idea how long he'd been out cold. *Is it the same night or the day after?* He had no clue. All he cared about was burying his mother.

It took a long time. He was weak, and he had no tool other than his own hands.

When he finally finished, he knelt and knocked his head three times on the ground, a tradition to show respect. Wiping the dirt, the blood, and the sweat from his face, he began his long journey back to Fuzhou.

Without money, he walked and hitchhiked, while begging for food. Once in a while he took oxen-carts and horse carriages. But most of the time he walked.

Several days later Wu Pan realized he would never get back in time if he didn't do something drastic. So he did—he tried stealing. The first two times he wasn't lucky. He was chased and beaten. The third time he took enough money to travel halfway back to his regiment. Then he had to repeat what he hated to do. By the time he arrived in Fuzhou, he was three weeks late and missed his chance to get to Taiwan.

Without identification, he was pushed back and forth from department to department. It was several days before he found a major who was patient enough to listen to his story. The sympathetic officer wore a black patch over one eye. With his help, Wu Pan finally received a boat ticket to Taiwan.

"Take this." Along with the precious pass, the major gave him enough money to live for two days. "The boat leaves tomorrow evening."

Wu Pan felt tears sting his eyes as he grabbed the officer's hand in gratitude. He hadn't cried when his mother was killed. He hadn't shed tears when the communists beat him into unconsciousness. He found his way to a cheap restaurant and ordered steamed buns. His stomach was empty; he hadn't had a real meal in weeks. The first bun disappeared down his throat without being tasted. Then he slowed and savored each bite.

The boat ride was blissful. For the first time in more than a month, Wu Pan slept in a real bed and didn't have to worry about his safety. The food was fantastic. He ate enough to make up for the past several weeks. But once he reached Taiwan, his good luck ran out.

Again, without proper identification, he was shoved back and forth within the bureaucracy. He couldn't locate his regiment. This time, nobody was willing to help him. Everything was in chaos. After several days of frustration and anger, he made a decision. *Deserter or not, I don't give a damn. If they don't want me, then sure as hell, I don't want them!*

Wu Pan was young and healthy. It was easy for him to get a job as a porter at the harbor. Lots of people were needed to transport goods and military supplies from the Mainland. His muscular body allowed him to make enough money to eat well and to share a shabby dorm with a dozen coolies. For almost a year he lived a simple, labor-intensive life. Then his luck ran out again.

On a warm autumn evening, he tripped on a wobbly ramp and tumbled ten feet onto the concrete below. A heavy wooden box toppled with him and cracked open. Bottles of wine exploded and glass shattered, cutting his face and body. He lay curled up on the ground and grunted in pain, holding his fractured arm and dislocated shoulder. The air reeked of wine.

A foreman rushed over. Seeing the broken goods, he yelled and kicked Wu Pan in the ribs. "Stupid pig! I'll see to it you are fired."

And sure enough, Wu Pan was laid off. A coolie had no rights and received no compensation for an accident. For three days he stayed in the dorm, and then his fellow coolies rented the space to someone else.

He left the only shelter he had. Unable to lift his arm, he couldn't work, so he picked trash and begged for food. Wu Pan grew weaker, and the possibility of finding a job grew slimmer. He was homeless and slept on the street.

Without a home, family, or friends, he was an easy target. Roving gangs bullied him from time to time. He was too frail to defend himself.

Chapter 43

— — — — — — —

"Bastards!" Birch fumed after Wu Pan had finished his story. He didn't know to whom he was referring. The Communist Party? The Nationalist Army and government? The street punks? All three were bastards. He'd heard two horrible stories on the same night—one friend had been beaten to death by the Communists, and the other had lost everything and almost starved to death under the Nationalist government.

"A tiger would be bullied by dogs when he ended up in a treeless prairie," Wu Pan quoted an old Chinese saying. He knotted his thin hands in his lap to keep them from trembling.

"Yeah," Birch agreed with a helpless sigh. Then he said, "No one is going to bully you anymore. Stay with us. We need...a driver. You can—"

"I can't."

"Why not?"

"Honestly, you don't need a driver."

"Yes, we do. Xiao Mei takes a bus to go to the market. She doesn't want to bother me. You can—"

"I'm bad luck. Look at me. My mom died because of me—"

"Don't be absurd." Birch waved a hand. "Dammit! We lived through the Japs' bullets. Sure as hell, we won't let peacetime break us."

"Birch, you don't have to do this—"

"Yes, I do!" Birch slammed the steering wheel. "If we don't take care of each other, no one else will."

Wu Pan put a hand on Birch's arm, his eyes glistening. "Thank you. As soon as I get back on my feet, I'll find a place to stay." Tightening his grip, he added, "I owe you."

———

The next fifteen months passed uneventfully. By March 1952, Birch had been running his flying club for over two years. He was often surprised by the deep satisfaction it gave him.

"Birch?"

He heard a familiar voice behind him and thought it was one of the mothers. Dressed in a khaki shirt and trousers, he was getting ready to leave the field on this Sunday afternoon. "Yes?" he answered, turning around. Instantly, he froze.

The woman standing in front of him was Mary!

He should have known. He'd smelled the familiar scent of her perfume.

"How are you?" she asked. "You…you look great." She seemed stunned. Her eyes traveled up and down his body.

Birch didn't reply. He was in shock. His eyes opened wide and stared at the face that had appeared in his dreams countless times. Mary didn't look a day older than when he'd last seen her.

Seven years. He hadn't seen her for almost seven years! Oh, he'd imagined meeting her so many times. He'd wanted to look for her and ask her to come back. He would have begged her to stay if he thought that it would help. But he hadn't done any of those things. Hurt feelings. Hard-bitten pride. Self-pity over his physical condition. The woman had taken a piece of his heart.

What is she doing here? Is she looking for me, to return that piece of my heart? Questions flooded his mind. One look at her face and he could barely breathe. His heart pounded as it had when they'd first met. The feelings he'd tried so hard to bury rushed back.

"Birch," said Mary, speaking in English. "This is Tony Zhu, my…

husband." She indicated a man standing next to her. Her right arm circled his arm, and her left hand rested on her bulging belly. A telltale pink stained her cheeks.

Birch's heart tightened as he realized she wasn't alone—she was with another man, and she was pregnant. He'd been so excited to see her that he hadn't noticed anyone else. Out of habit, he stretched his arm and shook hands with the man.

A boy came running toward them with a red model airplane.

"Johnny is Tony's son. Oh, no, no," Mary corrected, "our son. Right, darling?" She turned to her husband, a giant smile on her face. "Sorry, his Chinese isn't very good. Tony grew up in the States."

"I'm glad you're here to pick him up." Birch squeezed his words through numb lips. He hadn't spoken English since Danny's death. His face had turned to stone.

"Thank you, Birch. Johnny is crazy about airplanes," said Tony, readjusting his steel-rimmed glasses. He was a fine-looking man in his early-forties. "It took me awhile to find a good club like yours."

Birch nodded, not trusting himself to speak further.

With one arm circling Mary's shoulders, Tony touched her stomach. "Perhaps," he said cheerfully, "he'll join your club when he's old enough."

Mary smiled awkwardly. "Well, goodbye, Birch. See you next weekend." She walked away, hand-in-hand, with her husband, leaving the scent of her perfume behind. The boy with the red airplane bounced alongside his father.

Chapter 44

— — — — — — — — —

Birch stood perfectly still after they disappeared from view. He was shattered.

He loved Mary. She was part of the reason he'd survived. After so many years, he'd known that she wouldn't come back, but that hadn't stopped him from hoping. What if she changed her mind? Now, seeing her with another man and pregnant with his baby vanquished any hope of reuniting with her.

Birch sent off the rest of the children while in a haze. Once the last boy had left, he slumped to the ground as if someone had punched him in the stomach. He pulled the ring off his left pinky. Staring at the dazzling gold band he'd planned to give Mary, he felt its weight in his palm. What a fool he'd been!

Pain, betrayal, and loneliness swept over him. In exasperation, he took his frustration out on the jewelry. Raising his right arm, he threw it toward the edge of the woods. The moment it left his hand, he regretted it. The wedding band had belonged to his mother, not to Mary. It was his family's heirloom. Quickly, he stood up and ran after it. In his haste, he forgot about his disability, and fell, hitting the ground hard.

"Damn it!" For several seconds he could only lie there and suck one breath after another. His fist hit the earth a few times before he pushed himself up.

The ring had dropped into a ditch near the woods. If there was water, or if it was muddy, he would never find it. Luckily, the spot was dry, and the gold shone on top of the dirt. He slid into the ditch and picked up the ring, pressing his fist to his chest.

Seven years ago, he'd lain in a trench, waiting to die, yet struggling to survive. The combination of his promise to Danny and his love for Mary had kept him alive. Now, he had no way to fulfill his promises. He hadn't found anyone—not Jasmine, not Danny, not Jack. And the woman he loved had left him. His struggle to live, so important at the time, suddenly seemed meaningless.

Beyond his grief, Birch had reservations about the political situation. The war against Japan had ended long ago, but China was now torn between the Communists and the Nationalists. He couldn't even set his foot on the Mainland, where he'd spent years fighting. Birch seriously questioned his past. He was hurt in the present. And he had little hope for the future.

With shaky hands, he reached into his pockets, eager to light a cigarette. After going through all of them, he remembered that he'd left the pack in his bag. He was dying to smoke, but he was too drained to climb out of the ditch.

The sun sank below the tree line. A breeze stirred the nearby woods, making the cypress trees rustle and the pines sigh. The night was chilly with a sharp bite to the wind. Despite the uncomfortable temperature, hunger, and thirst, Birch just lay there. The house wasn't far up the hill, and all the lights were on, yet he had no energy to move. Not even when he heard Xiao Mei calling him.

The night was lonely and quiet. Occasionally a frog croaked, a bird sang, crickets bickered in the grass. Fireflies winked at him from the leafy shadows. Alone in the darkness, Birch thought of his loved ones, now gone. For years he'd put on a brave face for his father's sake, for his family's name, for his own pride as a hero. He was the courageous Tough Tiger to most people, and a hero, a leader, and Big Brother Birch to the young villagers. He was beloved Uncle Birch to his flying pupils. But underneath, he was a broken man.

Surrounded by blackness, witnessed by no one but the stars and a thin sliver of the moon, he wept. The tears he'd suppressed for years tumbled through his clenched hands. The last time he'd cried like this was back in jail when he realized Danny had left the chance of life to him. *Why did you take my place? Why didn't you let me die?* Folding his arms around his amputated leg, he curled up at the bottom of the ditch. Only in the wee hours did he fall asleep.

In his dream, he saw Danny walking toward him.

"You wasted your life for nothing," said Birch.

Danny hovered above him with a disappointed look on his face.

"I'm just a Paper Tiger, not a real Tiger as you and Daisy thought."

Danny stared at Birch with his gold-flecked brown eyes and shook his head. After a few moments, he floated away, a white scarf flapping behind him.

"Don't go, Danny!" yelled Birch. "I have so much to tell you, and we didn't even say goodbye!" He stretched out his arms, trying to grab his brother, but caught nothing except air.

His scream woke him and he lay shivering in the early-morning cold. Dew covered his face, hair, and clothes. The dawn turned the sky to gray.

A porch light was still on when Birch trudged home at daybreak.

"What happened?" Xiao Mei hurried toward him, staring at his stained clothing.

He was too drained to answer. Pieces of grass dangled in his unkempt hair.

"Thank God you're back. Hurry—"

"What's wrong?"

"General...your father—"

"What happened?"

"I don't know for sure. He fainted last night. I called Captain Wu, and we sent the general to the hospital—"

Birch spun round and headed to his car. His gait was gawky and uneven, but he limped as fast as his artificial leg allowed.

Xiao Mei leaped forward and caught his arm. "I'll go with you."

Chapter 45

—————————

"General Bai had a heart attack," said the doctor, his voice dark and foreboding. "He survived. But he's in bad shape. You'd…better talk to him. And…let him eat whatever he wants."

Birch stood perfectly still. His father had not been in good health for a while, but he was only sixty-two. "How long?" he asked.

"No way to be sure; perhaps a few weeks."

Birch sucked in a harsh breath. An acrid smell of antiseptics hung in the air, aggravating his sense of loss. He squeezed his eyes shut for a few seconds to calm himself, then with a sinking heart and a stone face, he walked into his father's hospital room.

———————

"Come with me." As soon as Birch walked away, Wu Pan took Xiao Mei's arm.

"What are you doing?"

"Just come with me." He tugged a little harder and led her down the hallway.

"What's going on?"

Taking a deep breath, Wu Pan grabbed her hands and looked into her eyes. "Marry me, Xiao Mei!"

"What?"

"Marry me," he repeated in a louder voice, assuming a militant stance with feet apart and shoulders squared. It had been fifteen months since Birch had rescued him from the dark alley. Now in his early thirties, Wu Pan was back in shape. His body was trim, his thighs lean and muscular. Emotionally, he was stronger than he'd ever been.

Xiao Mei pulled her hands away.

"Please!"

"I can't." Her voice was soft but firm.

"Please! General Bai is very sick. You can't—" he stammered. "You know you can't stay in the house alone with Birch."

She looked up, confused.

Frustrated, Wu Pan wrestled with telling her the truth. "There are rumors circulating. Don't you understand? They're gossips about you and Birch. He's famous. People like to talk about him, good or bad. If you stay here, if you're with him alone, there'll be more..." His voice trailed off sullenly.

"Dear God. But...but we're not..." In her simple white dress with turquoise stripes, Xiao Mei looked naïve, and much younger than her thirty years.

"I know. I know. But it doesn't matter what I think. People talk. Gossip can be nasty."

Her disbelief was mixed with contempt.

"Marry me, before General Bai is too sick. We'll ask his permission and his blessing."

She shook her head.

"Am I not rich enough?"

"You know me better than that."

"Then, why?"

She stared at him then lowered her head. "You know the reason."

"Dammit!" Wu Pan exploded. He spat out his next words without thinking. "Why do you want to wait for an impotent cripple? He's not going to get better."

"You scum!" Xiao Mei snarled, her eyes brimming with reproach. "What is wrong with you? Birch is so kind to you. If it weren't for him, you'd be dead. You told me that yourself. How dare you—?"

"No need to pretend, Xiao Mei. I know the truth." Wu Pan swallowed hard, his face red with embarrassment. "I've followed you a few times…even when we were in Chungking. Deer Antler. You've been buying the yang booster for years, haven't you?"

Her instinct was to deny it, but she was too stunned to think. Hot color flooded her cheeks, and all she could do was grind her teeth. Xiao Mei thought the secret was hers, except for Linzi. She'd asked the villager to buy the herb when they lived in Yunnan, and had sworn him to secrecy.

"It's been over six years," said Wu Pan with more confidence. He seized her hands again. "It hasn't worked, has it? He won't be the man—"

"He'll be okay. I know he will," protested Xiao Mei, wrenching away from him. "All the doctors said he wouldn't wake up. Look at him! Birch is a strong man. He's getting better every day. I can see it. He will—"

Wu Pan slipped through the opening she had left. "And when he's strong, when he's healthier, he'll marry someone else, someone of his class. Someone like Mary—highly educated, rich, with family status. Either way, you lose. You have no chance. He'll never be yours."

"It doesn't matter," shouted Xiao Mei. She took a deep breath. When she spoke again, her voice was low and shaky. "It doesn't matter if he is mine or not. I'll be happy for him if he marries someone else. I'm happy…as long as he's happy." Tears sprang to her eyes.

"Marry me, Xiao Mei." Wu Pan softened. "I'm active and healthy. I can make enough money to support us. I'm crazy about you." He gave an awkward grin. "I was taken with you the first time I tasted your cooking almost ten years ago."

Her lips parted, but no words came out.

Wu Pan fished a white handkerchief out of his pants pocket and dabbed the tear on her cheek. "We won't abandon Birch, if that's what you're worried about. I'm not an ungrateful person. He saved my life. I'll never forget that. I swear on my mother's grave that he'll always be a part of our lives. If he doesn't object, I'd love to be his sworn brother. You see, in this way, he would be family. He could be our children's godfather, if you like."

"I'm sorry."

Wu Pan threw up his hands in despair. "You're a stubborn fool. Don't waste your life, Xiao Mei. Don't wait for someone who will never be yours. Marry someone of your own class."

"My life is fine as it is," she said, chin set firm, shoulders squared. "I don't plan to get married. Not to you. Not to anyone else." She turned and ran away, leaving the former captain stunned and wounded.

Chapter 46

— — — — — — — —

"I haven't been a very good father," said General Bai. Lying in the hospital bed, he looked haggard, very different from his usual appearance. He was surrounded by a whole host of tubes and an army of machines. "I never spent much time with you when you were growing up. I thought it was your mother's job. A man's job was to provide for the family. I wish we were closer. I wish we'd had more heart-to-heart conversations. It's too late…"

"Don't say that, Dad," uttered Birch, sitting on a chair close to the bed. His father's sudden feebleness shocked and saddened him.

"Listen," panted the older man. Each breath became harder for him to take, but he had to talk before it was truly too late. "I'm proud of you. Your mother would be very proud, too. But Birch, if she were here, she'd be worried about you being alone. I wanted to talk to you, but I didn't know how to handle it. It's obvious you're lonely. Son, marriage is part of life. Don't—"

"Look at me, Dad. How can I think about marriage? I can't marry anyone."

"Not just anyone. I'm talking about Xiao Mei."

"I have nothing to offer her." Birch looked bitter and crestfallen.

"That's up to her to decide. She's in love with you. She's never said it out loud, but it's obvious. You've known each other for seventeen years. It's not easy for her to keep caring for you without asking anything in return, without a single complaint. Your beautiful girl-friend left you as soon as you were seriously injured."

"Don't mention her." Birch's voice betrayed his annoyance.

"Xiao Mei took care of you when you were in the coma. I never told you all the details, as I should have. It was hard. Even when I gave up hope, she'd never given up. If it weren't for her, you wouldn't be here."

"She deserves to find someone better than me."

"You know she doesn't want anyone but you. We tried to let her go. What did she do? She insisted on staying." General Bai coughed. "The title of wife is important to a woman. You may not know... There are those who gossip—"

"About her?"

"And about you! Why you're not married. Rumors about you keeping a servant girl as a mistress without giving her a proper title…"

"Bastards!" Birch fumed. He wouldn't feel outraged if it were just his reputation. But a woman's purity was unrivaled in Chinese society.

"People talk," continued the general. "You can't stop them. It's human nature. And we've given them reason to be nosy. How many families have brought a servant girl from the Mainland?"

Birch shook his head, looking miserable.

"And there will be even more talk now that I'm going to..." The general looked worried. Once he was dead, what kind of gossip would there be about a single man and a single woman living in the same household? "Let her in, Son? Give her a chance, and give her the title she deserves. You may not love her, but at least you care about her."

Birch nodded. He'd met Xiao Mei when she was a maid in his uncle's household. She was only fourteen. That image of the fright-ened teenager had never left his mind. His feelings for her were nothing more than a kind young man's sympathy for an unfortunate little girl.

"Life is a strange thing," General Bai continued. "Your mother and I had met only once before we were married. And look at us! We grew to love each other." He paused again, apparently thinking of his late wife. "Xiao Mei is a lovely woman. You shouldn't be alone after I'm gone. I'm worried—"

"Dad!"

General Bai lifted his hand. "Life has limited time. Don't waste it, Son." He stretched out his hand, the veins blue and thick beneath pale skin, and clasped Birch's arm. "I know Xiao Mei isn't the prettiest girl in the world. I know she's never had a formal education. And she's in a different class. In an ideal situation—"

"Those are not problems to me," replied Birch.

"Marriage between families of equal rank is fundamental in our society." The father squeezed the young man's hand. "But her devotion to you is unending."

"But—"

"Just think about it. Okay?"

Birch stared at his father. His forehead was etched with deep lines, and puffy bags of flesh formed beneath his tired-looking eyes. His sagging cheeks were dotted with age spots, and under the fluorescent lights, he seemed worn-out from worry.

Birch was filled with conflicting emotions. Although he had no romantic feelings for Xiao Mei, he cared deeply about her. She was family, and just like her name, she was *Xiao Mei—Little Sister*.

The room was quiet except for the electronic blips and bleeps.

"Okay, I'll think about it," agreed Birch at long last.

General Bai nodded and closed his eyes.

Chapter 47

- - - - - - -

General Bai's condition deteriorated quickly. He slept most of the time. Even when he was awake, he seemed dazed and worn out. Day and night, Birch remained at his bedside. Xiao Mei offered to help, but Birch declined. Although there was little communication between father and son, being together—a hand squeeze, a soft smile, a few words—gave them comfort.

No one had influenced Birch more than his father. His decision to become a fighter pilot had surprised everyone. Although he'd always been athletic, his mild demeanor was more like his uncle's, a scholar. It was his admiration for his father that had drawn him down the military path.

"Go home, Birch," said the head nurse on the fourth evening. "Get some sleep. We'll take good care of General Bai. Trust us."

Reluctantly Birch got to his feet. He tightened the blanket around his father and stared down at him for a full minute before leaving. He was drained and half-starved. He'd taken only short naps for several days. Xiao Mei prepared plenty of food, but he'd been too preoccupied to eat.

Daylight drew its last breath when Birch stepped out of the hospital. He drove with a somber expression as he watched the sky glow with dying embers of sunlight. Soon darkness would swallow any light of the day, just as it would swallow his father's life.

Their stone house was well-lit at twilight. The smell of delicious food hung in the air when he stepped out of the car. *Dad will never taste Xiao Mei's cooking again.* Leaning against the car, he pulled a pack of Luck Strikes from his pocket.

The early March evening was damp and chilly. He wore a short sleeve shirt and a pair of slacks. Goosebumps erupted on his arms. Yet he stood there and sucked in the smoke, trying to collect himself.

Birch was so immersed in his thoughts that he didn't pay any attention until it was too late. Several hands grabbed him from behind. He jerked and wrenched his left arm free. His elbow jabbed backward, and he heard a crunching sound. An agonizing scream followed.

More hands grabbed his arms. One attacker bear-hugged his waist, pinning him against the car. Birch squirmed, yanked, and kicked. A blunt object smashed the back of his head. Pain rocketed through his skull. He sagged, gasping. Within seconds, a handcuff slid around his wrists, a hood was slipped over his head.

They dragged and shoved him inside his car. He roared. His left leg snapped out in an upward strike. "Fuck!" someone shrieked and uttered a furious round of curse words. Birch struck again. Unable to see, he didn't find a target this time.

Before he could throw another kick, one attacker slammed his boot hard into his right knee. Pain shot up his amputated stump and knifed through him, stealing his breath. For one excruciating moment, Birch slumped as darkness whirled at the edge of his vision. They threw him into the backseat. The movement caused another burst of pain. Sparks exploded against a field of black. Before they shut the door, he heard a high-pitched cry of "*Shao Ye!*" and he felt a pang of sympathy for Xiao Mei.

Xiao Mei was in the kitchen when she heard the car coming. She wiped her hands, put on a soft smile, and opened the front door.

There in the driveway, Birch leaned against the car. His cigarette glowed in the semidarkness. Xiao Mei withdrew quietly, not wanting to disturb the Young Master.

A few minutes later she heard a long, horrible cry and a string of swear words. The noise stunned her so much that it took her a few seconds before she raced outside.

Four men were wrestling with Birch, trying to shove him into the backseat of his car. She watched Birch kick a heavyset man in the face. Before she could blink, the man slammed his boot onto Birch's right knee. Her heart sank. A scream lay trapped inside her throat. Only when they slammed the door shut did she find her voice and shrieked at the top of her lungs while running toward the car.

The heavyset man with a bloody nose attacked her. He slapped her across the face so hard she stumbled sideways, lost her footing, and fell. Her vision blurred and her ears rang. Blood trickled from the side of her mouth.

Xiao Mei gave an anguished cry of pain and watched helplessly as the car sped away. She slumped on the cold ground. Events were moving so fast they didn't seem real. *Who are they? Why did they kidnap the Young Master? What do they want from him? What will they do to him?*

A million questions rushed into her mind. *Street gangs abduct wealthy people for ransom money.* A wave of dizziness hit her. *Get help. Quickly!* She dashed inside and barely took a breath between sentences when she called the local police. But the man wasn't in a hurry to do anything even after she repeatedly urged him.

"Nothing I can do right now," he said. "It's late. Everyone is off work. As soon as someone shows up…"

Xiao Mei's emotions swung back and forth between anger and disbelief. Taking a lungful of air, she forced herself to calm down. *Who else can I ask for help?* If General Bai weren't sick, he would know whom to call. She didn't have the heart to trouble him, though. The father would be worried. And it would likely be detrimental to his already fragile health. She shuffled through the address book and dialed Chen Bin's number.

The engineer fumed over the phone. "What do they want? Did they say anything?"

"No."

"Four men, you say? What did they wear? Uniforms? Plain clothes?"

"It was dark. And it happened so quickly. I think they were in black suits."

"Black suits?" Chen Bin muttered a curse. "Let me make a few calls. I'll get back to you as soon as I can."

Chapter 48

▬ ▬ ▬ ▬ ▬ ▬ ▬ ▬ ▬

Birch didn't know who had kidnapped him until the hood was yanked off his head. He was suspended by the wrists; his feet barely touched the ground. He blinked a few times to bring the world back into focus.

The windowless room was brightly lit with fluorescent lights. Odors of blood, vomit, and urine pervaded the air, even though the floor seemed to be recently washed. A hose of some kind coiled like a snake in the corner of the room. The only furniture was a metal desk; on top lay a notebook, handcuffs, whips, pliers, scalpels, and a couple of electronic devices.

Two men sat at the desk. One was in his forties. A pair of wire-rim glasses accented his scholarly demeanor. His hand held a pen over a notepad. The other man was fit and much younger. He had sharp features with a rattlesnake's eyes. Both wore black suits. Behind them, a slogan hung on the wall: "Patriotism requires anti-Communism. No compromise in the anti-communist stance; No mercy to Communists or their followers or sympathizers."

Birch knew then that he was in the hands of *Jun-Tong*, the secret military police. Although he was still puzzled and irritated, he felt somewhat relieved. He was worried that he'd been kidnapped by a street gang. "What is wrong with you people? Whoever you want, it isn't me. I'm—"

"We know who you are," said the scholarly-looking man. He put down the pen, drew a pack of cigarettes from his top pocket, and stuck one between his thin lips. Flicking a lighter, he let the flame burn briefly before lighting the cigarette. "Major Bai Hua. Former fighter pilot in the Air Force."

"Then you know you've made a mistake."

"We never make mistakes," growled the snake-eyed man. "You're a traitor."

"Hell! What did I do?"

"We know what you've said and done."

"Like what?"

"You want to hear the evidence? Well, let me tell you." With one hand holding the cigarette, the "scholar" tapped the notebook with the other. "You helped a communist in Yunnan. You visited his family several times. They moved to a nice apartment because of you. We know everything about everyone."

"Then you know Ding Fang was killed by the Japs. He and his wife died for the country. His family deserves to be treated with dignity. If you—"

"You denounced the party and the government." Snake thrust an index finger and yelled, "Didn't you call the Army and *Jun-Tong* asshole—?"

"You are an asshole!"

Snake slammed his fist on the desk, making the scalpels jump and clink. "We can kill you, and killing you is as easy as crushing an ant."

"How dare you? I worked for the Nationalist government and fought the Japs for eight years. I was a decorated officer. My father is a member of the party. He—"

"Don't count on your old man to save you," interrupted Snake. "He's going to kick the bucket anytime—"

Birch strained against the bonds, making the chains rattle. Anger infused his face with color.

Snake shot to his feet. "Before we kill you"—he glared at Birch with his cobra-like eyes—"we'll peel a layer of skin from you first."

"Rot in hell!" Birch glared back at his interrogators.

A fierce exchange between them lasted almost an hour. At length, Snake lost his patience. He shed his suit and rolled up his sleeves to his elbows. "Let me take care of him." He picked up a whip and snapped it a few times. He added with vehemence, "He kicked the shit out of—"

The "scholar" raised his palm. A new cigarette dangled from his lips. His dark eyes were trained on Birch. "I don't want to do this. You were a great pilot. I've read all the reports. But I'm under orders. Help me here, Birch. May I call you Birch? Let's do this the easy way—for both of us. What do you say?"

"I have nothing to say. I've already told you, I didn't do anything."

The man scrutinized him. "Your timing couldn't be worse. Li Wei defected to the Mainland with his P-47 two months ago. He was in your squadron."

"He joined the squadron after my plane went down," said Birch. An acne-ridden face appeared in his mind. He'd met Li Wei a couple of times and heard the rumors about the escape. No one knew for sure why the young pilot took off. One thought was he'd been treated poorly here. But others guessed that by being a traitor to the Nationalists, he was trying to save his family that he'd left in the Communist-controlled Mainland. "How the hell—"

"You know the rule," the "scholar" said. "We won't let a single guilty individual walk free, even if we have to kill one hundred along the way."

"Screw your cold-blooded rules!"

Snake snapped the whip again. "I'll break him. It won't take long."

The man in charge blew out a cloud of smoke. "I can't help you if you don't help me." He tapped the ash off his cigarette. "You'd better come clean before I throw you to the lions." His brow furrowed as he waited. Without hearing an answer, he closed his eyes briefly before nodding his approval.

Snake walked with measured steps and stood before Birch with feet planted slightly apart, hands on his hips. "He'll crack before we use the fancy devices," he assured his superior over his shoulder. "No need to waste electricity."

Birch's instinct was to kick the son of a bitch. He was stretched to stand on tiptoes. His right knee was swelling and throbbing. But with the help of his strong arms, he could still deliver one powerful blow with his left foot.

But then what?

As the Communists on the Mainland eradicated the Nationalists, the government in Taiwan was just as worried about a Communist invasion. Martial law had been declared in May 1949. The rule was clear: It was better to capture one hundred innocent people than to let one guilty person go free. This attitude, along with a ridiculous incentive system that entitled the arresting officer to a significant portion of the prisoner's wealth, had led to imprisonment and executions of many innocent people. "White Terror" spread across the island.

Now, Birch's life was in their hands.

Years ago, Captain Zhang had said in the Japanese prison that there were no heroes, only survivors. Birch could not believe that his warning still held true. With enormous self-control, he fought the impulse to fight. If he wanted to survive, it was best not to provoke them. He balled his fists, counting to ten, and decided to keep calm and silent.

He wasn't afraid of death, but to die like this was meaningless. And if he did die, what would happen to his father? He would be heartbroken. What would Xiao Mei do? She would be homeless and all alone. Birch found himself caring about Xiao Mei's life more than his own. He had to do everything in his power to survive.

Unhurried, Snake unbuttoned Birch's shirt, revealing a white tank top. "One last time: who else is in your group?" he asked, sending a wad of saliva arching through the air. Without hearing an answer, he grabbed the neck of the undershirt, and with one fluid motion, ripped it apart. Drawing back a step, he lifted the whip.

Birch's lips pressed white.

"Wait!" the man in charge called out and jumped to his feet. The expression on his face changed discernibly as he stared at Birch's chest full of whip marks and old gunshot wounds. He shook his head, disbelief mixed with shock and awe. After a noticeable hesitation, he said, "The Japs did this?" It was half question, half statement. Then he mumbled to his associate, "Cut him some slack."

Snake was obviously disappointed.

Ignoring his subordinate, the "scholar" turned back to Birch. "Don't be stubborn, Birch. If you don't think of yourself, then think of your father. Is this what you want him to see at the end of his life? This is no joke. Don't be a hero. Tell us what we need to know so you can go home."

With that, he left the room, leaving Birch surprised and Snake dismayed.

———

Birch had been disappointed with the Nationalist party and disagreed with some of its policies, but he'd never done anything to undermine the government.

Who had tipped off Jun-Tong? They knew what he'd said. He'd complained only in front of his family and friends. *But how did the secret police find out?*

Birch couldn't believe any of his friends would give him up. They'd known each other for years, some through life-and-death situations. *Did someone tell others unintentionally?* A handful of them loved to drink. Who knew what they would say when intoxicated?

What if someone was in trouble? He hoped that none of his friends was in a predicament and had no choice but to indict him.

Well, if there is anyone I can trust completely, that person is Xiao Mei. No matter what happened, she would stand by him. She would never betray him. *That's a lot to say about a person.* Birch now realized that he'd paid so little attention to the gold mine right next to him for so many years.

Dad is right: If I can get out of here, I'll marry Xiao Mei. I owe it to her. I've got to protect her name. To hell with the doctors! I am a man. Watch me. And I can't let Dad leave this world worrying about me.

Hanging from the ceiling, he dreamed of being with his loved ones. Birch was so exhausted that he dozed off, despite the pain in the knee and the discomfort in his wrists and shoulders. Soon a nightmare plagued his sleep.

Captain Zhang pointed his nail-less fingers at him and yelled, "See, you Nationalists are animals, just like the Japs!" He lifted his right foot and kicked Meng Hu in the gut.

Birch slipped in between the two men to protect his fellow fighter pilot. *How come Meng Hu doesn't fight back? It's not like him.*

Then it hit him. Meng Hu was dead! He was killed by the Communists. As he grappled with the sad truth, Captain Zhang threw a bucket of water over his head.

Birch jerked awake with a start. He was drenched from head to toe. Snake stood a few steps away, a hose in his hand. "Keep your eyes open. No sleep"—he sprayed again—"unless you tell us who else is in your group."

The cold stream struck Birch in the face. He sputtered, choked, and gagged. To avoid the suffocating blow, he twisted his head and body. In the process he lost his balance. For a moment, he was suspended in the air. The handcuffs cut deep into his flesh. His already sore arms seemed to be wrenched from his shoulder sockets. Every joint, muscle, and sinew in his body screamed and protested. He kicked his feet to regain a standing posture on his tiptoes. The blast lasted a couple of minutes, but it felt like hours. When it was over, he gasped for air. It took everything he had to withstand the cruel treatment.

Dad thought Taiwan was safe. If I had stayed on the Mainland, at least I would be killed by the former enemies, not by so-called comrades. Birch felt insulted and aggrieved by the injustice. *How come Dad is so different? He's a member of the Nationalist party.* Struggling to stay awake, his mind wandered into the past.

In 1940, his father, a colonel at the time, had captured three Japanese communications officers. He kept them as his personal prisoners, but never once tortured or mistreated them. Instead, he visited them regularly and debated with them about the course of the war. As a graduate of the University of Tokyo, he spoke their language well.

Never being treated equally by their own superior officers, the Japanese captives were touched by his benevolence and impressed with his intelligence. Little by little, they were swayed by his point of view. They became convinced that a country with great people like Colonel Bai would win the war. After a year of such gentle persuasion, the three Japanese agreed to help the Allies.

Colonel Bai dressed them in the Nationalist uniforms and brought them into his office as communication specialists. The turncoats helped him to decode their countrymen's messages. Detailed data such as the number of airplanes, their altitude, and destination, significantly aided the Allies in counterattacking the Japanese raids. Without the valuable information, there would have been many more Allied casualties.

His father had lost so much, yet never lost his benevolence and *Yi*—morality, duty, decency. *But at the end of his life, Dad must face another heartbreak.* The thought set off another round of shivers in him that pierced his wet clothes and speared icy chills straight into his bones.

Birch was kept awake throughout the night. Whenever he dozed off, Snake hit him with more water. The room was already cold, and now it became unbearable. If the Japanese torture chamber was an inferno, this place was an icy underworld.

His teeth chattered nonstop. Tremors of overexertion seized his biceps, triceps, thighs, and leg. Only his will to survive, to see his father and Xiao Mei, kept him fighting.

Early next morning, a heavyset man replaced Snake. His nose was swathed, and dark blood flecked the white bandage. The left side of his face was discolored with a huge blue and purple bruise. One eye was swollen shut.

An unmitigated hatred in his other eye alerted Birch. He guessed that this must be the man he'd kicked. But no matter how much he tried to stay vigilant, the lack of sleep for days caught up with him. His eyelids grew heavier and heavier. At length, his head lowered to his chest. He was half asleep when a blow to his right knee jolted him awake. For a moment, he spasmed with pain.

His knee seemed afire. Warm liquid ran down his pant legs. He realized that he'd just soiled himself. His face twisted. He'd been holding for hours. But in his slumber and with the sudden shock of pain, he'd lost control.

The heavyset man turned around, picking up the hose. "Filthy traitor," he barked.

Cold water slammed between Birch's legs. He hardly heard the man; his pain and the humiliation were too great.

Chapter 49

Xiao Mei waited. She paced in circles in the living room. Her left thumb pressed the small scar on the back of her right hand. *God, help me. Guanyin, show your mercy. Birch has been through hell. Don't let anyone hurt him. Please!* Again and again, she prayed to the God and the Goddess of Mercy.

As she lay slumped on the sofa, open-eyed, waiting and praying, the phone finally rang. She jumped up and yanked the receiver off the cradle after the first ring.

"Someone tipped off *Jun-Tong.*" Chen Bin sounded grim.

"The secret police? Why? What did he do?"

"That's not relevant. What's bad is that they think he conspired against the government. They blamed him for Li Wei's leaving. Xiao Mei, we'll try our best, but frankly, I'm afraid we can't do much. It's all about connections and knowing the right people. We need someone in an influential position. Too bad General Bai is sick. Are you sure he can't make a few calls?"

"He's in bad shape, Chen Bin. We shouldn't tell him. I'm worried—"

"Okay. We'll keep trying. Du Ting is making more calls right now."

Xiao Mei stood still after the phone clicked off. *Conspiracy against the government is the worst crime.* She'd seen slogans like "Exterminate conspirators, traitors, and communist spies" on every street corner.

Citizens were encouraged to spy on one another and then inform the secret police. She'd heard rumors of people being arrested, tortured, or killed. Never in a million years could she have imagined Birch in such a dire situation. How could the government lash out at its own people, at its own hero?

What if they're hurting him right now? The thought sent a shudder through her.

Focus! You've got to think. Biting her lip, she tried to concentrate.

Who could tip off the secret police? Birch is so kind to everyone. He doesn't have enemies. Then her eyes widened. *Unless...?* A small gasp escaped her mouth. Could it be Wu Pan? Could he be so angry at her that he would hurt Birch? He hadn't shown up for work in days. She shook her head, unwilling to believe.

What if it's true? Anger surged through her. *How could he do this?* Xiao Mei ripped the phone from its bracket and dialed Wu Pan's number.

"Hold on," an old man answered. She heard his husky voice shouting for Wu Pan. The phone in the office was the only one in the complex.

Several minutes later, a gruff voice came on the line. "Yes?"

"Wu Pan, the secret police snatched Birch last night," said Xiao Mei. She'd cooled down; she knew she had no evidence and couldn't stand the idea of sending Wu Pan to his doom, if he were innocent. There were always people listening and spying on others. "Please help."

"Holy shit! You're sure it's *Jun-Tong?* If it's the secret police, we're screwed. They have power. What do you expect me to do?"

"Try something—"

"Look, Xiao Mei. I would if I could. Believe me. Birch saved me. I'd love to return the favor. But be realistic. I'm nobody."

She couldn't tell if the coldness in his voice was real or in her imagination. *Could he actually betray the Young Master? How could anyone be so ungrateful? How could he stab Birch in the back when Birch has been so kind to him?*

The questions disturbed Xiao Mei. *It's my fault if Wu Pan has indeed gone this far.* She felt a twinge of guilt. *If he'd made it in the first place, then he could retract his statement.* Clinging to a sliver of hope, she blurred out, "If you get him out, I'll…I'll…" Still, she couldn't bring herself to say the words. Her hand tightened around the phone.

"What?"

She unclenched her teeth. Her voice came out barely above a whisper. "I'll marry you." Tears sprang to her eyes.

"You're kidding!"

"No. Just help him!"

A bitter laugh came across the line. "Haven't you heard, Xiao Mei? They will kill one hundred innocent people to find a single guilty one. A place like that is easy to go in, but hard to get out."

By now the room was awash with sunlight. But Xiao Mei trembled. She didn't know who hung up first. Her mind was in turmoil, her emotions in a tailspin.

Desperate, she grabbed the family address book. Frantically, she called anyone with a number. Some replied politely that they would look into the situation, while others didn't even hear her out. She was just a servant. And no one was able or willing to confront the secret police.

An overwhelming sense of helplessness engulfed her. As she collapsed to the floor, a name flashed into her mind. *Mary!* Birch's ex-girlfriend came from a wealthy and influential family. Even though her father had died, she might have connections. Xiao Mei grabbed the phone for the hundredth time and called the engineer again. "Chen Bin, do you have Mary's telephone number?"

"Mary? Oh, how did I forget about her? Her cousin is the deputy chief."

"Of the secret police?"

"Yes. I'll give her a call right away."

"No!"

"Why not?"

"If you know where she lives, I'll go to her. I'll talk to her, woman to woman."

"Good idea. I'll take you there."

Chapter 50

— — — — — — — —

They took Birch down on the third day. Immediately, he fell to the floor. He had lost all feeling in his limbs. Snake and the heavyset man seized him under his arms. The two men dragged him face down out of the room, his limp body hanging between them. An iron door clanked and rattled before they tossed him onto the floor. Then the door clanged shut.

It was raining. The wind blew through a small, shattered window, bringing in the frigid air. There was a narrow bed in the room. Birch stretched his hand and immediately felt a thousand pinpricks stabbing his arm. He simply couldn't reach the top of the bed; it stood as tall as the Hump.

Shivering, he lay on the cold concrete floor. His eyes were dark and deep-set. His face was shriveled. A foul stench rose to his nostrils. He wasn't sure if it came from the room or from his clothes.

An all-encompassing despair came over him. He'd given everything to serve his country: his mother, his sister, his cousin; his brother and friends; his aunt and uncle; his girlfriend; his leg and his ability to be a father; his confidence as a man. And finally, his freedom and his dignity. What had he gotten in return?

Birch lost the battle with his iron-clad self-control. He was in hell.

A famous phrase ran through his mind—to live in the worst adversity is better than to die under the most satisfactory circumstances.

The idiot who came up with that saying didn't know a damn thing about hardship. It would be better to die a hero in that trench, oblivious to the pain, the guilt, the injustice, the degradation. Starved and beyond exhaustion, his body trembled with pain, cold, and fatigue. His mind whirled. *This is it.* He'd had enough. He was ready to let go.

Then he heard her voice.

"*Shao Ye,*" Xiao Mei called out. "Be strong. You can do it. Life is hard. It can be very painful. Being alive can be harder than dying… But you're a hero. Don't forget what Major Hardy said. A real Tiger doesn't give up easily. You're a real Tiger!"

When did she say that to me? In my coma?

Images swam into focus: She squeezed his hand and shook his arm. Her almond eyes stared at him with concern and affection. She smelled of the jasmine flower on her blouse.

Xiao Mei would be heartbroken. She didn't save me from the coma only to see me die here. Danny didn't give up his life only to watch me give up. And Dad still needs me. The kids in the flying club were waiting for their Uncle Birch. He couldn't let them down.

Xiao Mei! He reached for her, but she faded away. So he followed her into the merciful corners of unconsciousness.

———————

Two weeks later the secret police released Birch without any explanation. A simple shout of "Get out" was all they said.

A pinkish-gold dawn lay like a ribbon along the eastern horizon when Birch stepped out of his cell. He tilted his head up, closed his eyes, and drew a deep breath of the fresh air. His face was etched with fatigue. His limbs felt like they weighed a thousand pounds each. With aching muscles and joints, he dragged his foot and staggered across the compound toward the entrance.

"*Shao Ye!*" Xiao Mei stood at the other side of the gate. She was in a lily white sundress with a gray cardigan sweater. A navy blue jacket was draped over her arm. Her eyes trained on him as she twisted the end of her pigtail around her index finger. Chen Bin and Du Ting stood next to her.

Birch hobbled toward his friends.

The two former colleagues each grabbed an elbow to steady him. Du Ting took the jacket from Xiao Mei and wrapped it around him. "Welcome back," said Chen Bin, knocking him with a fist. "You look like hell."

Birch grimaced.

"Son of a bitch! They hurt you."

Birch waved off their concern. "Anyone else in trouble?"

Du Ting shook his head.

Chen Bin shrugged and said, "No one we know of."

Birch let out a pent-up breath of relief. He looked up and saw the glint in the servant girl's eyes. "Xiao Mei, come here." He stretched his arms.

She reached out. But before grabbing his hands, she hesitated. As she faltered, he pulled her into a tight embrace. The tears she had fought for days rushed out.

"It's okay. I'm all right." Birch patted her on the back and let go only after her cry subsided. With the help of his left hand, he lifted his right arm and wiped the tears from her cheeks. His eyes had sunk into the dark circles surrounding them, yet now they brimmed with tenderness as he stared at her. "I vowed I'd do the right thing, if I could get out." He paused to catch his breath. "You've been with us for so long. It's time—"

Xiao Mei stilled. "Oh, no! Don't chase me away. Please!" Looking up, she threw him a glance that was half-scared and half-appealing.

"No, no, no! That's not what I'm talking about." Towering over her, Birch picked up her hand.

She was shivering. Her thin hand was as cold as his.

"I've been a fool. Forgive me, Xiao Mei. Would you like to stay in the family? Forever, I mean. If you don't mind my...my condition, will you marry me?" He swallowed against the dryness of his throat. "I'm not the best husband a girl could dream of, but I promise, in my limited ability, I'll make you as happy as I can. Will you be my wife?"

Her eyes snapped wide open. "*Shao Ye?*"

"Don't call me Young Master. Call me Birch. And if you don't mind that…that I can't give you any children, then be my wife."

Xiao Mei stared at him. "Birch," she said in a near-whisper and lowered her head. The sound of his name painted a shy smile on her lips.

"I'll be damned," exclaimed Du Ting.

"I was going to ask her if you didn't," Chen Bin joked. "Her dishes are out of this world."

"Seriously," Du Ting said, "it's about time." He put a hand on Birch's shoulder. "If it weren't for Xiao Mei, you would've rotted in there."

"Yes, she saved you."

"I'm nobody," protested Xiao Mei. "It was…Mary."

"Mary?"

Xiao Mei nodded. "She pulled some strings—"

"No," Chen Bin countered. "We started a petition. Xiao Mei stayed on the street day and night. She got more signatures than all of us combined."

Birch pressed her hand to his lips. "Dad will be so happy." Worried about his father, he said, "If you don't mind, we'll get married tomorrow. I'll arrange a formal ceremony later. You know, I just want to get Dad's blessing before—"

Xiao Mei's face fell. She opened her mouth, yet only a strangled sound came from her throat. Tears rolled down her cheeks again.

Her expression put Birch on alert. A sense of foreboding tightened his chest.

"General…Dad…" She still couldn't bring herself to deliver the heartbreaking news.

"I'm sorry, Birch." Du Ting put a hand on his shoulder. "General Bai passed away two days ago."

Birch felt the earth crumble beneath him. His bravado collapsed. And the physical pain and fatigue he'd suffered caught up with him. He swayed. Both Chen Bin and Du Ting grabbed him under his arms.

"I'm so sorry, *Shao*…Birch." Xiao Mei circled her arms around him. Her cheek touched his chest. Her tears wet his dirty shirt.

A great emptiness opened up inside Birch. His father had been his only family member for almost a decade. *But I wasn't there for him. I didn't even say goodbye.* It struck him that he'd never been given a chance to say goodbye to any of his loved ones. *Not to Mom. Not to Daisy. Not to Jasmine. Not to Danny. Not to Uncle or Aunt.* Such a realization chilled him to the bone. The sun had spread its glory, but failed to warm him. His entire body recoiled as if someone had laid a finger on an open wound.

"Take it easy." Du Ting squeezed Birch's arm. "General Bai went peacefully. All of us were there. Xiao Mei kneeled and bowed on your behalf."

Birch nodded, tears glinting in his eyes. Then his breath stopped, trapped between his lungs and his throat. "Did he know?" he asked with an unnatural tremor in his voice. "Dad was worried about me, wasn't he? Oh shit, I was the reason—"

"No!" Xiao Mei cut him off. "He didn't know. I didn't—"

"That's right. Xiao Mei never told him. He was unconscious most of the time. And when he was awake, she made up an excuse for you."

"It's not your fault!" Xiao Mei emphasized.

Birch took a shaky breath. His expression turned contrite. "Dad wanted us to get married. I was such a fool. He'd be so happy." He brushed a strand of unruly hair from her face as he murmured apologetically, "Sorry, Xiao Mei. We'll have to postpone. I can't—"

She put a finger to his chapped lips.

Chapter 51

Three months later, a simple ceremony took place at the marriage registration office. Chen Bin and Du Ting were the only guests. It was very different from a traditional wedding, which was elaborate and loud. Birch was still in mourning, and Xiao Mei didn't care about formality.

She was ecstatic. Her eyes glowed with childish excitement. The muscles of her face ached from smiling. Marrying Birch, a decorated hero and the only man she'd ever loved, had been an impossible dream.

She'd wished and dreamed but never seriously thought it would come true. Marriage between a maid and a master was unheard of, unless she was the second, the third, or the fourth wife. Staying in the household as a servant had been her realistic goal.

Xiao Mei loved their marriage vow. She'd never heard the pledge before. Birch said it was the western way. Danny had told him about it, and he loved it. She agreed with him. It was better than the traditional bows to Heaven and Earth, to the ancestors, and to each other.

That night, sitting on the edge of their bed, Xiao Mei kept twisting the ring on her finger. She liked the feel of it. It symbolized her union with Birch. Now she was part of the family, part of him. *I'm no longer an outsider.*

She blushed, her face the color of the red cheongsam encasing her petite body. She closed her eyes and inhaled the intoxicating smell of the jasmine flowers pinned to her chest.

Although Xiao Mei was excited and couldn't wait to be intimate with the man she had loved nearly all her adult life, she was shy. Women were taught to be submissive and obedient. Biting her lip, lowering her head, she waited patiently for her newlywed husband to initiate the next move.

There was a long awkward silence.

Xiao Mei peeked over at Birch and saw his hesitation. She let out a soundless sigh. Within seconds, she righted her mood. *I love him more than he loves me. So I have to do more, to try harder.*

Despite her determination, she didn't know what to do. Sex had been a taboo for thousands of years in China. No sex education. No talking about it. Not even a whisper. All she knew was that when a man and a woman got married, they slept in the same bed and made babies. *How?* The closest descriptions in literature were like "they had a blissful night" or "they turned the clouds into rains." *What did that mean?*

Fortunately, her biological instinct kicked in, and her unsuppressed love guided her. She turned to face him.

The room was bathed in the golden glow of candlelight. Soft shadows crossed Birch's face. He was still as handsome as when she'd first met him. Only time took away his youthfulness, and life had added hardness to his facial appearance, attested to by a jagged scar at the bottom of his chin and another faint one under his left eye.

Behind his rugged good looks, Xiao Mei often discerned unimaginable suffering, as well as steadfast strength. Every time she watched him struggle, it pulled on her heartstrings. *It's my fault.* If she hadn't selfishly awakened him, if he'd never come out of the coma, he wouldn't have had to suffer. Her guilt was as strong as her love.

She lifted her arms and placed her palms upon his face. The tips of her fingers grazed his cheeks and chin. Then her cheek touched his. Rubbing against his skin, she savored every second, treasuring every inch against his flesh. Joy filled her. She'd dreamed about this moment for so long.

She reached out to unbutton his shirt. Another rush of heat

flushed her face, and her heart raced frantically.

Birch leaned over the nightstand and blew out the candles. "Let's—" He motioned to the ones closer to Xiao Mei.

By the dancing candlelight, she could see the skin grow taunt across his cheekbones and a hint of sadness appear at the corners of his mouth. She understood his hesitation. Birch was conscious of his appearance and embarrassed about his physical imperfection. He'd been a picture-perfect man before the war.

Xiao Mei felt a tug of sympathy. After all, his battered body was the reason that Mary had left him.

She didn't blow out the candle. Instead, she brushed open his shirt. When she saw the first scar below his right collarbone, she lifted her hand to it. Her fingers skimmed the rough skin. With tenderness she placed her mouth on the scar. She heard his sharp intake of breath and sensed his quiver. Immediately, her head shot up, her startled gaze flying to his face. "Are you still in pain?"

His jaw shifted.

"Then—"

He didn't answer. But his eyes revealed discomfort. His shoulders sagged.

Xiao Mei felt the sting of tears. She placed her lips on the scar again. Wrapping her arms around him, she kissed him all over his chest and felt his tremors. When she finally lifted her head, tears filled her eyes. "Birch, your scars are badges of courage and bravery. I love you, everything about you. I wish you'd never been injured. I wish you'd never gone through the hell you've been through." She seized his large hands, wrapping them tightly in her small ones, pressing them onto her lips. "But your scars are part of you and the kind of man you are. You're a tough man. A real Tiger!"

Birch's eyes flew open.

"No need to hide the scars from me," she continued. "Especially now that I'm yours. We're one and all. 'For better, for worse, in sickness and in health, to love and to cherish.' Remember?"

Xiao Mei poured her heart out. She'd had no right to speak to him in this way when she was his servant. Now that she was his wife, she could say what she'd yearned to tell him for years—"Your wounds are my wounds." In a soul-filled voice, she added, "From now on, let me share your pain."

Birch knew Xiao Mei had been infatuated with him for years, yet her strong emotions shocked him. He was even more taken aback by her boldness. Her willingness to love and her eagerness to comfort touched him deeply. For the first time in ages, he felt a heart-to-heart connection with another human being.

Xiao Mei, this seemingly shy and obedient girl, moved him to the core. For years Birch had refused to let anyone reach him. He was afraid of being rejected and hurt again. He was petrified to find out whether he was impotent as a man, as the doctors had predicted.

An unexpected warmth welled inside him. Although he didn't feel sexual desire, as a decent person, he had a sense of duty and responsibility to be a good husband. He decided to take charge. *Be a man*, he urged himself. *You took her as your wife. Promised to make her happy. So keep your word. You've got to try.*

While he wasn't skilled, he knew there was more than one way to satisfy a woman. He was determined to try his best to repay the kindness to his wife.

So he cupped her chin in both his hands. His eyes traveled over her face. Xiao Mei was pretty in an unassuming way. Her almond-shaped eyes were always pure and kind, and they glowed whenever she looked at him. She had a soft smile. What she lacked in extraordinary beauty was made up for in her sweetness and sincerity. With two waist-length braids, she appeared much younger than her thirty years.

Birch fused his mouth with hers. This time he felt her tremble. He pulled away and watched hope leap to life in her eyes. Traces of tears still remained on her face. Nevertheless, she was lit up from the inside. The redness on her cheeks deepened under his intense stare. In an instant, she was transformed into a blushing teenager. He'd never seen such unfettered joy or passion.

Her bliss became his incentive and motivation. He eased her onto the bed and stared down at her. In the soft candlelight, her eyes were clear, brimming with emotions—tenderness, yearning, love. Her penetrating gaze reached out and touched his soul. Even in silence, her words echoed loudly in his mind—*We're one and all.*

Birch couldn't wait any longer. Bending down, he kissed the salty tears off her cheeks. In a little while, he unbuttoned her cheongsam. His lips grazed her neck, trailing down her shoulders and exploring the shape of her body. He was surprised that, unlike her work-roughened fingers, her skin was smooth. She tasted like the jasmine flower she wore.

He touched her breast and felt the muscles spring to life under his fingers. A jolt of desire shot through his veins when she moaned. His heart slammed against his chest as her upper body arched and her fingers dug into his hair, pulling him closer to her.

Nothing turned a man on more than a woman's desire. A tingling sensation, foreign yet primal, coursed through his body. His blood seemed to burn as arousal hardened his muscles. The erogenous parts of him that had lain dormant for years now came to life.

When he entered her warm body, he emitted a low growl. His eyes lit up, and a look of pure ecstasy passed over his face. To his astonishment, he tasted the pleasure he'd thought he could never experience.

With each smooth thrust deep inside her, he was carried to new heights of sensation. His breath became faster and harsher as their moans grew louder. When the final moment came, he buried his face in the hollow of her neck to stifle a loud cry of release that ripped through him.

At thirty-eight, for the first time in his life, Birch tasted the intense sexual pleasure of being a man.

Chapter 52

▬ ▬ ▬ ▬ ▬ ▬ ▬ ▬

The next two months passed in rare contentment.

On this August morning, a ringing telephone dragged Birch out of a deep sleep. Lying in a tangle of sheets, he let out a low, satisfied sound. Hand stretched, he tried to wrap Xiao Mei back into his arms and found her side of the bed empty. He opened his eyes to see her talking on the phone in the faint light.

"Slow down. What? I can't understand you. Wait, please don't hang up." Covering the mouthpiece, she turned to him with a look of disbelief and fear. "It's Chen Bin. He's talking nonsense. I think…I think he's drunk. You'd better—"

Birch bolted upright and snatched the receiver. He listened intently for a moment. Then his jaw dropped. "Where are you? Tell me. Let's talk," he pleaded. His hand tightened around the receiver. "Chen Bin, don't hang up. Dammit. Let me help you!"

The line went dead.

Birch looked up. His face crumbled with helplessness.

"What happened? Did you understand him?"

He nodded. His eyes were now wide open, but they'd lost their luster.

"Is he drunk?"

"Yes, but that's not the problem. Du Ting…" Birch's Adam's apple bounced a few times before continuing, "Du Ting is dead. He—"

"What happened?"

"His wife—"

"I know she was left on the Mainland."

"Chen Bin said something I didn't quite catch. If I understood correctly, she was forced to remarry, so she jumped into a river."

"Oh, no!" Xiao Mei covered her mouth with her hand. "And Du Ting?"

"He jumped…from a tall building, I think." In a tormented voice, he cried, "God, how many of us have to die? Danny is gone. Meng Hu was beaten to death. Du Ting killed himself. Chen Bin might be next—"

"Where is he?" Xiao Mei interrupted.

"I don't know. He's drunk; kept saying that Du Ting had jumped. And that he should have followed him. They've been best friends for years." Birch looked dazed, his face white. But his uncertainty lasted only seconds. Flinging back the sheets, he fumbled for his clothes with his shaky hands. "I have to find him. I won't let him—"

"I'll go with you."

———————

It was drizzling as they drove toward Taipei. Dawn had turned the sky gray, and a thin scrim of mist covered the land.

When they arrived, Chen Bin's apartment was dark and locked. Birch knocked on the door, softly at first and then harder. No one answered, even after they pounded for several minutes.

"What can we do?" asked Xiao Mei.

"I know several bars where he likes to go."

The usually busy city seemed deserted as the rain had driven people off the street. At each bar there was no sign of the engineer. By mid-morning, Birch was in pain and limping badly. Rainy days were always hard on his injuries, and his recent imprisonment and water torture had made it even worse.

"Stay in the car, Birch," begged Xiao Mei. The drizzle had become a downpour. Streaks of water hammered the car's roof and windshield.

"Let me get out and check. Don't step in the rain. Please!"

Birch shook his head. He squeezed her hand before opening the car door. Xiao Mei hurried to his side and grabbed his arm. The wind-driven rain fell almost horizontally and rendered the umbrella useless. It wasn't a cold day, but her wet clothing clung to her body, making her shiver. For the next hour they kept looking.

Around noon they returned to Chen Bin's apartment. The door was still locked.

"What now?" Xiao Mei asked, her voice sliding out of control. She was worried about the engineer as well as Birch's leg. Water dripped from their clothes, forming small puddles around their feet.

Birch sat down outside the door and closed his eyes. "Let's think for a moment." He took some deep breaths and then slowed his breathing. After a couple of minutes, he opened his eyes and said, "Let's go to the police. Find out where Du Ting jumped. Chen Bin said something about following his best friend. Maybe he's there. I hope it's not too late."

It was mid-afternoon by the time they found out where Du Ting had committed suicide. The former tail gunner had jumped from his lawyer's office in the center of the city. Birch and Xiao Mei ran to the building and took the elevator to the sixth floor. The gray-haired lawyer was startled to see the drenched couple.

"Which window did Du Ting jump from yesterday?" Birch asked. Seeing the lawyer's stunned expression, he added, "I'm his friend."

The man pointed to a corner window behind his desk.

Birch rushed over and spotted a figure on the ground directly below. *Dear God! Is that Chen Bin?* He felt an ice-cold spike drive through him. "Did…did anyone else jump?" he asked.

The lawyer shook his head, still perplexed.

The couple dashed downstairs. Birch's teeth chattered, and he knew it wasn't from the rain.

Chen Bin lay curled up on the wet sidewalk. His eyes were closed. His face, once chubby and boyish, had an unhealthy, gray pallor. His Nationalist uniform, with a medal pinned to his chest, was soiled and soaked. Two empty liquor bottles lay beside him.

"Chen Bin?" Birch dropped to his knees, grabbed his friend's arm, and shook him a few times.

A faint groan escaped from the engineer as he rolled over on his side and smacked his lips. Birch almost choked with relief. His friend was still alive. He leaned over and picked up the motionless figure.

"No!" cried Xiao Mei, worried about her husband's leg.

"Open the door," Birch ordered. The stench of vomit on Chen Bin's clothing rose to his nostrils, but he kept a tight hold. Tears mixed with raindrops dripped down his cheeks. Xiao Mei jumped to her feet to help Birch carry the unconscious man into the car.

They raced to the hospital. Later, a doctor told them that Chen Bin's blood alcohol content was dangerously high and that he had to remain in the hospital. Knowing Chen Bin was in good hands, they returned home. The clouds parted and a portion of a full moon lit up the sky. Xiao Mei warmed some leftovers, and they ate in silence. Exhausted from the day's events, they took a hot bath and went to sleep.

Chapter 53

The next morning Birch woke up screaming Danny's name.

August was always hard for him. Danny's birthday was the thirteenth of the month; he'd been killed two days before he would have turned thirty-one. Both Daisy and Jasmine had died several days after his birthday. Birch himself had been shot and left to die on August thirteenth.

He'd hoped this year would be different, now that Xiao Mei was by his side. But Du Ting's death brought back the nightmares.

"Shhh… It's okay," Xiao Mei said in her soothing voice. "It's just a dream." Her petite body pressed tightly against his back, her arms wrapping around him. Softly she stroked his chest, his arm, his face.

Little by little, the trembling that held Birch captive subsided as her lips grazed his back and neck. He watched early morning sunlight dance around the edges of the window where the thick velvet drapes were drawn, and he began to relax.

As soon as he was fully awake, he called the hospital and was told that Chen Bin was out of danger, but still in a deep sleep. At breakfast Birch gave Xiao Mei a quick rehash of the conversation. Afterward he walked outside and sat on the back porch for a long time.

It was a sunny day. The sky was a vivid blue with scattered clouds left in the wake of the swift-moving storm from the day before. The torrential rain had cleansed everything. A crystal vase full of forget-me-nots stood on the patio table. The air smelled of wild-flowers, delicate and subtle.

Xiao Mei left him alone, but she kept bringing fresh coffee. On his fourth refill, he started to talk.

For the first time, Birch voiced his reservations about the war. He didn't expect Xiao Mei to comment, but he had to let off steam.

"Was it really worthwhile?" he asked. "Was the sacrifice justified, especially for Danny and Jack? They could have spent their lives in the mountains of California, hiking and rock climbing. Instead, they came to China and died in a foreign land."

He banged the cup onto the saucer. "I could have stayed in America like other rich boys. I could have had expensive clothes, luxurious cars, and a big house."

"Yeah, your life would've been easy sailing," echoed Xiao Mei, taking a chair beside him. Her long braids were gone, and a short bob seemed to give her more maturity.

"I thought that kind of life was selfish. Hollow and purposeless, you know." Absentmindedly Birch kneaded his right thigh. "But look at the path I chose."

Xiao Mei leaned closer and started to massage his leg. "Most people, including me, had no choice but to follow what life offered. With all the options, you picked the most dangerous one. Dad was so anxious every time you took off, especially when you flew over the Hump."

"It was awful. Over fifteen hundred airmen died. Those mountains are too high. The weather was almost always bad. We didn't have reliable charts or radio navigation. On sunny days, we could see reflections of the wreckage. It was hard not to wonder when it would be our turn."

"You and your colleagues risked your lives to keep the military supplies coming. Flying the Hump was invaluable." Her voice was soft, yet carried an undertone of intensity. "Remember how Mother was killed? How Jasmine's parents died? How my family and the entire village was slaughtered? How Jasmine was raped and tortured? How you had no choice but to…kill Daisy?"

Birch's voice stuck in his throat, so he nodded. His hands balled into fists.

"Without you, Danny, Meng Hu, Du Ting, or Chen Bin, what kind of world would we live in today? A lot more people would've been tortured, raped, or killed. You and your friends protected them. You protected me."

Xiao Mei caught his fists between her palms. "Because of all of the wounds on your body, I have none. It's because you lost one leg that I have both of mine. Can't you see? You endured unbearable pain, so I didn't suffer. And I'm only one of the thousands of people you saved. Birch, you didn't endure hell for nothing." Tears filled her eyes. "You went through hell for me. For us! I'm forever grateful to you."

Her strong words gave him the solace he'd craved. They validated his choices and contributions and gave meaning to the life that he questioned. Once again, Xiao Mei had reached out and touched his soul. His chest swelled with warmth.

"And because of Danny, we're able to sit here." Xiao Mei squeezed his large hands. "He wanted you to be happy, my dearest Birch. Think about it this way. You wanted to take his place. If you had done that, would you like him to regret his entire life?"

Birch shook his head. "But I fought for this country. Eight years. Now I can't even set foot on the Mainland. I'd be killed if I did. And even here, in Taiwan, the Nationalists put me in jail." Birch still stung from the injustice of the event and struggled to hold his temper. "Meng Hu is dead. Du Ting is gone. They fought the Japs for years. Now they're dead in this godawful peaceful time." Anguish seized his face, and he grimaced. "I don't even know whether Meng Hu had a boy or a girl. I...I was going to be the godfather."

Unable to speak, Xiao Mei kept holding his hand.

"Danny and Jack will be forgotten on the Mainland. Or worse yet, they'll be labeled enemies of the country. Enemies! The Communists won't honor any American as a hero. How unfair! They died for China." Birch crumpled, as if the weight of the world was upon him.

The United States had sided with the Nationalists during the Civil War. So by default, they were enemies of the Communists.

They were double enemies because they supported South Korea in the recent Korean War. Mainland China backed the North Korean Communist.

"I understand your frustration," said Xiao Mei, staring hard at him. She pulled his fists apart and laced her fingers within his. "Let me ask you this, Birch: What would you do if you could turn back time, now that you know the outcome?"

Birch lifted his head and probed the depth of her eyes, blinking at her words.

"I bet you'd still choose to be a fighter pilot. You'd trade anything in the world to be Danny's brother and Meng Hu's friend. Even if you knew your friendship would end too soon. Even if you knew you'd be heartbroken in the end. Am I right?"

His eyes moistened.

"You must accept the past, good or bad." She ran her thumb over the ridges of his knuckles, making slight circles. "This is far from a perfect world. Even a Tiger has limited influence."

"So, we're helpless," he groaned, resentment stiff in his voice.

"Not true. We can't change the world, but we can change the world around us. That's what you told us. You're doing it now. Why can't you see it?" Xiao Mei scooted forward. "I know why you started the flying club. It's more than teaching kids about planes. You set it up to honor Danny. I heard your conversation. He said in his old age he wanted to start a flying club."

Birch nodded, and then he blurted out, "That's it!"

"What?"

"Forget-You-Not! That's the name—"

"That's a perfect name for the club."

This name delighted Birch. Then and there he vowed to tell the children all the heroic stories that he'd tried to bury in his memory. *No matter how hard it is, I have to do it so that the younger generation will know the truth.*

He decided to invite his former colleagues to join him. It would give his friends a purpose and renew their camaraderie. *We have to help each other. No more meaningless death.*

"See, you're doing a great thing. Don't beat yourself up."

"How come I didn't see it clearly?"

"'The onlooker sees most of the game,'" Xiao Mei cited a proverb. Lifting his hand, she kissed his palm. "You're too emotionally involved."

"You're not an onlooker. For God's sake, you lost your entire family."

"But I didn't fight the Japs face to face, or fly those death-defying missions. I never watched fellow soldiers die in front of me. I wasn't shot at. I don't have scars all over my body, and I didn't lose a leg. I wasn't tortured or left to die in a mass grave. I didn't have to kill my loved one in order to save her from humiliation and shame."

She stood up. Her small hands clasped his well-built shoulders. "Birch, you've experienced horrific things. It's understandable that you can't always think rationally."

———

Birch stared at the petite woman before him. Xiao Mei was slim and barely four feet, ten inches tall. Her body was encased in a lilac cheongsam with a side slit to show off one slender leg. He parted his knees, pulling her onto his lap. His arms looped around her waist. "How on earth did you get to be so wise?" Amusement flicked in his eyes.

"Jasmine's mother taught me how to read and write. Don't forget, I've lived a long time in two intelligent households. I listened. I paid attention and learned."

"You have an incredible memory. I know that."

Xiao Mei nodded. "Actually," she said, her lips curved upward, "I have to thank you."

"Me? What did I do?"

"You told us—the villagers and me—so many stories. Remember? Those were informative and educational."

He smiled.

"Also, after I read to you for months—"

"Oh, I heard you," exclaimed Birch.

"Really?"

"I didn't know until I was in jail." He stroked her hair, his eyes soft. "Your words saved me again, Xiao Mei."

She looked satisfied. "I benefited from it, too. I started reading regularly. Not many days went by that I didn't read. There were plenty of books in the house."

He narrowed his eyes. "I had no idea that you are so well-read." He skimmed a knuckle down her jaw. "You were only fourteen when I first met you."

"To me, you were a Tiger, and will always be a Tiger."

"You know, Danny said I should marry you."

"He did?"

"At first he joked about it. He said we'd have delicious food for the rest of our lives. Then he stopped teasing and told me that you were real and solid."

Xiao Mei bit her lip, flattered by the Flying Tiger's remark.

"But he wouldn't guess this. You bailed me out more than once. God, you...you're unbelievable." He leaned over, giving her a peck on the cheek. "Why didn't you talk to me like this before?"

"My silly *Shao Ye*." Her dancing eyes gleamed with wicked wit. "How could I? We stood on different grounds. You were my Young Master and a larger-than-life hero. I was a petty *Ya Tou*. My job was to serve you. I tried so hard to be a perfect servant so that I could stay in this household. Oh, Birch, you can't imagine how much I wished I could talk to you like this."

She drew a shaky breath. "I wanted to hold you when you screamed." She wrapped her right arm around his neck, lifted her left hand, and touched his face. "Remember the time I went into your room? I almost got myself fired." She chuckled and ran a finger along his cheek. "Oh, as God is my witness, all I wanted was to touch you like this so that I could ease your pain."

Birch grabbed her hand, but Xiao Mei didn't allow him to stop her. She unfastened the top three buttons of his shirt and slid her hand under his clothes. Her smooth palm caressed his bare chest in a slow circular motion. She watched him close his eyes, drowning in her soft touch. Her heart reached out to him and then sang a sweet song. For many years Xiao Mei had wished and prayed that her young master would live a better life. She was happy that she was able to help him begin the healing process.

Her hand glided over the scar below his right collarbone. She heard him suck in a quick breath. This particular injury had become his soft spot ever since the first night they were together. She dropped to her knees in between his legs. Undoing the rest of his shirt, she buried her face in his broad chest. Her arms curled around his waist, pulling him closer to her. She nuzzled his bare skin, inhaling deeply, savoring his masculine scent.

Xiao Mei kissed the scar and felt his flesh tense. She heard his muffled moan and knew it wasn't due to embarrassment anymore. She kept on kissing him all over his body, reveling in this strong man's bliss.

Her sweet seduction was intoxicating. Every touch and kiss from her seared into his soul. Before long, Birch peeled her away and scooped her into his arms like a giant lifting a rag doll. He looked down, bathed in the glow of her eyes and the flush on her cheeks. Their gazes locked. He felt warmth in the pit of his stomach. "Those goddamned doctors," he cursed under his breath. "If I knew—"

Xiao Mei didn't allow him to finish. She pressed her lips to his. Holding her tightly, his mouth fused to hers, Birch rushed to the bedroom.

And there, the imperfect couple made perfect love again.

Part Three

From the Ashes

Chapter 54

- - - - - - - -

The next three years were quiet and peaceful. Birch still missed his loved ones very much, especially when he was happy. He wished his younger brothers and sisters could experience a joyous life. He still suffered nightmares from time to time. The pain and regret were like beasts lurking in his subconscious, always wanting to break out. But now, someone was there by his side when he woke up screaming from night terrors. Xiao Mei's soft touch and soothing voice gave him comfort. Her embrace meant the world to him, and with the help of the loving woman, his emotional wounds began to heal.

The morning of August 13, 1955 started bright and pleasant. It was the day Birch had been looking forward to all year long—his club's annual event.

He let loose a whistle when he caught sight of Xiao Mei stepping out of their bedroom. She wore an ivory-colored silk cheongsam, her petite figure wrapped in an exquisite, body-hugging dress.

"You look beautiful," he commented.

"And you, my dear *Shao Ye*"—Xiao Mei liked to call him *Young Master* every so often—"you're the best-looking man in uniform." Her radiant smile clearly showed a woman in love.

He kissed her on the cheek. "The guests are coming soon. Otherwise…" He pressed his lips to hers. Even after three years of marriage, Birch couldn't get enough of his loving wife. He often joked that he was trying to make up for those years they should have had together but were denied.

Xiao Mei touched his cheek with her palm. "I'll still be here tonight, my Hungry Tiger." Her eyes brimmed with delight, but her face was a little pale.

———————

"I've told you the stories before. I'll tell you again today and in the future." Birch began his speech with his booming voice. In his early forties, he was composed and handsome. Six medals were pinned to the left side of his chest.

In his backyard, dozens of children and veterans, including Chen Bin, sat around three long tables covered with white tablecloths. Birch stood at the head of one table. "We shouldn't forget the people who have sacrificed their lives to protect ours."

He pointed to two gentlemen sitting to his right. "First, let me introduce our special guests, Mr. Deng and Mr. Tu. They are reporters from *The China Post*." He extended his arm and shook hands with them. "Welcome. Thank you for coming. We hope you'll enjoy our special event."

The newsmen tipped their heads.

Birch turned to a gangly teenager seated to his left. "Today, Xiao Hu will tell you the stories." His suntanned face glowed as much as the boy's. "Let's give him a big round of applause."

Little Tiger stood up with the help of a cane. A pair of toffee-brown slacks covered his artificial leg. At eighteen, he was almost as tall as his instructor. "Thank you, Uncle Birch. This is such an honor. I can't believe…" He was so thrilled his voice trembled.

Birch patted the young man on the back.

Little Tiger nodded with gratitude. Taking a breath, he started the story. He was so proud when he defined the Flying Tigers' victories. He stopped briefly after he recounted the rescue of Danny Hardy by Jasmine, Daisy, and the villagers. His voice cracked as he described the death of the two girls and the other civilians. His face flushed as he recited Birch's rescue of the Flying Tiger and how the two men became sworn brothers. He was full of pride when he recounted the airmen's courageous missions. Tears gleamed in his eyes when he spoke about Danny's self-sacrifice and Birch's near death experience.

The audience shot to its feet and applauded when he was done. Most people had tears on their cheeks or in their eyes.

Birch stood up and took Little Tiger in his arms. His eyes were moist. This ceremony was always emotional for him. Today, apart from sadness, he was proud. Letting the younger generation know the stories was his goal, and he was successful.

While still holding the young man on his left arm, Birch turned to the crowd and waved his right hand. The group followed his cue—everyone started to sing. Chen Bin and a few other veterans punched their right fists into the air as they sang.

Use our flesh and blood
Lay down our life
Protect the country from the enemies
Safeguard the freedom of our people
We are a team made of iron
We have brave hearts

The patriotic wartime song was inspiring. There was an atmosphere of excitement, and the clapping lasted a long time.

Finally, Xiao Mei announced, "Lunch is ready. I need a few volunteers to bring the dishes out." Before she walked away with several helpers, she turned to Birch and flashed him an intimate smile. Her eyes glowed, but her face again looked pale.

Chapter 55

━ ━ ━ ━ ━ ━ ━ ━

Birch stood up and raised a glass of rice wine. He waited until everyone had followed his lead and then made a toast. "To Danny, Jack, and all the American airmen! We'll never forget their bravery. We'll always appreciate their sacrifices. And to Jasmine, Daisy, and all the villagers who risked their lives to save the Flying Tiger. These heroes and heroines will forever live in our hearts."

He clinked the glass with those nearby, and then raised it to the sky. "Happy birthday, brother! I wish…" His voice caught on a lump lodged in his throat and cracked to the point that he couldn't finish.

"We wish that Jasmine, Daisy, and Jack are with you," Xiao Mei continued toasting for him. "And that you are having a marvelous birthday."

Birch gave her a grateful nod.

"This is such an important event. Eye-opening and touching," Mr. Deng, one of the reporters, said during lunch. "We heard about your imprisonment. Such a terrible injustice! I'm so sorry. That's another reason we want to be here—to let the public know the truth." He shook hands with Birch again. "Thank you for what you've done for the country, and for the kids. I'm honored to meet you."

Mr. Tu, the other reporter, snapped a few more pictures of the ex-fighter pilot.

All Birch could do was nod in appreciation.

"May I ask you something?" Mr. Tu put down his camera. He took a stack of black-and-white photos from his bag and flipped through them. "I collect wartime photographs and try to gather as much information as I can." The reporter handed one photo to Birch. "Most of them showed Japanese atrocities. But I found this in a trading market. What the man said bothered me. He said, 'The Japs were helping farmers for a change.' Now, I've never heard stories like this. Wonder if you know anything. Did the Japs help Chinese farmers?"

Birch studied the yellowed photograph. A group of six Japanese soldiers stood in a rice paddy, all of them bent over at the waist except for one, who stood, shading his eyes. "I've never heard anything like this."

"Could it be propaganda?" suggested Chen Bin.

"The Japs tried to convince everyone that they would provide peace and prosperity. Some of the posters looked quite convincing. But this seems to be a snapshot." Birch turned the photo over. "What does it mean?" he asked. The scribbles in the back were in Japanese.

"It says Hong Kong"—Mr. Tu pointed to the word—"and Sadao Endo, a name. No idea which one is he. How come only his name is labeled?"

"Perhaps he took the photo?" Chen Bin guessed.

"Hold on. Did you say Sadao Endo?" Since the name was in Japanese, it took Birch awhile to understand Mr. Tu's accented pronunciation.

"Yes."

Birch burst into laughter. "Sorry," he apologized to the startled onlookers. "I know who he is. He was a fighter pilot, an ace in the Japanese Air Force." He paused, eyes blazing. "Believe it or not, Sadao Endo was the first pilot Danny and I shot down together."

The group erupted, amazed by what they'd heard.

Chen Bin exclaimed, "I remember! It was a couple of months after you and Danny started working together."

Birch beamed, unable to suppress his delight and pride.

"Oh, my goodness," cried Xiao Mei. "I remember it, too. You and

Danny came back home several weeks afterward and told Dad about the dogfight. I heard the conversation. Both you and Danny were so animated. Dad couldn't stop smiling."

Birch grinned. "It wasn't easy. Even though we shot him down, he got us a few times, too."

"The two of you looked happy, of course," said Xiao Mei, "but… funny at the same time." She turned to more listeners gathered around them, pointing to her left elbow. "Each of them had a cast on his left arm. Dad joked that they could pass as twins."

"Danny's canopy flew off," Chen Bin added, "and your plane looked like Swiss cheese." He raised his chin an inch. "But we patched them up in no time."

"We were thrilled to score our first victory together. But we had no idea that Sadao Endo was an ace."

Mr. Tu tilted his head, trying to remember something. All of a sudden his eyes widened. "Wait a second." He flipped through the stack of photos again and fished out another one. It was an aerial shot. Three fighter planes were in the frame—the one in the middle was spiraling downward while two Tiger Teeth-painted airplanes flanked it. The reporter turned the photo around and pointed to the inscription. "It says 'the last moment of Sadao Endo.'"

Birch took the picture and studied it.

The planes were too far away to see detail except for the closest one. The canopy was gone. A sheet of paper of some sort was plastered onto the pilot's face. A long white scarf flapped behind his neck in the wind.

"This is Danny. When his canopy flew off, the map on his lap was lifted by the wind and covered his face. He was blinded for a moment."

The gathering cheered.

"It was our first strike on Hong Kong. Twelve B-25s and ten fighters," said Chen Bin, tears forming in his eyes. "Meng Hu and Du Ting were there, too."

Birch nodded. "We caught the Japs by surprise. When the boys dropped the bombs, the area below us came alive with smoke and debris. Some Japanese fighter planes came up, trying to reach our

B-25s. That's when Danny and I swooped down."

"It's a fighter pilot's job to protect the bombers," Chen Bin explained to the kids.

"Together we found our target and finished him. At the end of the day, we lost one bomber, but guess how many enemy planes did we leave in smoking ruins around Hong Kong that day?"

The people looked at him, their eyes wide open, eager to hear the answer.

"Twenty!" Chen Bin said with pride in his voice.

The crowd was in awe.

Mr. Tu grinned, and then rubbed his chin, still looking confused. "Forgive me, but I don't get it. Are we talking about the same Sadao Endo?"

"I know what you're thinking. How come his name is listed on this snapshot, which has nothing to do with an air fight?"

Everyone nodded.

"Well, Hong Kong is where we shot him down. I know the Japs looked for his wreckage later on. This is what they were doing."

A satisfied smile broke across Mr. Tu's lips. "It's hard to believe that there is a fascinating story behind this simple snapshot. Who knew?" He wrote a few lines on the back of the photo.

"The man who tortured Jasmine was named Sadao." Xiao Mei narrowed her eyes. "I know it can't be the same man. I couldn't help but wish it was the same person, though."

Birch said, "I had the same wish. You're right. It can't be the same man—one was an army officer, and the other was a pilot. But Danny said it was fate. In a small way, we had our revenge."

"Oh, I wish Danny could see these photos." Xiao Mei sighed.

"He'd be thrilled." A wistful look came over Birch.

———

"Uncle Birch." A six-year-old boy stepped in front of the adults, interrupting the conversation. He was too young to be a member of the club, but he had come with his father, a veteran.

"What is it?"

"I thought the Japs looked like devils. How come they don't have fiery eyes and huge mouths?"

"They don't look like devils. In fact, Japanese look like Chinese. They have relatively flat facial features."

"So, how come they are called *Ri Ben Gui Zi—Japanese Devils?*"

"It's what they did that made them devils. They invaded our country and killed a lot of people."

Nodding, the youngster asked again, "Uncle Birch, what does it feel like to get shot at?"

Birch hesitated, trying to find a way that a child could relate.

"Do you like injections at the doctor's office?" Xiao Mei knelt down and put herself at eye level with the boy.

"No! I hate the needles. They hurt."

"Okay, being shot by a gun feels like being stuck by a needle thousands of times."

The kid gasped. His hands flew to his gap-toothed mouth. Then, bit by bit, he moved his hands and lifted his arm. His tiny fingers grazed over Birch's shiny medals. Staring at the ex-fighter pilot with his curious eyes, the boy asked in his childish voice, "May I see your scar?"

Xiao Mei turned to her husband, concern in her eyes. The pallor of her face seemed even paler.

The boy's father scolded his son for being impolite.

But Birch hesitated only a moment. Slowly, he unfastened the first three buttons and opened his uniform, revealing a white tank top and the wound below his right collarbone. He sat up straighter.

The boy stepped closer and looked intently at the scar. Then he reached up and blew a few gentle puffs of air. "That's what Mommy does when I have a booboo."

Birch felt a lump lodge in his throat. He tucked the boy under his arm.

"Next time I'm in the doctor's office," the kid declared, his apple-like cheeks flushed, "I won't cry. When I grow up, I want to be a brave man just like Uncle Birch."

The youngster's innocent words melted Birch's heart. He pulled the boy closer and pressed his mouth to his forehead. When he finally looked up, he cleared his throat and said, "Let's clean up and get ready to fly."

Flying was the highlight of their ceremony. It always brought tears to his eyes when he watched the forget-me-nots' blue petals float down from the sky. It had taken Chen Bin and him a few tries to figure out the best way to drop the flowers.

As everyone cleared the tables, a girl ran out of the house. "Uncle Birch," she shouted, waving her arms. A look akin to panic appeared on her youthful face.

"What's wrong? Is someone hurt?"

"Yes. Hurry. Auntie Xiao Mei—" The girl didn't get to finish. Birch ran toward the house.

Inside, Xiao Mei leaned over the kitchen sink. Her face was as pale as chalk.

"What happened?" Birch asked. His voice filled with anxiety.

"I must eat something—" She threw up again.

"Oh, God! We have to see a doctor."

"No, no. We're in the middle—" Xiao Mei waved a hand.

"Don't worry." Little Tiger urged, "Go to the hospital, Uncle Birch. We'll be fine. Take care of Auntie Xiao Mei." The teenager stood tall and looked mature.

"Go!" Chen Bin stepped into the kitchen.

Birch scooped Xiao Mei into his arms.

Chapter 56

▬ ▬ ▬ ▬ ▬ ▬ ▬ ▬

Birch sat on a chair in the hallway, his head hung low, eyebrows pulled together. How had he missed the signs? All morning he'd seen the pallor on Xiao Mei's face.

He wrung his large hands until the joints cracked. He felt terrible, not just for what had happened on that day, but looking back, he realized what a poor husband he'd been. Xiao Mei had been taking care of him her entire life.

I've never even told her that I love her!

His mouth curved into a frown at the thought. Birch loved Xiao Mei, but as a typical Chinese man, he didn't express his feelings. *This must change!*

He paced up and down the hall in front of the closed exam room. The quick tap of his cane thudded heavier with each step and echoed in the corridor. *What would I do if she was seriously ill?* No matter how sick she was, he was determined to take care of her as she'd cared for him.

Finally, a young doctor stepped out of the exam room. His mouth curved into a wide grin. "Congratulations," he chirped, shaking his head. "What a miracle!"

Birch rushed inside. When he saw the euphoric glow on Xiao Mei's face, he believed what the doctor had said. Settling on the edge of the bed, he wrapped his long arms around her. His broad-shouldered body virtually swallowed her petite figure. When they finally let go of one another, Birch said, "I can't believe this. I'm going to be a father!"

Xiao Mei nodded. Excitement made her look younger than her thirty-three years.

"I'll be a father," repeated Birch.

"I wish Dad were here," she said.

"He'd be thrilled," Birch agreed. Without his father's support, they wouldn't be a couple, let alone parents.

"So, which would you like to have, if you could choose? A boy or a girl?" Xiao Mei asked.

"A girl."

"Really?"

"Yes. I'll name her Phoenix." Birch thought about the conversation he'd had with Danny in prison. He'd hoped his daughter would grow up like the mystic bird, rising from the ashes of the horrid war, becoming an incredible woman like Daisy or Jasmine.

"Bai Feng Huang? That's a lovely name."

"So—" He put his right hand on her stomach, reveling in the newfound happiness. "What about you?"

"A boy," she answered without a trace of hesitation.

A boy was so much more important than a girl in China. A boy would carry the family name and lineage, while a girl would marry into another family. Traditionally, without a son, the family was viewed as ended since a daughter couldn't keep the family name going.

Having one child was already a miracle. The odds of having another was slim. So her reply wasn't a surprise. Yet, Birch asked again, "Why?" He was in a playful mood. His large eyes blazed.

"A boy will be like you—tall, handsome, brave, kind. He'll be a Tiger, just like his dad."

Her answer caught Birch off guard. That wasn't what he'd expected. Xiao Mei never ceased to amaze him. He placed a warm kiss on her flushed cheek. "His name?"

"Bai Dan Ni."

"That's the same name I told Danny I would give if I had a son." Birch gave her an appreciative nod and rubbed her stomach. "No matter whether it's a boy or a girl, you shouldn't do chores from now on."

"I know. The doctor warned me. We need to hire—"

"No."

"No? Then how—?"

"I will do everything. I'll clean. I'll cook—"

"You? When was the last time you cooked?" A sweet grin turned her mouth up in amusement.

"Uh…never."

"See," she lilted, patting his cheek.

"I'll learn." Birch gave her his most charming smile. "Any man who can fly a plane can learn to cook."

"No doubt. But a man should do important things. Now that the reporters visited us—"

"Taking care of you and the little Phoenix, or Dan Ni, is the most important thing."

Her grin wouldn't go away. Out of habit, her right hand twisted the wedding band on her ring finger. She'd been doing this regularly since they were married.

"Xiao Mei, I'm so sorry." Suddenly Birch looked downhearted. "I've been selfish. You've been taking care of me all your life. And what have I done for you? Nothing." He lowered his head; his shoulders sagged.

"My dearest Birch, don't be silly." Stroking his cheeks and chin, she said, "Has a day gone by that you haven't seen me smiling?" An impish grin bloomed on her lips. "I like a Hungry Tiger, you know."

Birch touched his wife's rosy face. "I told Danny you called us Hungry Tigers. He liked the nickname. We were so hungry." A wistful look came over him. "We talked about your dishes constantly."

"Danny would never guess what a Hungry Tiger means to us now." Xiao Mei elicited a smile from him, trying to lighten the mood. The redness on her cheeks deepened.

Birch didn't smile. He was still lost in memories. "The day before…

he said he wanted to stay in Daisy's room when we came back home."

Her eyebrow formed an inquisitive arch.

"I could tell he was torn."

"What would Danny do, if Daisy survived? Do you think he would have fallen for her?"

"I wondered about that, too. Jasmine loved him so much and died for him in such a painful way. Danny would never forget her. But how could he refuse Daisy's love if she had survived? It would have taken time, though."

"Well, at least now he doesn't have to face such a dilemma."

"Hopefully he's in Heaven. And he's a big brother to both of them."

"Or a husband to both!" Her smile changed into a playful grin. "Now that he's a god, and they're angels. Growing up in our society, Jasmine and Daisy wouldn't mind sharing him."

"Would you mind sharing me?" Birch teased.

"No."

"Really?"

"Don't forget, I was a *Ya Tou*. The best hope for a servant like me was to be your second wife. For the longest time, that was my dream. I wished you'd marry a girl like Mary—attractive, educated, having the same family status as yours. Then one day you'd feel sorry for me, and take me as your concubine."

Birch's eyebrows furrowed. "How much did I hurt you?"

"No, my silly *Shao Ye*, you didn't hurt me. I was willing, even as your servant for the rest of my life. I had choices. You and Dad gave me freedom. You wanted me to have my own family. Remember? I chose to stay."

"God, why didn't I marry you earlier?" Birch shook his head, muttering under his breath, "Those damned doctors! We wasted so much time."

Out of the blue, Xiao Mei looked uneasy. "You...you have to forgive me. I..." she stammered, "I've been keeping a...secret from you for a long time."

His eyebrow rose in bewilderment.

"The doctors weren't too far off the mark. I...I..." Xiao Mei looked at him with a sense of guilt. She picked up his hand and pressed it to her mouth. Kissing his palm, she murmured something like, "I'm sorry."

"What are you talking about?"

"Wang Hong told me of an herbal remedy. Deer Antler—"

"Deer Antler?"

"Yes, it's a…Yang tonic. I asked several herbalists. Wang Hong was right. So I added it regularly to your diet ever since you woke up. Forgive me, Birch."

"Why didn't you tell me?"

"Would you have taken it?"

"I don't know… No, I take it back, I wouldn't have. My pride would have gotten in the way." Birch brushed a loose strand of her hair from her cheek. His eyes roved over her face like a physical touch. "Deer Antler is expensive. How on earth could you afford it?"

"I used all my salary. I used to take off after payday. I—"

"Oh, yes. I remember."

"I even lied to Dad."

Birch's eyes rounded.

"He asked me what I was doing." Xiao Mei lowered her head and whispered, "I lied to him. Told him I needed to go to the Buddhist temple to pray for my family. The truth is that I wanted to buy the herb far from our house—"

"You were afraid?"

"People like to gossip. I didn't want them to talk about you."

Birch touched her cheek. "You had no idea that you'd be my wife one day."

"That didn't matter. I just wanted you to be happy and healthy. To be the strong man you should be."

He cradled her face and drew her close to kiss her lips. "Have I ever told you how much I love you?"

"You don't have to. I know. I feel—"

He opened his arms and folded her in his embrace again. "I love you very much, my Xiao Mei!"

Chapter 57

▬ ▬ ▬ ▬ ▬ ▬ ▬

Birch and Xiao Mei had a girl. As they wished, little Phoenix grew up happy and healthy. The joy of being a father never ceased touching Birch's soul. Whenever he looked at his daughter, he would see Daisy and Jasmine. Her voice, as sweet as a jingle bell, bore a striking resemblance to Daisy's. And like Jasmine, two dimples emerged every time she smiled.

To the Bai family, life was good and time slid by in true contentment.

But the passage between Taiwan and the Mainland remained blocked.

Birch held on to the hope that he would move back to Yunnan one day. He was always prepared to take on the demanding task once the opportunity presented itself. *I'm going to find Danny. I'll bring him back to the U.S. to his family.* He recited those phrases, reassuring himself.

In the back of his mind, though, he was worried that he would never get the chance. That was why he'd put so much energy into educating the younger generation, including the kids in his flying club and his daughter. When Phoenix was old enough, he took her hiking and taught her rock climbing. He told her the family's stories. He spoke to her half in Chinese and half in English.

His concern wasn't unwarranted.

The door to the Mainland never opened before persistent coughing and shortness of breath sent Birch to hospital in 1964. The diagnosis was grim—emphysema. Years of smoking had created serious damage to his lungs.

"I have to go to America," Birch said to Xiao Mei soon after he was released from the hospital, "to meet Danny's parents and sister." He'd always hoped that he could find Danny's remains before he took the trip, but in light of his failing health, the task was urgent.

Xiao Mei nodded, and then with a note of concern, added, "You're not well. You shouldn't—"

"I can't wait anymore," interrupted Birch. He coughed and then took two deep breaths. With one hand holding Xiao Mei's and the other stroking Phoenix's hair, he continued, "I have to *fu jing qing zui*. It's long overdue."

"I know what that means," the eight-year-old Phoenix chirped. Then she looked up with her innocent eyes and asked in a small voice, "Daddy, are you really going to carry brambles on your naked back to ask for forgiveness?"

"No, silly girl." Xiao Mei gave one of Phoenix's pigtails an affectionate tug. "The saying comes from an ancient story."

"But I am going to offer a sincere apology," said Birch. His eyes were sunken with dark circles surrounding them. His gaze, however, was steady and unfaltering.

Phoenix made a series of little nods. A relieved smile blossomed on her lips, creating two dimples on her cheeks.

———

Soon the family was on their way to America.

Birch barely rested during the flight from Taipei to San Francisco. "Danny invited me to go home with him," he said. "We planned to leave as soon as the war was over. Now I'm on my way. I wish it were him sitting here instead of me!" He almost choked on the words. It had been twenty years. Danny's death still left an emptiness inside him that would never be filled.

Xiao Mei took his hand.

"I've dreamed of going home with him so many times. How thrilled—"

"Danny would be happy, knowing you're on your way to visit his family," Xiao Mei said.

"I was hoping I could bring his remains home. I owe him that much."

"It's not your fault. If you could have stayed on the Mainland safely, you would have found him." She squeezed his hand. "With or without his remains, the best part of a good man stays with us forever."

Xiao Mei held his hand and talked with him until the wee hours of the night. "Close your eyes, Birch. Rest for a while. You're not well."

Birch nodded and sought a more comfortable position on his seat. He was thin with hollow cheeks. But his eyes remained open even after Xiao Mei had fallen into an exhausted sleep. Gently he tucked a wayward strand of her hair behind her ear. Then his gaze shifted to the little girl slumped between them.

Phoenix was in a deep sleep. She wore a simple sundress the color of apricots and a pair of black, open-toed sandals. She looked adorable. Birch pulled the blanket that had fallen to her stomach up to her chin. Leaning down, he brushed his nose against her soft black hair.

Danny said he'd also name his daughter Phoenix. How might Phoenix Hardy look? Would she have the same brown eyes as Danny? He rubbed a hand through his hair and heaved a tired sigh.

Feeling restless, Birch picked up a journal from his carry-on. He'd kept a diary during the war. The last three volumes were with him now. Written partly in English and partly in Chinese, they recorded the years he'd befriended Danny. He planned to read them to Danny's family, if permitted.

Turning on the overhead reading light, he gazed at the leather journal. With trembling fingers, he flipped through the pages. The papers were yellow with age, but the writing was well preserved. Over the past decades, he'd read the journals to his club many times. He was always emotional whenever he held the books in his hands. They felt much heavier than they were.

Taking a deep breath, Birch read the first entry.

June 7, 1944

Yesterday started badly. I didn't sleep much the night before. The Japs kept dropping bombs around our base, as they've done regularly for weeks. In the beginning, we all got up to seek shelter. Lately, we're so tired that some of us sleep through the raids.

Two nights ago, Meng Hu was so drained that he refused to get up, even when I dragged him. Danny didn't want to move, either. Somehow I managed to pull him out of bed. We spent most of the night in the bunker, half-sitting and half-lying on the cold ground.

When we came back in the morning, to our dismay, we learned that Meng Hu had been rushed to the hospital. Luckily, his injury wasn't too serious. When we visited him, he joked that next time around he'd listen to me, an older and wiser brother. Four months younger, he's also a Tiger.

Then he turned to Danny: "You're one lucky son of a gun. Have you seen your bed?"

Danny nodded. We've already seen it. Standing in front of his bed, Danny had looked stupefied. The mattress was covered with debris. If we had stayed in the dorm that night, he might have ended up in the hospital, or worse yet, the morgue.

Since we've always kept the base dark at night, the raids haven't done any significant damage. Nevertheless, they've kept us on edge and deprived us of quality sleep. I started to wonder how we could fight anyone without much rest. Clearly, that was what the little weasels were aiming for—driving us to exhaustion and insanity.

Apparently, Danny didn't have any better luck sleeping. His bloodshot eyes told the story. He was uncharacteristically quiet during breakfast. I thought he was just tired. After the meal, though, he turned to me with his infectious grin, as if his sleepiness had just vanished. "Hey, Big Brother, dare to moonlight with me?" Seeing my confusion, his smile broadened. As usual, this little brother enjoyed teasing me.

"Count me in. There is no job you can do that I can't." I lifted my chin, returning the same grin.

I often wonder how we get along so well. Both of us are Tigers. We're competitive, but we've never let our competitiveness get in the way of our jobs or our friendship. Is it fate? God or whatever deity took pity on us—after he lost Jack and I lost Daisy and Jasmine, we deserve each other as brothers?

"We'll give the Japs a dose of their own medicine," he said, entirely too excited. "We'll bomb the hell out of their base tonight."

"No shit?" *Our planes are not adequately equipped for night flight. Otherwise, we wouldn't let the little bastards bully us like that.*

"The moon will be full tonight." *He couldn't seem to suppress his delight.*

"And it'll be a clear night." *I was instantly pumped up. Now I understood why his drowsiness had disappeared so quickly.*

So that's what we did last night. We flew a couple of hours northeast to Wuhan. The Japanese didn't expect an aerial attack, so the airport was well-lit. We released the bombs on our belly racks and dumped everything we could carry on their base. Boy, did we give them a surprise! The sleepy-eyed Japs had no chance to fight back.

"Enjoying the light show?" *asked Danny.*

I could hardly pull away from the sight. "Now let's see who is having a restless night," *I hollered into the radio, unable to contain my satisfaction.*

"And I'm hoping this will give them nightmares..."

As we were leaving the area, we found two Japanese transport vessels upstream toward Wuhan on the Yangtze River.

"Hey, Danny, I bet you're thinking what I'm thinking."
"Absolutely!"

So we nosedived together, each lining up on a boat, and then fired. A hail of bullets ripped the vessels to shreds, blew gaping holes in the hulls, and sent pieces of wood flying in every direction.

We made a few passes, spraying all of the ammo we had. As we were leaving, I stole a glance and saw the boats on their way to the bottom of the river.

"We should do this more often," I said over the radio on our way back to our base in Hengyang. Despite the fact I only dozed off for twenty minutes in the afternoon, I was so fired up that I felt I could take to the air like this forever.

"Pray for more clear nights."

"Hey, Danny?"

"Yeah?"

"For what it's worth, it's nice to listen to a younger brother once in a blue moon," I joked and immediately heard Danny's hearty laugh. Every now and then I catch him off guard like that, and he really enjoys my sense of humor.

"For what it's worth, care to fly to the moon with me?"

Through the windshield, I'd been watching the dazzling full moon. It looked as if we were flying directly toward it. "Hell, yeah!" I answered.

While we cruised, I turned sideways and looked out of my right window. And there he was! Moonlight glinted off the side of Danny's aircraft. It glowed, luminous against the dark sky. I was mesmerized by the tranquility of the sight.

All the chaos and ugliness faded away. No blood. No pain. No death. Only a silver bird gliding gracefully across the velvet sky. No, not one, but two. Side by side, we soared toward the moon.

At that instant, I prayed to God again as I've done countless times that my brother and I would fly together like this for the rest of our lives.

Birch managed to read with relative calm until the end. The last sentence caused hot tears to glaze his eyes. A great rush of emotion erupted inside him. Love. Longing. Grief. Guilt… He leaned against the headrest, closed his eyes, and breathed a heavy sigh.

Chapter 58

━ ━ ━ ━ ━ ━ ━

Through a maze of streets, a taxi took Birch's family to a quiet suburb of San Francisco. It had been more than two decades, but the address was etched in Birch's mind. He hoped that Danny's parents hadn't moved away.

On purpose, he hadn't called or written a letter before the visit. He didn't want to give them a chance to refuse him. He had to apologize and ask for their forgiveness face to face.

Tucked into a grove of sprawling oaks, the house was surrounded by well-maintained landscaping. This two-story stone house had appeared in Birch's dream countless times. Danny's father had built it in the 1930s, and judging by its appearance, it had been remodeled over the years.

As soon as they stepped out of the taxi, Birch smelled the intoxicating fragrance of jasmine in the air. It was a balmy Sunday morning in May. Bright sunlight splashed across the newly mowed lawn. A boy about twelve was playing basketball in the driveway. Seeing the family, he dropped the ball and walked toward them.

The boy was tall. With attractive features and dark brown hair, he bore a striking resemblance to Danny. His smile was as sweet and welcoming as the warm spring morning. His eyes, brown with gold flecks in the irises, lit up with curiosity and glowed when he grinned at them.

Birch was mesmerized by the boy's eyes. A feeling of déjà vu came over him. He thought he was looking at Danny.

"Hi," the youngster greeted them with an easygoing manner, "are you lost?" He switched to speak in Chinese. "I can speak Mandarin. Maybe I can help you."

"Thank you," answered Birch, his voice trembling. "We're looking for Danny Hardy's family. Is this—?"

"Yes. Danny Hardy is my uncle. My name is Danny Greene."

Taking a large stride, Birch closed the gap between them and held the boy at arm's length. "My name is Birch Bai. I'm…your uncle's brother." Lifting his hand, he stroked the youngster's short hair.

"Holy cow!" exclaimed young Danny. "I know who you are. Oh, my God!" Turning his head toward the house, he yelled at the top of his lungs, "Mom, Dad, come quickly. Uncle Birch is here."

Birch couldn't hold back anymore. Unchecked tears streamed down his cheeks as he dropped to his knees. He cradled the boy, who was named after Danny, in his arms. His heart swelled when he felt young Danny's small hand patting his back and shoulder.

A moment later the front door flung open. A couple in their forties rushed out.

Dressed in a pale pink T-shirt and tight blue jeans, Susan Hardy was athletic. She walked with a spring in her step that reminded Birch of Danny. Her hair in ungoverned ringlets bounced around her shoulders. She brushed stray curls that were tossed by a slight breeze from her cheek as she stared at Birch with a stunned incomprehension in her eyes.

At age fifty and being sick lately, Birch was thin and frail. His face was gaunt, a web of wrinkles suspending each eye. He couldn't possibly be the young, energetic fighter pilot in the photos Susan had seen more than twenty years earlier. Yet, the incomprehension lasted only a second before recognition set in.

Her eyes widened. "No, it can't be. Jesus!" she murmured, shaking her head.

"It's me. Birch Bai." Birch released the boy. Still kneeling, he bowed down toward Susan. "I'm so sorry," he said, his forehead touched the grassy lawn, using the Chinese way to express his sincerest apology.

Both Xiao Mei and Phoenix followed him.

"Oh, stand up. For goodness's sake, stand up. Please!" Susan took several large steps. Along with her husband, she pulled them to their feet one after another.

Birch swayed as he stood up. He leaned heavily on his uninjured leg. Xiao Mei held him by his arm.

"Are you hurt?" asked Susan. Before hearing the answer, she instructed the boy, "Go, Danny. Find Dr. Watanabe."

"No need." Birch managed to wave a hand. But young Danny had already started running. "Come back," Birch called after him.

"Better let a doctor take a look," Susan said with concern in her voice.

"I'm going with him." Phoenix ran after Danny.

"Well, let's go inside." The tall man grabbed Birch's arm and looped it over his shoulder. "I'm Jeff Greene, Danny Hardy's brother-in-law. Pleased to meet you, Birch. I've heard so much about you."

Once sitting in their living room, Birch began to tell the story. "Danny was the bravest man I've ever met. To this day, it's still hard for me to think of Danny as...gone. He was so full of life." Birch took a shaky breath and finished by saying the thing he should have said to Danny more than twenty years ago: "He was the best brother one could ever have had!"

Tears filled Susan's eyes as she held Birch's cold hands. "Danny said the same thing... He told us everything in his letters."

"But I wasn't..." Anguish darkened Birch's tone. "I didn't protect him as a Big Brother should have. I let him down. I—"

"Don't talk like that. Danny went willingly to China."

"I should have died with him. We vowed—"

"No, don't keep saying that!" Susan shook his knotted hands as if trying to liberate him from his self-loathing. "I wish Danny were still alive, but at least you survived. At least one of you lived through that hell."

She opened her arms and hugged him. An involuntary sob escaped her trembling lips as she whispered near his ear, "Oh, Birch, you're my Big Brother as well. *Da Ge*, I wouldn't want you to have died with Danny!"

For many years Birch had dreamed of hearing Danny calling him *Da Ge—Big Brother* in his mind, but he knew it was only his imagination. Now hearing Danny's sister say the words sent a shock through his body. He held Susan in his arms as if he were hugging Danny.

Finally she said, still sniffling, "Oh, I wish my parents could hear this. They passed away—"

"I'm so sorry," said Birch. Then his eyebrows furrowed. "When did that happen? Soon after Danny...?"

"No. Mom died of a stroke ten years ago. She hadn't been in good health since Danny was listed as missing in action. She kept calling his name in her last hours. She—"

"I'm so sorry!"

"Dad died a year later. Both of them had never recovered from... He kept asking me to find out what happened to Danny. He'd be so proud if he—"

"They didn't know anything?"

"Well, we were told his plane went down with yours in Yunnan. Later, we learned that you were in a coma, but there wasn't any news about my—"

"No." For a moment, Birch's face held nothing but perplexity. "I reported as soon as I woke up. I wrote a long letter to you and your parents several weeks after that. I—"

"Yes," interrupted Xiao Mei. "I mailed it. It was this thick." She used her thumb and index finger to indicate the thickness.

"Thirty pages!"

Susan shook her head. "We never received anything from you, nor heard anything about Danny. Before today, I didn't even know you woke from the coma. I didn't know you survived."

"Dear God!" Birch plowed his fingers through his short hair. His guilt had blinded him and prevented him from considering an alternative reason as to why they'd never replied. After all, international mail was unreliable during that chaotic time.

"Both Mom and Dad wished I could go to China one day, to find out what happened to Danny, to bring him home. They'd be so thrilled to meet you—"

"I'm terribly sorry!" Weighed down by newly-formed guilt and regret, Birch paused to draw several deep breaths. "I've always assumed that you and your parents were angry with me. You blamed me for not saving Danny. Oh, Susan, I've imagined you yelling at me for twenty years."

"Birch! How can I blame you? You've done nothing wrong. I've always wanted to thank you. You meant the world to my brother. In fact, I did send you a couple of postcards after we heard you were in a coma. We wished your recovery and good health."

Birch shook his head and closed his pain-filled eyes, preventing anyone from seeing the depth of his emotion.

"Seeing you now is like a…dream." Susan rubbed her right palm up and down his arm as if making sure he was real. "You're part of Danny. You're family!"

Birch's voice failed him, so he gave a nod.

"Would you like to have something to drink?" Jeff offered. "Water? Coffee? Anyone care for a beer?"

"Coffee, thank you."

As they shared more stories, Susan blurted out, "Do you need something for pain?" She pointed at Birch's leg. The kids had come back without finding the doctor.

Birch realized that he'd unconsciously reached down to rub his knee.

"He doesn't take pain relievers." Xiao Mei spoke for her husband. "In fact, he hasn't used them for almost twenty years."

"Because of Danny's death?"

"Yes."

"Why did you punish yourself like that?" Susan held Birch's hand again. "You knew my brother better than anyone. He'd hate to see you in pain."

Tears of profound love trickled down Birch's face. Today, in front of his long-lost family, he allowed himself the freedom to express his deepest feelings.

"Uncle Birch?" Young Danny walked toward them. He'd been playing with Phoenix in the backyard.

"Yes, Danny?" A tenderness welled inside Birch as he spoke the name.

"Phoenix told me you brought gifts for us. May I take a look?"

"Of course." Birch nodded.

Xiao Mei opened a suitcase. It was filled with all kinds of food—candies, nuts, and cookies.

"Wow! This is like Christmas, only better." Eagerly the boy picked up a package. "May I?"

"Wait," Phoenix called out, choosing a different package. "This is my favorite." She peeled the wrapper and stuck the candy in young Danny's mouth.

The adults exchanged affectionate looks.

Xiao Mei opened the other suitcase, revealing a big box with a picture of an olive green airplane.

"Whoa!" the boy exclaimed.

Birch took a radio-controlled airplane out of the box. "Twenty years ago Danny gave me a plane like this. We talked about a flying club."

"Daddy had it painted." Phoenix pointed to the tiger face on the nose of the aircraft. "He said it looks like the ones he and Uncle Danny used."

"This is so cool!" Young Danny's face lit up with undiluted joy as he touched the airplane. "Can it really fly?"

"Sure."

"Too bad. I don't know how to…"

"I know. I know," Phoenix said, jumping up and down. "I know how to fly. I'll show you."

"Really?"

"Yes. Daddy taught me. And a lot of other kids, too."

"I started a club. It's called—"

"Forget-You-Not," the young girl cut Birch off, eager to share her knowledge.

"Forget…you…not?" Susan repeated. Understanding the significance, she reached out and touched the back of Birch's hand.

"We have lessons every Sunday, and we have a big, big event each year." Phoenix flung her arms wide. "We hear stories of Uncle Danny, Uncle Jack, Auntie Daisy and Jasmine." She stood tall and proud. "When I grow up, I'm going to look for them with my daddy."

Susan crouched down in front of Phoenix and folded her into her arms.

Moments later Phoenix asked in her small voice, unsure of herself, "Can Danny go with us?"

"Certainly."

Birch picked up a gaily wrapped package. "This is for you." He handed it to Susan.

"For me?"

"Open it."

A magenta silk scarf appeared when she removed the wrapping paper. "Oh, my goodness!" Susan looked up. Astonishment mingled with comprehension and appreciation. "You…you gave—"

"Yes, I gave a pink scarf to Daisy and a red one to Jasmine."

"Danny told us in his letters. He said Daisy had the pink scarf when she…" Susan stopped, touching Birch's hand again to show her compassion. "The image of Daisy vanishing right in front of him…haunted him. He wrote about the scarf many times. He said pieces of it floated down the gorge like raindrops. It'd appeared in his nightmares often."

Birch's throat jammed with emotion.

"Danny always seemed so…carefree," said Xiao Mei. "Nothing seemed to bother him. I can't believe he also suffered such guilt like Birch."

"A lot of veterans suffer nightmares and depression. Danny also said that he didn't know how to repay the girls' kindness. I guess, giving you a chance to live was his way to show his gratitude."

Unable to speak, Birch nodded.

"Will you?" Susan asked as she held out the scarf.

Birch took it and gingerly wrapped it around his younger sister's neck.

"Thank you!"

"There is another one," said young Danny, pointing to another package.

Birch picked it up, hesitated a moment before handing it to Susan with both hands. "I'm sorry," he said, his face grim.

A white scarf came into view. It wasn't new and had smudges of blood that couldn't be completely removed. Susan stared at it in confusion. Then one hand curled over her opened mouth in disbelief.

"Danny left it to me." Birch squeezed the words out past the dryness of his throat.

Susan pressed the scarf to her chest and closed her eyes.

"Jasmine gave it to him on his twenty-eighth birthday," said Birch.

"I know. She had to tear his old one to wrap his wounds."

"Danny always had this and the red scarf around his neck. He left it to me the night before..."

"Birch had it when he was shot," Xiao Mei pointed to the scarf. "That bullet hit his right shoulder."

Susan stretched it open. There was a hole in the middle. She held the precious gift close to her for a full minute before beckoning young Danny. Wrapping the scarf around his neck, she said, "Remember the white scarf your Uncle Danny had?"

The boy nodded, touching the scarf.

"This is it! Take good care of it." She turned to Birch and Xiao Mei. "Today is special. Next time he wears it...will be the day we find Danny or Jasmine."

Chapter 59

A knock on the door interrupted their conversation.

"It must be Dr. Watanabe." Jeff stood up. A moment later, he came back with a short Japanese man.

"I am sorry I am late," the newcomer apologized with a strong accent. Outfitted in a black suit and yellow tie, he was in his late-thirties, a medicine bag in his hand.

"Dr. Watanabe, thank you for coming." Susan turned to Birch. "Dr. Watanabe is our neighbor and a friend. Danny left a note for him to come by." She turned back to the short man, beaming. "This is my long lost brother, Birch Bai."

Birch stood up. He didn't like to interact with Japanese. In principle, he understood that not all people in Japan had participated in the war or the atrocities, but emotionally he had difficulty facing them. Seeing a Japanese always reminded him of the horrors he'd experienced, but being a civilized person, he held out his hand.

The doctor smiled and tipped his head in a polite bow. Looking up, he stretched his arm. But before he touched Birch's hand, out of the blue, he paled. The smile faded into a look of astonishment. "Brother? Birch?"

His eyes bulged. His hand froze in midair. "I…I have to go." His small frame seemed to shrink visibly as he took a step backward. In haste, he bumped into Jeff who stood behind him. "Sorry." He ran toward the door as if all the devils in hell were at his heels.

Recognition dawned on Birch, too. "School Boy?" he called after the Japanese man.

The name bolted the doctor into place. Then, frantically he resumed running.

Birch called out again, raising his voice.

This time the man turned around. He looked like a hunted animal who had just realized the last route to freedom was closed. Without further hesitation, he dropped down and crawled back on his hands and knees. Stopping right in front of Susan and Birch, he lowered his head to the floor.

The group took a collective gasp. Jeff herded the kids out of the house in a hurry.

"You are School Boy," said Birch. A wave of nausea hit him as he reconciled this polite, well-dressed man with the thin young guard he remembered from the prison.

Dr. Watanabe kept banging his forehead on the wooden floor. "I am sorry. So sorry, so sorry…"

"What is going on?" asked Susan, bewildered. "Who is…?" Suddenly, her eyes widened. "No!"

"Yes." Birch nodded. "He was one of the guards."

"In the prison?"

Birch dipped his head. He squeezed his eyes shut, wishing to block the sight of the former guard. Emotions swirled inside his chest.

For a few moments, the surroundings faded away, and he was back in the grim prison cell. Haunting images flooded his head: Danny's pain-twisted features and bleeding leg; Mr. Ding's bruised forehead and broken eyeglasses; Captain Zhang's nail-less fingers; the teenage prisoner's headless body; Jackal's sword dripping blood; the mass grave.

Voices he would never want to hear again sounded loud and clear in his ears: Danny's agonizing screams, Mr. Ding's pleading words, Captain Zhang's curses, the poor teenager's wail, the gunshots, the buzzing of the flies around the bodies.

He could still smell the foul odor of sweat and urine. He felt the smoldering heat. He tasted blood and death in his mouth. Birch had lived in that prison for seven weeks, and out of dozens of people there became the sole survivor. Now, he was forced to face their shared enemy.

What could he say to the former guard for all those dead souls? Raw emotion sent Birch into a tailspin. He didn't know what to do. One thing he did know, though, was that no matter what he said or did, nothing would bring those people back to life. Nothing would bring Danny back.

And out of all the guards, it was School Boy he was facing, which made it even more complicated. Birch quivered, maintaining his composure by a thread.

Susan stood up, grabbed the Japanese man by the collar and slapped him with her open palm. "How dare you to come here? And pretend to be our friend?"

Dr. Watanabe continued to kneel as he protected his head from another assault.

"Stop, Susan." Birch grasped her arms. "He wasn't the bad one. He helped us."

"I *am* the bad one," the doctor shrieked. "I am guilty!" Still kneeling, he straightened his upper body. "I...I shot...I shot Danny."

"You did what?" asked Birch. The knuckles on the back of his hands bulged, turning white.

"I am the guilty one. I killed Danny."

Birch picked up his cane, raising it high above his head. The urge to hit the little man swelled like a tornado about to unleash its destructive power.

"No. Birch, no!" Xiao Mei begged, closing her hand around his bicep.

"I had no choice." Tears poured down Watanabe's face. "I was ordered to do it. I am so sorry." His nose was running, spittle flew from his mouth. "As God is my witness, I did not want to kill him. I liked Danny. He taught me English. My uncle lived in the States. I have always liked Americans. I am a U.S. citizen now."

Birch clenched the cane. His arm shook so hard the stick wobbled in the air. A war waged inside him. A soul-deep ache stirred within him, demanding him to punish the man. It took incredible discipline not to send the cane down.

More tears flooded down the Japanese man's cheeks. "I came to the U.S. I became a doctor. I wanted to redeem myself." He angled his face toward Susan. "The moment your brother died, the soldier part of me died as well." Putting a hand on his chest, he added, "I swore on my mother's grave that I would become a doctor one day. I would save lives to repay the lives I had destroyed."

The cane came down without touching the man kneeling before him. The tidal wave of anger ebbed. Birch believed him. There was no reason for him to lie. He'd confessed on his own. In this middle-aged man, Birch could see School Boy, who had kindly offered Danny the precious pain reliever and the food. He took the medicine bottle out of his pants pocket and shoved it to the doctor. "Danny had always appreciated your kindness." He then told everyone the escape plan and how Danny had persuaded others not to kill School Boy.

The doctor listened. By then his torrent of howls had weakened to a snivel. Holding the medicine bottle before his chest, he bowed to Birch, using the Chinese way of showing his sincerity. "Thank you!" Then he turned to Susan. "I did not mean to lie to you. But how could I tell you the truth? I was too ashamed."

"Dear God! Did you know who we were before you—?"

"Yes. I picked the house close to yours. I did not mean anything malicious. Please, believe me. I just…"

"Did Danny say anything before…before…?" asked Birch. "Tell us the truth."

"There were seven of us and seven prisoners. I was facing Danny. I was so shaky that I could not steady the rifle. I was only eighteen. I had never killed anyone. Danny…laughed. He said, 'Medicine bottles fit better in your hands than a gun.'" Lifting his hands, the doctor studied his palms and the small bottle cradled within them.

Birch cringed, and then sensed Xiao Mei's hand on his back, soothing him as she'd always done.

"He looked so…calm. His gaze was steady. I could not believe anyone would be so calm…in the face of death."

Closing his eyes, Birch tried to hide his emotion. *Danny was calm because he was willing to die for me.*

"We fired," Dr. Watanabe said in a detached tone. "I saw him go down. Even then I could still hear him…speak…" he stammered, putting his hands over his ears as if to block his hearing. "He was talking in Chinese. His voice was low and weak, but it scared the hell out of me. I dropped the rifle. The prison chief kicked and punched me. Then he walked toward Danny and…" the doctor faltered again, his Adam's apple sliding up and down. "He used his sword."

Birch felt the wound in his heart being ripped open. For twenty years he'd wondered about Danny's death. *Who killed him? How did he die? Did he say anything? What was he thinking at the time?* Now, he'd finally learned the truth, and the gruesome details cut through his soul. Grief swelled inside him, an ache powerful and all-consuming.

Trancelike, Susan slumped back onto the sofa and sat there trembling. Birch put his arm around her shoulders. The room was quiet except for the sound of weeping and sniffling.

Birch broke the silence: "What did Danny say?"

"Honestly, I do not know. But I believe he was reciting a poem. There were words like wind…and water…"

"Oh, Christ!" said Birch, tears returning to his eyes. "*Feng xiao xiao xi yi shui han. Zhuang shi yi qu xi bu fu fai,*"

"That is it. My Chinese is terrible, but I know a few words."

Birch turned toward Susan. "It's a phrase from an ancient story. I don't think any translation can truthfully convey the sense of heroism, the sad feeling, and the dignity of a warrior staring in the face of death."

He sat up straighter. "To translate it directly—" His throat ached with the effort to hold back tears as he repeated the exact words that he'd spoken to Danny more than two decades earlier. "It says: Wind rustled across the desolate land. Water in the river turned icy and cold. In this gloomy day, a warrior, knowing he wouldn't return alive, walked straight forward without so much as a backward glance…"

Another heavy silence descended on them.

Finally, Susan asked, "Did anybody else say anything?"

"They all shouted," the doctor answered, "'Down with Japanese Devils. Long live China.'"

Birch nodded. The slogans were common during that era. "What happened to Jackal?"

"Jackal?"

"The prison chief."

"He retired from the military after the war. I was told he took a job in charge of a small jail down south. He—"

"He didn't receive any punishment for brutalizing and killing the prisoners?"

"No. Military personnel who had committed worse atrocities were never punished. But several years ago I heard he was killed during a riot. He was so cruel to the inmates."

"Sounds like the saying is true," Xiao Mei said and sighed in relief. "*Shan you shan bao. E you e bao—what goes around comes around.*"

Birch didn't like this saying. If it were true, then Danny wouldn't have ended up in an unmarked grave. Hundreds of thousands of innocents, including Daisy and Jasmine, wouldn't have died painful and unnecessary deaths.

Yet he didn't have the energy to argue. The idiom tried to persuade people to conduct virtuous deeds for the sake of having a good ending. In his philosophy, though, no matter what the result, being a decent person was what motivated him. And Danny had done just that.

The reality was cruel and ironic. A great man like Danny had died. The person who'd participated in his execution had not only lived, but also became an American citizen. The United States and Japan became allies. China, the very country Danny and Jack had fought for, was divided. Birch still couldn't set his foot on the land he'd spent eight years fighting for.

Doubts which had troubled Birch for a long time resurfaced. *Did we do the right thing? What was the purpose of our sacrifice? Was it truly worthwhile?* His mind reeled. He felt himself doubting everything they'd done and the very principles for which they'd stood.

"I am so sorry," Dr. Watanabe apologized again. "Please forgive me."

Blinking hard to beat back the tears, Susan gripped the doctor's arms. This time she pulled him upward. "Oh, for that bottle of pain reliever you gave my brother—" Yet she couldn't say the forgiving words.

"Give us some time," said Birch. Then he added, "Danny would be happy knowing that you listened to him and became a doctor."

Dr. Watanabe nodded gratefully as he left.

The trio sat huddled together, embracing and nursing their wounds.

The kids returned home, and young Danny cradled the tiger-faced airplane as if he were holding a baby. The white scarf was wrapped around his neck. Phoenix, a head shorter, held the transmitter in her small hands. Her scrawny chest puffed up. Side by side, they walked into the room, talking and laughing. Their youthful and innocent faces lit up like summer sunshine. Along with their smiles, they brought fresh air. Even though they'd met only several hours ago, they seemed to have become instant best friends.

More like a brother and a sister, Birch thought. Suddenly, his eyes, shiny with the recent tears, widened. The dark thoughts, which had almost choked him a moment ago, loosened their grip as a revelation hit him. In a moment of clarity, he understood— across time and space, out of all the ugliness and the unfairness, an extraordinary friendship had formed and thrived; love endured and prevailed.

Such an invaluable bond was worth dying for.

The two brothers had used their lives to attest to the concept of Yi—morality, duty, loyalty, decency, and brotherhood. No matter how difficult, Birch would keep this principle alive, for himself, for his best friend, and for the next generation.

Sweeping his hand from left to right, he asked, "What would Danny do if he could see us now?" A wholehearted smile graced his lips. Feeling Danny's spirit close, he raised his voice. "I bet he would grin from ear to ear."

A tentative smile broke through Susan's grief. "And his smile would light up the universe."

Tears clung to her long eyelashes, but love came to life in her eyes—golden-brown eyes, just like Danny's.

Interview with the Author

Did you plan to write *Will of a Tiger* when you wrote *Wings of a Flying Tiger?*

No, I didn't. I started writing this book several months after I finished *Wings of a Flying Tiger*. During that time I kept on thinking and imagining what might have happened to the characters in the first book after their rescue of Danny Hardy, the American pilot. Those characters became so real to me that I wanted to know how their lives turned out to be. So I started researching, not only about The War Against Japan, but also Chinese history afterwards.

The more I learned about the survivors of war, the more I realized how much adversity they had faced, especially for someone like Birch Bai. Surviving The War Against Japan might have been the beginning of his long battle. On top of physical disability, emotional grief, and survivor's guilt, he had to deal with the dreadful political reality—the Chinese Civil War and the separation of the country.

Is it true that the Japanese military questioned an American POW about the atomic bomb?

Yes, it was true. After the first bomb was dropped on Hiroshima, the Japanese questioned an American pilot who was captured on August 8, 1945 for information about the nuclear weapon. Under torture, he "confessed" that the U.S. possessed one hundred more atomic bombs. Ironically, this forged number might have swayed Japan toward making the decision to surrender.

When did Taiwan lift Martial Law? And when were the exiles in Taiwan allow to visit Mainland China?

Martial Law was lifted in 1987. In the same year, after a 38-year blockage, the Communist government on the Mainland opened the door to the people of Taiwan. This benefited many, especially former Nationalist soldiers, who had been separated from their families on the Mainland for decades.

Did anyone actually search for the remains of those American airmen who perished in China?

Yes! There were individuals and organizations that vigorously searched for the remains of the Americans who died for China during The War against Japan. In a number of cases, the remains were found and transported back to their hometowns in the States.

Did you or your family serve in the military?

No, I didn't have any military experience. Nor did most of my family. However, my grandfather, Yang Duanliu, served as the Director of the Audit Office of the Central Military Commission in mid 1930s. He was an economist and a professor at Wuhan University. Because of his immense knowledge in economics, he had given lectures to Chiang Kai-shek, the leader of the Republic of China. He was the only admiral who was allowed to wear plain clothes in the Nationalist Military. When I wrote General Bai, I thought of my grandfather: gentle, intelligent, principled, and disciplined.

Why do you like to write wartime stories?

My mother asked me a similar question when I was young. She was curious about why a quiet, shy girl liked to read books about war. I didn't have any answers at the time. I didn't even know the reason. Now looking back, I can see it clearly. I was born a very shy and fearful person. I was afraid of pretty much everything—darkness, height, insects, snakes, strangers, public speaking... It was because of my shyness and fear that I loved reading wartime stories. I looked up to heroes. I admired their courage and their spirit. I read books about those extraordinary people so that I could be inspired by their heroic acts and hopefully learn from them.

Growing up in a family of professors, I've always loved reading. Even before I was born, my parents and grandparents bought books for me. However, during the Cultural Revolution, the Red Guards came to our home and took most of the books away. I read the few leftovers again and again because there weren't many books available—for almost ten years the libraries were closed and the bookstores had nothing except political works. You can't imagine how hungry I was for books!

But I was lucky to have a wonderful father. My hometown, Wuhan, is one of the "Three Furnaces" in China. We had no air conditioning or electric fans. In the hot and humid summer evenings, we sat outside. Surrounded by neighboring kids, my father told us stories—from Chinese masterpieces to Western classics, including some of the most heroic tales such as *Romance of the Three Kingdoms, Water Margin, The Great General Yue Fei,* and *Spartacus.* Those summer nights influced me in many ways.

So as a writer, I write what I love to read: heroic tales with touching love stories. And I'm happy to say that I'm no longer a shy or fearful person. Check www.irisyang-author.com for more information.

Acknowledgments

My deep appreciation to Anne Crosman, who volunteered to edit the manuscript. A retired journalist of thirty years, she was patient and thorough. Together we went through the manuscript word by word, line by line. I'm forever grateful for her kindness and help.

Many thanks to Marywave Van Deren and Gary Jacobson for showing up unexpectedly to offer much needed guidance.

I'm grateful to three writing groups led by Naxie Reiff and Rodger Christopherson, Sy Brandon and Jim McMeekin, and Gary Every and Robin Harris. Their feedback made my book better, and their praises kept me going. I'm thankful to Megan Aronson, David Kanowsky, and Dana Best for reading the story to the groups. Thanks to Sedona Public Library and Cottonwood Public Library for their invaluable resources.

My heartfelt thanks to all the readers of my first novel, *Wings of a Flying Tiger*. Special thanks to those who went out of their way to support the book: Greg Curtis, Jim Wilfong, Ed Bustya, Carolyn Francis, Phil Sullivan, Melinda Collis, Brian Daniel, Manije Irani, Bertie Boston, Judy Glasser, Jeff Howard, Becky Coltrane, Paul Falk, Tom Tate, Roy Murry, Les Gee, Susan Sage, Emit Blackwell, Mary Anne Yarde, Colleen Story, Linda Hill, Barbara Bos, Cheryl Holloway, Clarissa Devine, Gale Zasada, Karen Bernard, Meg Stivison, John Genord, Anna Casamento Arrigo, Rebecka Jager, Jolene

Pierson, Doug McDaniel, Ginny Storey, Ellen Rosher, Lou Sideris, Celeste Barrett Rubanick, Tom Murphy, Jade Vincent, Valerie Thompson, Jay Bower, Hayley Gross, Paul Steffy, Susan Birdsey, Susie Alvarado, Allyson Tilton, Janet Flowers, Michael Norwood, Katie Tsui, Yan Li, Yuli Wang, Cheng Wang, Xiaoying Yin, Leon Zhang, Jing Isabel Liu, Alex Zhu, Hang Liu, Cathy Kimball, Fred Mao, Frank Liu, Min Cheng, Zhe Liang, and Garry Guan.

My sincere gratitude to David Ross and Kelly Huddleston at Open Books. Once again, they made my dream come true.

Finally, I give thanks to my family. I'm eternally grateful to my mother Zhou Chang and father Yang Hongyuan for their love. My special thanks to my sister Jin Yang, daughter Jessie Xiong, and best friend Libby Vetter for their encouragement and support.

Made in the USA
Middletown, DE
31 July 2019